Readers  love
KATE MCMURRAY

The Stars that Tremble

"Kate McMurray picked up my imaginary gauntlet and smacked me with it. This book was fantastic."

—Live Your Life, Buy the Book

"McMurray has written an endearing and poignant love story between two fantastically vulnerable men… This one is a must read for my fellow hopeless romantics."

—MM Good Book Reviews

"…part of the reason why I enjoy Kate McMurray's books so much is because even if her plot has fantasy, over the top elements, her guys more often than not behave close to how real people would behave."

—Reviews by Jessewave

The Silence of the Stars

"*The Silence of the Stars* by Kate McMurray is a sweet and gentle story that hides a bit of a punch as it explores the effect of PTSD in a relationship."

—Prism Book Alliance

When the Planets Align

"I stayed up waaaaaay too late reading this and now I have one of those nasty book hangovers we all hate to love."

—The Blogger Girls

"So from the playground to the prom, from Iowa to New York, the journey to happiness is told in wonderfully clever words and is delivered in another great book by Kate McMurray."

—The Novel Approach

By KATE MCMURRAY

Blind Items
Four Corners
Kindling Fire with Snow
Playing Ball (Multiple Author Anthology)
The Stars that Tremble • The Silence of the Stars
A Walk in the Dark
What There Is
When the Planets Align
The Windup

Published by DREAMSPINNER PRESS
http://www.dreamspinnerpress.com

The
WINDUP

KATE McMURRAY

DREAMSPINNER PRESS

Published by
DREAMSPINNER PRESS

5032 Capital Circle SW, Suite 2, PMB# 279, Tallahassee, FL 32305-7886 USA
http://www.dreamspinnerpress.com/

This is a work of fiction. Names, characters, places, and incidents either are the product of author imagination or are used fictitiously, and any resemblance to actual persons, living or dead, business establishments, events, or locales is entirely coincidental.

The Windup
© 2015 Kate McMurray.

Cover Art
© 2015 Aaron Anderson.
aaronbydesign55@gmail.com
Cover content is for illustrative purposes only and any person depicted on the cover is a model.

ISBN: 978-1-63216-967-9
Digital ISBN: 978-1-63216-968-6
Library of Congress Control Number: 2014959927
First Edition April 2015

Printed in the United States of America
∞
This paper meets the requirements of
ANSI/NISO Z39.48-1992 (Permanence of Paper).

Acknowledgments

Writing a series is a large undertaking, and I have some people to thank for giving me the push I needed to write it. First and foremost, this series would not have happened without Damon Suede, who said to me in a hotel bar during a conference that if I wanted to write a series, it should be about baseball. Obviously. So thanks, Damon, for the idea and for your continued friendship and support. I'd also be remiss if I did not acknowledge the guidance from Marsha, who read some early drafts and is good at telling me when I've gone astray, and most especially Laura for her great feedback and enthusiasm. Thanks, too, to my agent, Saritza Hernandez, for being my tireless advocate, and to the whole team at Dreamspinner for making this series a reality.

A big thank-you goes to my Facebook friends who answered my call of "Baseball puns! Go!" with a lot of fantastic book title ideas. And all the love to my fans who have been poking me to write more baseball stories. This book is for you.

Chapter 1

IAN HAD been back in New York City for three whole weeks before he had a panic attack.

It happened one evening after he went to visit his mother. He felt off balance as he descended the front stoop of his childhood home, a gorgeous brownstone in Park Slope, Brooklyn, that Ian's family had bought for peanuts back when the neighborhood was home to gangs and drug dealers instead of yuppies with strollers. When a ponytailed woman in yoga pants nearly ran over his foot with her double-wide stroller, Ian was not entirely convinced the neighborhood had improved. He had to admit, though, that it was prettier than it once had been, that the renovated old brownstones on Sixth Street had taken on a new sheen. The cherry trees lining the sidewalk were a nice touch, certainly.

So it was good to know that his mother was in a good place, even if he still basically hated the house. He'd spent the early part of the evening lounging on the same brown-and-cream plaid sofa that had sat in the living room since 1984. Then he'd had dinner at the scuffed table in the dining room, and it had all been routine, except not quite. Ian's father had not been there. And that was cause for rejoicing.

His father's decision to leave Ian's mother and move to the suburbs was part of why Ian had moved back to New York to begin with. The paycheck his new employer had dangled before him was an even bigger incentive.

Although none of that mattered now that he was back in the relative safety of his nostalgia-free block on Eighty-Fourth Street, the Upper West Side of Manhattan being the farthest from Brooklyn he could move while still being reasonably close to the new job. Now his breathing had suddenly become a labored thing and his heart was beating faster. A vague disquiet plagued him, one he couldn't quite put a finger on. He hadn't been in New York long enough to establish a routine to deviate from, so that wasn't the trigger. He was a few miles away from his childhood home, so that couldn't be it either. Maybe it was just the noise of the city, louder than the neighborhood in the Chicago suburbs he'd just left, or the taxi that whooshed by him when he put his foot on the street to cross it. Maybe it was job stress. Maybe he had no business being back in New York.

He jaywalked, cutting across Eighty-Fourth Street to get from the north side to the south, where his building sat, and he could see the gold numbers above the glass doors that led inside, but then they went blurry. Armand, the doorman, took a step away from the door and shot Ian a quizzical look. Then, bam, right in the middle of the goddamn street, the panic attack seized him and all was lost. His vision went fuzzy, his heart rate kicked up too fast, and he gulped for air, but nothing was going to stave this off.

"Sweet Jesus," he heard someone—probably Armand—say, and then a hand wrapped around his arm and yanked him into the building. Swiftly he was pushed into one of the ugly red chairs in the lobby, and a man—again, probably Armand, who was earning a larger holiday tip with each passing minute—shoved Ian's head down so that he was hunched over, his head between his legs, and Armand was muttering, "Breathe. Just breathe."

Though the symptoms eventually abated, the unease didn't.

"I don't even know what I'm panicking about," Ian said softly to a furrow-browed Armand.

"You and everyone else in this neighborhood," Armand said.

As he rode the elevator up to his apartment, Ian tried to remember what his mother had said. "Get out there. Meet new people. Make some friends." Re-entrench was the implication. She wanted Ian to make New York his home again, even though he didn't see how it ever could be. He'd work this job for a year or two and then he'd be off to the next one.

Besides, he *had* friends.

Once he felt almost normal again, Ian called Josh, not for advice but just to say hi. Unfortunately he ended up unloading instead. Not about the panic attack—Josh knew enough about Ian's anxieties to frequently compare him to a yappy little Chihuahua on speed, but he didn't need every symptom of Ian's anxiety catalogued, certainly—just about the visit with his mother and the whole speech about what an asshole his last boyfriend had been and how he really should meet someone new.

"You know," Josh said, "there was an article in the *Times* last weekend about how gay sports leagues are the new hookup spot. More so than bars."

Ian rolled his eyes. "Here we go with the baseball league. Josh, I already told you—"

"Not that the bar scene is dead, but we're a little old for it, don't you think?"

"What I think is that you're married to a very nice man who would not appreciate—"

"Seriously, sign-ups are on Saturday and you really should come. If not for me or the love of the sport then because the league will provide you with about a hundred opportunities to hook up with some guy."

Ian laughed despite everything. "I bet this article also had some stats about how many deeply committed, loving relationships had resulted from gay sports leagues."

"There may have been a mention of that."

"I don't want a deeply committed relationship."

Josh made a raspberry sound into the phone. "Oh, honey. I hope you end up on my team. I've got just the guy for you to meet."

"In that case, forget it."

"Ian. Honey. Please. Just come to the sign-ups. See what the league is about. If you hate everything about it, fine, but I think you'll have fun."

TY TOSSED a baseball up and watched it arc through the air before he held out his hand to catch it. He did it again, enjoying the satisfying slap each time the ball hit his palm.

"Showing off?" Josh walked over, a stupid grin on his face.

Ty snatched his baseball out of the sky. "Someone has to," he said.

Josh crossed his arms over his chest. He scanned the scenery. They were standing at the periphery of one of the East River Park ball fields, next to a card table they'd set up for league sign-ups. A colorful banner advertising the Rainbow League, New York's premier LGBT amateur sports league, hung from the front. On this particular cool spring afternoon, they were signing up new players for summer baseball. Ty hadn't had much else to do that afternoon, so he'd volunteered to help with registration. Somehow he'd been left there by himself for the past twenty minutes while Josh and a few other volunteers had thrown a ball around on the field. Ty was bored out of his mind.

At least Josh had come back. He walked over to the table and flipped through the binder that served as their roster.

"You know," Ty said, "there's this thing called the Internet. Much as I like sitting out here in the sun, we could have saved time and manpower by getting that damned website up."

"Hey, I argued that we should," Josh said with a shrug. "This was Will's directive."

"And where is His Majesty?"

"He just got here. He's trying to get Nate and Carlos to play a real game instead of just tossing the ball around. They don't seem to be having any part of it."

Ty sighed. "Sounds about right."

"Whatever." Josh pressed his palm against an open page, the sign-up sheet for his and Ty's team, the Brooklyn Hipsters. "So, look, with Bryan gone and that Adam guy going MIA, there are two slots open on the team. Everyone else re-upped."

"Good." They'd had a great team the previous season, and after a few seasons in the league, Ty had come to loathe adjusting for new players. New guys were too unpredictable.

"I'm hoping my friend shows up while we're manning the table so we can get him on our team before someone else gets him," said Josh. "Once it becomes knowledge that he's actually played baseball, everyone will be fighting for him."

Ty cocked an eyebrow and shot Josh what he thought of as his best sexy insouciant look. "Actual baseball experience."

Josh was unfazed. "We played together in high school."

Ty tossed the ball in the air again. "Ha. And here I thought you were going to tell me he'd been a pro. If playing in school is the only measure, I had actual baseball experience before I joined the team."

"You played T-ball in elementary school."

Ty just smiled. "We have Mason, though. Much to the envy of everyone else in the league." Actually, most of Ty and Josh's teammates had some kind of baseball experience. Nate and Carlos—who, along with Mason and Josh, were Ty's closest friends on the team—had played on the same Little League team when they were kids, for example. Joe and Shane had played college ball.

"Sure," said Josh, "but it's nice to have more than one person on the team who knows how the game works. As opposed to some other people."

"Hey, just because I don't give a shit about pro baseball doesn't mean I'm totally ignorant." Ty really pulled out the Texas when he said that, so it came out sounding like "tote-ly ig-nant." He cleared his throat. "So where is this baseball god?"

"Dunno. He wasn't that keen on joining, but I tried to persuade him that it would be worth it for the hookup opportunities. He seemed intrigued."

Ty laughed. "Well, sure. Who wouldn't be? I saw that article in the *Times*. Allegedly the New York gays are all joining sports leagues instead of going to bars. Which is horseshit, as anyone who has been in Hell's Kitchen lately knows perfectly well." Ty considered that for a moment. "Although I guess I did make it my mission to, er, work my way through the entirety of the Queens team last season."

Josh took a sip from his water bottle and narrowed his eyes. "How did that work out for you?"

Ty shrugged. "Well enough. Every team has to have a token slut. I'm happy to fill that role."

Josh shook his head. "Did Bill James say that?"

"Who?"

"Hey, Josh!"

Ty turned and saw a blond guy making his way across the park. He was, well, he was pretty good-looking, actually. Slender in an athletic way. Jaw that looked like it could cut glass. Package nicely highlighted by the dark jeans he was wearing. "This your secret weapon?" Ty asked.

Josh looked smug.

Ty tossed the ball again.

"Hi," the guy said as he arrived. "I made it."

Ty took a moment to really scope out the man. He'd started cataloguing his merits when Josh slapped his arm.

"Stop that!" said Josh. "So. Ty, this is my friend Ian from high school. He just moved back to New York after many years away and blah blah."

"And blah blah?" Ian said. "That's my whole backstory?"

"This," Josh went on, "is Ty. He's second base."

"And I Don't Know is on third," said Ty, holding out his hand to shake.

Ian shot him a wry smile. "Nice to meet you." He shook Ty's hand.

Ty supposed that this would be the moment in the movie when the music swelled, or the moment in the novel when the characters touched and electricity passed between them, but even though Ty was absolutely attracted to Ian and had already begun his strategy to get the man naked, nothing like that happened. They merely shook hands, casual as you please, as if this were a business transaction.

"I don't get a cute tidbit of information?" Ty asked Josh. "Just 'second base'?"

Josh shrugged. "What do you want me to say? Ian, this is Ty. He's from Texas, as I imagine you've gathered from the accent. He's been in New York about ten years. And he fancies himself the team slut."

Ian laughed. "Nice. Every team needs one."

"That's what I told Josh."

Josh crossed his arms over his chest. "So, you're here," he said to Ian. "Are you signing up or what?"

"Is Ty here as a sample specimen? Are all the guys on the team this hot?"

Ty guffawed. "Look at you, indirectly flirting with me. It's the slut thing, right? The fact that I'm easy makes me intriguing?"

"Sure," said Ian. "The ginger hair doesn't hurt."

"Josh, let's sign him up right now."

"Can you play third base?" Josh asked.

A matter of minutes later, Ian had registered for the league and was on the roster as the new third baseman for the Brooklyn Hipsters. "But living in Brooklyn is not a requirement, obviously," Josh explained. "That's just the way they do the team designations. There are eight teams in the league."

"All gay men?" Ian asked.

"No, some teams have women too."

"The Mermaids, man," Ty said.

"They're kind of our rivals," Josh explained. "The all-woman team representing Coney Island. Totally ruthless, those women."

"I see," said Ian, looking a little dazed.

"So, quickie rundown? Each team has a twelve- or thirteen-man roster which includes every position plus a couple of pitchers and a backup utility player. We do all our games here at this park." Josh pointed at the perimeter of the park. "You'll play one game a week, probably, at least until the play-offs, which happen at the end of the season in October. After each game, both teams go to this bar in the East Village for postgame drinks."

"The owner of the bar is sort of the league mascot," Ty chimed in.

"So that's it. And it's just fun." Josh gushed a little.

Ian laughed. He had a pretty great laugh, Ty could admit. And his voice was low and had a husky quality to it, like he'd smoked once upon a time. "I don't know why you're giving me the sales pitch *after* I've signed up. You got me, Josh."

"Did my presence sweeten the deal?" Ty asked, mostly out of curiosity. He certainly hoped it had.

"Maybe a little."

Josh rolled his eyes. "I see how this is. You're already fucking, aren't you?"

Ian sputtered. "Okay, first of all—"

At the same time, Ty said, "That's not what's going—"

Josh let out an exasperated sigh. "All right. Well. Welcome to the Hipsters, Ian. We practice in Prospect Park every Sunday too, just to make sure we don't completely suck. I'll e-mail you the info."

"Fair warning, though," said Ty. "Our manager, Scott? He's kind of a dick and super competitive. And according to the calendar, we're playing Hell's Kitchen first."

Josh grumbled.

Ian's eyes went wide. "What's wrong with Hell's Kitchen?"

"Will manages the Hell's Kitchen team. He's the guy over there with the mustache, pretending to play catch with the skinny guy in the yellow T-shirt."

"Pretending?" asked Ian.

"He's probably berating that poor guy," Ty said. "Will is constitutionally incapable of having fun."

"He *is* a tiny bit competitive," said Josh.

"Sure, if by 'a tiny bit' you mean 'sacrifices children and small woodland creatures before each game to ensure victory,'" said Ty.

"A couple of those other guys are on our team, though," said Josh. "That's Nate and Carlos throwing the ball back and forth over by the backstop. Nate's the best pitcher in the league."

Ian shook his head. "This is a lot of information all at once, guys. But thanks, I think."

"You will learn the ropes quickly," Ty said. "Just come to practice next week and we'll, uh, ease you into it."

Ian narrowed his eyes. "Are you coming on to me?"

This guy. Ty was definitely interested. "I was making a sexy pun, yes."

"Geez Louise," said Josh. "I kind of suspected this might happen when I introduced you two, but the league certainly doesn't need any drama. So, you know. Fuck if you want, but keep it off the field."

Poor Ian looked startled by that. Ty laughed. "And you, Joshua, never start any drama, of course."

"I'm married!" Josh said.

"I don't see how that makes you immune to drama."

Josh huffed. "Well, whatever. Welcome to the team, Ian."

Will suddenly barked at the five guys standing on the field, snagging everyone's attention.

Ty laughed. "Abandon all hope, ye who enter here."

"You said that guy's *not* on our team, right?" said Ian.

"You learn fast," Ty said.

ACROSS THE field, Nate fiddled with his glove while he avoided Will's gaze. It wasn't too hard, especially now that poor Jake had shown up. Will sometimes held back when yelling at players he didn't know well, but if you were on his team, all bets were off. Jake was now bearing the brunt of Will's aggression with a resigned expression on his face.

Carlos picked up three balls and started juggling them. "Check out the fresh meat talking to Ty and Josh."

Nate looked over at the registration table. There, indeed, was a guy Nate had never seen before, and Nate could tell by their body language that he and Ty were flirting madly with each other.

"I bet it would have been nice knowing that guy," said Nate.

Carlos chuckled. From the other side of the diamond, Zach yelled, "Practicing your ball-handling skills, Carlos?"

"You know it!" Carlos shouted back.

"Ball handling? You're doing it wrong!" said Aiden.

"I'll handle your balls later, *papi*!" Carlos said. He pursed his lips and made a kissing motion.

"You're all clowns!" said Nate, mostly to deflect from the fact that watching Aiden and Carlos flirt drove him bananas.

Carlos tossed the balls high in the air one at a time before catching each one. He said, "You see the game last night?"

"Caught the end of it." Nate didn't have to ask which game. For two guys who had grown up in the Bronx, there was only one baseball team worth anything. "Hell of a hit Gardner got in the ninth."

"Yeah, it was a beauty. What do you think of the new catcher?"

Nate could already see where Carlos was going with that. "As a player or as a man?"

"Either. Both."

"I wouldn't kick him out of bed."

Carlos motioned to Aiden and hurled one of the balls at him. Aiden caught it deftly. "Lourdes said he came into her nail salon last week. One of the other girls gave him some crazy trippy manicure."

"That's the thing catchers are doing now, I guess."

"Can you imagine Joe getting a manicure?" Carlos said, mentioning the Brooklyn Hipsters' catcher.

Nate laughed. "Nope. Well, maybe with black polish."

"Oh, oh, new guy is signing on the dotted line over there."

Sure enough, back at the registration table, the blond guy appeared to be filling out the registration form.

Aiden jogged over to Nate and Carlos. Carlos stared at him, starry-eyed. Nate wanted to throw up.

It wasn't that he was jealous. Well, okay, that was a lie. Nate was extremely jealous. Carlos should have been with Nate, not that asshole Aiden—who, sure, was handsome, but man, he was a dick. Nate had no right to complain, though, since he had never said a word about his feelings for Carlos. Although, Christ on a cracker, it wasn't like Carlos and Aiden were even doing more than flirting at this point. Nate had gotten an earful already about how much Carlos wanted Aiden and how frustrating it was that Aiden hadn't made a real move yet.

"Who's the new guy?" Aiden asked, gesturing toward the registration table.

"Ty's next victim," said Carlos.

"Do you know if they filled the rosters for all the teams yet?" Aiden asked.

"Probably not if they're still letting that guy sign up," said Carlos.

"We'd get more people if Will would just get the goddamn website done," said Nate.

"Sshh!" said Aiden. "Don't anger the beast."

Nate rolled his eyes. He didn't want to incur Will's wrath any more than anyone else, but he was not in the mood to deal with Aiden. Maybe he could bow out of this gracefully. "Do you think we really need to hang around much longer? Ty seems to be getting the job done over there."

Nate, Carlos, and Aiden watched for a moment. When Josh gestured toward them, they all turned and pretended to be doing something else.

"Eh, probably not," said Carlos. "Did you need to be somewhere else today?"

Nate didn't really have to be anywhere in particular, but he didn't want to hang around here if he was going to have to watch this bullshit. "I've got some work stuff."

Carlos looked at him as if he were trying to communicate telepathically. Nate and Carlos had mostly volunteered because they found out Aiden was going to be here, and Carlos wanted an excuse to spend more time with Aiden. Nate, apparently, was a sucker. Carlos wanted someone to lend him some courage to ask out Aiden, and here was the opportunity for the two of them to be sort of alone.

"I think we're all going to Barnstorm whenever this wraps," Aiden said.

And now alcohol would be involved. Nate schooled his face to not betray his frustration. "I should probably go get my work done. Give the new guy my regards."

Carlos gave Nate a halfhearted hug and then turned the full force of his attention back on Aiden. Nate gave them both a little wave before he left the field.

Damn it.

Josh snagged him before he could leave, though. "Nate is the pitcher I mentioned," he told the new guy. "Nate, this is my friend Ian. He'll be our new third baseman."

"That's great! I heard Adam moved to Chicago."

Josh scrunched up his face as if he found the mere thought of Chicago distasteful. "Are you headed out?" he asked Nate.

"Yeah, I... have a thing."

"Okay. Well, we'll see you at practice next week."

"Sure. Nice to meet you, Ian. Don't let Ty scare you off."

"I'm not scary," Ty said. He turned to Ian and shook his head. "I'm really not."

Ian laughed. He tugged on Ty's sleeve playfully.

Nate wanted to scream. Instead, he gave those assembled a quick nod and then made a beeline out of the park.

Chapter 2

TY WOULD never be able to give a satisfying answer for why he kept a photo of Ryan propped up on his living room bookcase. Invariably, whenever someone came to his apartment for the first time, he or she would notice the photo, make some comment on the man's attractiveness, and ask who he was. Well, sometimes a trick would ask, "This your boyfriend?" No, Ryan was not his boyfriend, definitely hadn't been for coming up on a decade, and even then, putting any kind of definition on their relationship probably would have been a stretch. Ty was over it, had moved on. And yet he had never quite been able to put that photo away.

Ty had once been completely besotted with Ryan. Ryan hadn't returned the sentiment.

The photo remained as a reminder of… something. The past. Ty's old life, maybe.

He went to the closet near the front door of his apartment and dug out his cleats and equipment bag. The cleats still had last season's dirt caked in between the spikes. "Classy, that's me," he muttered before carrying them to the sink and using a butter knife to knock some of the dirt off.

As he changed into a T-shirt and an old pair of sweatpants, the image of Ian popped into his head. Josh's friend had certainly gotten his attention. But he'd demurred when Ty had tried to invite him home after they had drinks together at a Lower East Side bar.

Dressed for practice, Ty grabbed the cleats from the sink and slung his bag over his shoulder. He walked the few short blocks from his apartment to Prospect Park and followed the meandering path to the ball fields. Scott and Josh were already there trying to organize their team of wayward would-be athletes into some kind of formation for warm-up exercises. And sure enough, there was Ian right in the thick of it.

He really was very cute. Ty hadn't met a lot of grown men who were natural blonds. He liked that Ian was one, because it made him look youthful and bright. Ian's hair was just long enough to demonstrate its waviness, and his facial hair was so light it was basically invisible. Ty had already asked over beer if the carpet matched the drapes and was satisfied when Ian blushed furiously. But also, Ty noticed, the worn-looking baseball pants Ian wore showed off his ass to spectacular effect, and things were loose enough in the front to indicate he wasn't wearing a cup. Ty appreciated that but wondered how wise it was to forgo it. The team was pretty good, but it only took one bad hit to send a ball at one's crotch, as Ty knew firsthand. And Ty certainly wanted Ian's dignity preserved, if only so he could gaze on it later, preferably with his cock buried in Ian's ass.

And with that, Ty's jock got pretty uncomfortable.

He hiked up the waist of his pants and marched forward, dumping his bag with everyone else's on the bench behind home plate. As he was tightening the laces on his cleats, Josh jogged over.

"Scott is actually in a halfway decent mood today," Josh said. "You're late, though."

"No, I'm not. I'm exactly on time." Ty held up his wrist and showed Josh his watch. "Scott always starts practice ten minutes early to shame those of us who arrive on time. Practice was scheduled to start at 1:30. It is now 1:28. So Scott can suck my dick."

"Tyler!" Scott shouted. "Get your ass over here."

Scott annoyed the hell out of Ty, but he knew what he was doing as far as coaching went. The Hipsters had recruited him as their manager three years before, and though he was a hardass, he'd also made all of them play better. Not that it even mattered, since the whole point of the league was to have fun, but winning was nice.

Mason came running toward the bench and threw his bag at it. It landed at Ty's feet.

"Shit, I'm late. Am I late?" Mason said, panting.

"Only if you also live in whatever Bizarro time zone Scott does."

Ty grinned at Mason, who was basically the Hipsters' secret weapon, an ex-Yankee who had quit the pros after a minor injury and then come out in spectacular fashion. He'd been a media sensation when he'd first joined the Rainbow League—the *Post* in particular had taken no small amount of glee in reporting his every move—but that had mostly died down now. *Post* readers had short attention spans, Ty supposed.

Mason yanked on his cleats with practiced efficiency, and then he and Ty jogged together over to where the rest of the team had gathered. Scott started shouting and led them through calisthenics. Ty regretted taking up position next to Mason, who was by far the better athlete. All of his movements were practiced and smooth. Ty felt like a jerky, ungainly beast and struggled to keep up. In between squats he glanced over at Ian, who, of course, was following along with Scott's dictates as if this were the easiest thing he'd done all day.

When that bullshit was over, Scott lined everyone up for batting practice. Ty held back for a moment so he could sneak into the line behind Ian.

"Hello," Ty said a little lasciviously.

Ian gave him a sly half smile in return. Oh, yeah. Ty felt pretty confident that Ian was into it. "So this Scott guy is kind of a slave driver, huh?" Ian said.

"Yeah. He's an asshole, but he's a good team manager. Before he came along, we mostly just came to practice as a pretense to get a beer afterward. Now we actually play baseball."

"A baseball team playing baseball. How novel."

"I know, right? Anyway, don't sweat it. Scott is all bluster. You whiff the bat over one of these pitches and he'll let it go. So don't beat yourself up if you miss."

"Who says I'll miss?"

"No one. Just—"

"New guy!" barked Scott.

"Guess I'm up next." Ian took the bat Nate held out for him and walked up to the plate. He hit the first pitch and the ball sailed over Scott's head and nearly beaned Carlos, who had been daydreaming in the outfield.

Of course.

Scott grinned. "All right, new guy. You can stay."

WHEN PRACTICE finally wrapped, Ian was bone-deep tired. If all practices went this way, he could cancel his gym membership.

Ty had flirted with him in his overbearing Texas way all through practice. Ian appreciated the attention but couldn't decide if he wanted to get involved with a guy like Ty. That they were teammates seemed sort of immaterial; Ian got the impression that a lot of his teammates were either dating each other or other guys in the league. Well, that or, like Josh, they were married to outsiders. Ian adored Josh's husband, but athletic he was not.

A few of the guys had plans after the game, so they left with a promise to see Ian at the first game, scheduled for that Tuesday evening. Even though his things were packed up, Ty lingered as if he were waiting for Ian. Which he probably was.

Ian did think Ty easy on the eyes. He was tall and broad, with a crazy amount of orangey-red hair. He was currently sporting a sort of scraggly chin-strap beard the same fiery color. He had an insane number of freckles on his face and arms and presumably the rest of his body, and okay, Ian was pretty curious about where else Ty had freckles. Ty had a broad chest that tapered to a narrow waist and a tight butt that seemed to invite Ian to squeeze it. Ian had a flash of the two of them in bed, Ty above him, Ian's legs wrapped around Ty, Ian's hand tightly squeezing that ass.

He coughed.

There was something sexy about the Texas twang too, about the slow, relaxed cadence to his voice. He had a lazy smile, he looked good even in sweats, and though the bad beard was a little bit of a problem, it was something easily overcome.

So what the hell was Ian's problem? Ty was hot and he was clearly interested in Ian, and hadn't Ian let Josh talk him into joining the team so he could meet new men? Hell, if he was going to be stuck in New York for the next while, he might as well make the most of it. There was not a single goddamn reason for Ian to resist Ty's advances.

And yet.

He tried not to freak out when Ty stepped into his personal space and casually tugged on the hem of his T-shirt, but the proximity jangled something inside Ian and the gesture disturbed him. It shouldn't have. That was the anxiety talking. He could do this. He'd been with plenty of men before, some even hotter than Ty—albeit not many—and he hadn't had a meltdown in those instances. He knew that being in a new place—sort of; he'd grown up in Brooklyn but hadn't actually lived in the greater New York metropolitan area in, what, fifteen years?—had him on edge, that he was jittery and anxious because he was still getting his bearings. Introducing chaos in the form of a new man, even one as attractive and charming as Ty, was not really something Ian could handle just then.

Ty said, "So there's this gay bar on Fifth Avenue."

"In Park Slope?"

Ty's grin went wry. "Don't sound so astonished. Didn't you grow up in Park Slope?"

"Yeah, but dude. When I was a kid, my mother wouldn't let me walk as far as Fifth Avenue because she was convinced I wouldn't come back."

"The neighborhood is pretty different now. Although it is just the one gay bar, and it's much more low-key than the places in the Village or Hell's Kitchen. Couples bring babies there."

Ian crinkled his nose. "Is this supposed to sell me on the place?"

"We can go somewhere else. I just figured that since we are both gay men and I'm trying to get into your pants, a gay bar might have the right vibe." Ty raised an eyebrow as if he were waiting for a response.

"Ty, listen—"

"Just come with me for a beer. Which train do you need to get home?"

"From here? Whatever goes to Atlantic so I can transfer. I live on the Upper West Side."

Ty frowned but then pasted the grin on again. "Hell, you could walk to Atlantic from this place. Come on."

And so Ian felt himself swept along with Ty and a few of the other guys from the team—Nate, Carlos, and Mason, if Ian was remembering everyone's names correctly, plus Josh—and they were walking west toward Fifth Avenue. As they walked, Mason said he liked the bar well enough, though it wasn't really the sort of place you went to pick someone up. "Too much domestic bliss in Park Slope these days."

"By that he means everyone is married with babies," Nate explained. "Even the gays."

"What is the world coming to?" said Ty.

Ian was curious about the relationship between Nate and Carlos but couldn't quite figure it out. They were flirty with each other and walked very close, but Carlos mentioned some guy named Aiden at least three times on the walk to the bar, so maybe they were just friends and not a couple.

"Look," Ty said, nudging Ian with his elbow. "I have made my intentions clear, but no pressure. Think of this little outing as team bonding. Okay? If you're not feeling it, I get it."

"It's not that I'm not feeling it." Ian couldn't think of how to explain himself without sounding insane. "We just met."

"Sure, okay."

"Trust me, I appreciate that you want to, uh, get in my pants. I just don't move that fast."

"Fair enough. Can't say I'm not disappointed, but I respect that."

Ty dropped the subject. They got to the bar a few minutes later. It must have just opened, because it was largely deserted. Their little party of six snagged a table and got prompt service from the beefy bartender, who paid extra attention to Ty.

Ian squirmed in his chair, uncomfortable for reasons he couldn't identify, until he realized that he had already begun to feel a little possessive of Ty. Just because he wasn't ready to sleep with Ty didn't mean he wanted someone else to snatch him up and close the door to the possibility. Fortunately, the bartender left to tend to his other customers and Ty's attention seemed to hone back in on Ian.

They spent a pleasant evening drinking and eating fatty bar food. As the beer seeped into Ian's bloodstream and warmed his tired bones, he felt looser, more relaxed, less like Ty's touch might throw him into a panic attack.

And, God, Ty. He just sat there with all that red hair and the freckles and the stupid beard and was happy and handsome and pretty damned fuckable, and Ian kept thinking that he sure as hell wanted to fuck Ty, except he also really didn't. Sex was invasive and messy—not just literally. Although, Christ, Ty doing something as stupid as licking salt from his fingers was enough to send Ian into some kind of aroused fugue state, where all he could see was the rough tip of Ty's tongue and his pretty pink lips, and what if instead of his finger, he was licking Ian's dick?

"But then, Ian always did have a stick up his ass," Josh said suddenly.

Ian turned toward Josh. "Huh?"

Josh rolled his eyes. "While you were off daydreaming, I was telling Nate and Carlos about that time in high school I tried to get the GSA to organize a protest because Mayor Giuliani had introduced some kind of plan for the city that we thought would be bad for the gays, and you didn't want to do it because you were terrified we'd get arrested."

"That would have been half the fun," said Nate.

"There was also the time we got fake IDs so we could go to gay bars," Josh went on, "but when the time came to actually go, Ian here bailed because he had homework."

Nate barked out a laugh. "I bet you were the life of the party in high school."

"I'm not that bad anymore." To Ty, Ian said, "Really. I was terrified of everything as a kid. I got over most of it."

"What is it you do, exactly?" Ty asked. "Professionally, I mean."

"Hotel management," Ian said.

"He's too modest," said Josh. "You all are looking at the most sought-after hotel consultant in the country."

"Hardly," said Ian. "Basically, I help out struggling hotels. I usually go find a hotel that's got some big problems, work there for a year or two to help them fix the problems and climb out of the hole, and then I move on to another hotel."

"Like that guy on TV who yells at everyone," Ty said.

"Yeah, kind of. Except he does the show, what, like over a weekend? You can't fix a hotel in danger of closing in three days."

"You must have to move a lot," said Mason.

Ian shrugged. "I like to travel. What about you guys? Surely you all do things that aren't just baseball. Even you, Mason."

Ian already knew Josh was an English teacher at a private school on the Upper East Side. Mason said, "I work for a sports website and report on stories about gay athletes."

Which made sense. Ian imagined a gay ex-Yankee would have feelings on the matter.

Nate explained that he worked for an educational software company and Carlos worked as a lawyer for a nonprofit.

"See, it takes all kinds to come play for the gay sports league," Josh concluded.

"I guess so," said Ian. "What about you, Ty?"

Ty shrugged. "Marketing."

"Really? What do you do in marketing?"

"Design stuff."

O-kay. Ian nodded and pretended he understood. As Mason launched into details about a profile of a gay Olympic swimmer he was working on, Ian stared at Ty and wondered why he'd suddenly gone from flirty to silent. Was he ashamed of his job?

Rather than try to unpack that, Ian filed it away for later. He didn't even want to ask if Ty was okay lest that send him further into whatever quiet place he was currently inhabiting. Instead, Ian waited until Mason cracked a joke and Ty laughed before really rejoining the conversation.

When the bar started getting crowded and the fatigue and drunkenness made Ian feel like he'd fall asleep at the table, he stood and said he should get going.

Ty stood as well. "Hey, I'll walk with you for a few blocks and point you toward the subway. Yeah?"

"Sure," Ian said.

They said good-bye to everyone and wandered outside. It was dark by then and cold enough to necessitate slipping on a jacket. Ian pulled on his hoodie, but Ty had just short sleeves. He rubbed his arms.

"Aren't you cold?" Ian asked. "You want my sweatshirt?" Not that it would have fit, as Ty was quite a bit broader than Ian, but it seemed polite to offer.

"I'll survive. I don't live far from here." Ty pointed up Fifth Avenue. "I'll walk up to Park, but then I gotta turn and head home. Really, all you have to do is keep walking up Fifth and then you'll see the Barclays Center, plain as day and twice as ugly. The subway's right there."

"Okay. Thanks."

"And I just wanted to say, you know, offer still stands if you decide I'm not totally heinous and you might like a roll in the hay."

"I don't think you're heinous. I'm just...." Ian laughed. "I haven't really outgrown my uptight phase as much as I'd like to believe, I guess."

Ty laughed too. "I feel you. Just, I'm lusting pretty hard here. Don't keep me waiting too long."

Ian smiled and briefly touched Ty's hand. "When I get over myself, you'll be the first to know."

Chapter 3

THERE'D BEEN a time in young Ian's life when he'd come home from school, put a tape in his Walkman, and crank the volume up until it felt like the music was playing directly from a speaker in his brain. He'd unroll the liner notes from the album and read all lyrics carefully, as if the meaning of life were hidden somewhere in all those words. He listened to a lot of mopey songs in those days; he was a total sucker for the token slow song on the otherwise slamming hard-rock album.

He hadn't understood much as a kid. He'd figured out fairly early on that there was something not quite right about himself. When he was really young, he'd been picked on quite a bit, which he took as evidence he didn't belong. He was quiet and studious, though not shy as such. In fact, he had no problem offering his opinion in the rare moments when he had one; he just didn't have much was worth saying out loud most of the time. His father had given him a hard time for being so quiet and delicate, and though Ian knew better now, when he was a teenager, he viewed that as a character flaw in himself.

Ian had played baseball to prove to his father he was "normal," even if normal was something he never really felt or understood. He came out to his high school classmates. He found a small amount of acceptance, a balm to the unease that never quite went away. But he was too afraid to date. Even when boys showed interest, he begged off. It was too terrifying. What if sex hurt? What if he got a disease? No matter how hard he pined or how much he longed, it was easier to keep everything as it had always had been. He didn't want to do anything that could mess up the life he was building for himself, least of all the escape hatch called college.

So even though he'd come a long way since then—he'd had a number of boyfriends, and he'd had sex in basically every position he'd been able to imagine—it was still really hard to let go of his need to maintain control and order. And nothing invited more disorder than sex, in Ian's experience.

He hated that he thought about this instead of his work all Tuesday afternoon. He spent most of the day in his office at the New Amsterdam Hotel, a once luxurious hotel that was in a horrendous state of disrepair thanks to neglect and bad management. The new owners had offered him a very large sum of money to turn the hotel around, but it was going to be an uphill battle. He'd earn his exorbitant salary, for sure.

If he could get his head out of his ass.

It wouldn't be happening that day. The closer it got to game time, the more Ty dominated his thoughts, to the point where Ian was almost convinced he should just go through with it and fuck Ty to get him out of his system. Did that even really work? Sure, maybe the sex would be terrible and then Ian could dismiss the whole problem and move on with his life, but what if it was good?

By the time he got on the subway going downtown, he was a frazzled, panicky mess, not liking the turn his life had taken. Curse Josh for making him think he could step so far out of his comfort zone.

Still, he liked his teammates. He liked Ty, which was why he was tying himself in knots over a stupid baseball game. He imagined that most of those teammates he liked were focused on whether they would win the game and not whether they would sleep with the second baseman.

He got to East River Park about fifteen minutes before the game was supposed to start, and most of his teammates were already there, Ty included. Ian debated the relative merits of avoiding Ty until he had his head screwed on straight or just saying hi and getting it over with.

Ty solved the problem for him by approaching before he got all the way to the bench where everyone was congregating. "Hi, there," Ty drawled, sounding like John Wayne.

"Hi. We ready to play this game?"

"Not at all. The Hell's Kitchen team was the best in the league last season, and we will very likely get our asses handed to us. But welcome to the league." Ty put his hands on his waist and grinned. He looked pretty good in the team uniform: crisp gray baseball pants and the purple T-shirt that designated their team. The team name was scripted in white above the team logo: a drawing of thick-rimmed glasses and a beard. "Hipsters, geddit?" Josh had said when he'd handed Ian his T-shirt the week before. Each shirt had the player's last name and a number on the back. So the shirts were silly, but Ty made it look good, the fabric stretching across his pecs, the sleeves straining against the muscles of his arms.

"Can you turn around?" Ian asked.

Ty tilted his head quizzically but obliged. And, yup, the view was just as good from the back. Man alive, but Ty had a great ass.

"Thanks," said Ian.

"Checking out the merchandise?" Ty asked.

"Working up the courage to invite you back to my place later."

Ty turned back around and grinned. He had a spectacular smile—straight white teeth, nice lips, little crinkles on the sides of his eyes. "I knew you'd come around."

"Still working myself up to it."

Ty nodded. "You're kind of neurotic."

"I'm aware."

"I dig that. It's cute. And kind of a challenge. I usually don't have to work so hard to get laid."

Ian laughed. "Let me guess. You just walk into a bar and smile, and men come running."

Ty shrugged. "More or less."

"Let's play ball, okay?"

"If that's a double entendre, I think this will be a very fun night."

"It wasn't, but so noted."

The Hipsters were at bat first. The pitcher for the Hell's Kitchen Devil Gays, a guy called Jake, threw like he belonged in the majors, and only Mason was able to get anywhere close to hitting the ball, and even then, he hit it foul. By contrast, Nate let Hell's Kitchen get three hits and a run on his watch. The rest of the game went much the same way, with the Hipsters working their asses off to hit the ball and keep Hell's Kitchen from getting runs, but the game finally, mercifully ended two hours later with a score of 6–1.

Through the whole game, Ty flirted, Ian attempted to flirt back, and their teammates gave them a hard time. "Ty's all sweet talk," Nate confided. "Don't fall for it."

"No, I know what I'm getting into." The first thing Ty had said to Ian was that he was the team slut, right?

"Okay, just making sure. Ty's usually pretty good about only going after guys on opposing teams, so you know."

Ian understood that to mean that Nate didn't want anything Ty and Ian did to mess up the team. Ian wanted to assure Nate that it wouldn't, but he didn't think he could keep that promise.

The game wrapped, and they shook hands with their opponents, though some team members gave hugs instead of handshakes. It was clear that a lot of these guys knew each other well and had played together for years. It highlighted how much Ian was the new guy.

But then they walked over to Avenue B. Barnstorm looked like a fairly traditional pub on the outside, even with the rainbow flags hanging from the awning. A sign on the door said "Closed for Private Event," but judging by how the Rainbow League players plowed on inside, Ian guessed it was closed for them.

A bear of a man held court behind the bar and greeted everyone amiably as they walked inside. He had graying hair and a round belly and looked to be in his fifties. "That's Tom," Ty explained. "He's owned this bar for about a million years. Or, well, since the nineties, I guess. His lover died of AIDS almost twenty years ago and left him a pile of money, so he used it to open this place. He donates a chunk of his profits to an AIDS charity."

"Oh, that's...." Ian had no idea how to react to that. "I mean, that sucks about his lover, but it's nice that some good came from it."

"Tom is the best guy," Ty said. "Total sweetheart. He offers the space to us for free three nights a week—in exchange for us buying enough booze to drink ourselves silly, of course."

"It's a nice space," Ian said, and it was. Wood paneling covered most of the walls, but the lighting was warm and welcoming. Photos hung all over the walls, mostly of historic athletes, and one entire wall was dedicated to the Rainbow League, including framed T-shirts.

"Those are retired numbers," Ty explained. "When a player we all like has to leave for whatever reason—he moves or gets injured or whatever—we retire his number and hang it on the wall."

"Only players you like?"

"Well, yeah. Why would we celebrate guys we don't like?"

Ian laughed. "I enjoy the strange nihilism in this league. Sometimes it seems like there are no rules."

"Come on." Ty playfully hit Ian's arm. "It's a hobby league. We all do this entirely for fun. I'm pretty sure some of these guys only play the game to hang out at the bar afterward. None of us ever expected to play baseball professionally. Well, except Mason. Poor guy."

Ian glanced over at Mason, who was talking to Tom and laughing at something. Mason intrigued Ian. Here was a tall, muscular, super masculine black man who Ian supposed could look intimidating if you didn't know him—Ian had come to see that he was a friendly, jovial guy who would never intentionally hurt anyone—who had played for the goddamn New York Yankees. Ian remembered reading about Mason in the news when he came out, and had a lot of admiration for the man.

What a weird world he had stumbled into.

TY FOLLOWED Ian over to the bar, where they each ordered a beer and settled into a stool. Ty was feeling like this evening would go the way he wanted it to go—either he'd work his way into Ian's apartment uptown or he'd talk Ian into coming with him to Brooklyn—but Ian was awfully skittish. It made Ty doubt that pursuing something with Ian was really worth it. Ian was hot, but did Ty really want to be with someone that neurotic?

Would it mean Ian was a tiger in bed?

Ty hated wrestling with this decision. Because Ian had the blond hair and the square jaw and the long torso and the little butt, and Ty had been fantasizing pretty much all day about getting Ian out of his clothes and making him scream with delight instead of clenching like he was right now.

"So that was a game," Ian said.

"Yeah. We don't usually lose that badly. But Will is crazy competitive and his whole team has become infected with the same spirit somehow. Not that it even matters. This is all so low stakes."

"You care, though."

"Sure, a little. Winning is fun. But losing doesn't affect anything except whether or not you play a few extra games at the end of the season."

Ian nodded. "So what made you get involved with the league?"

It was a good question. He couldn't remember exactly. "I know Tony through work. You know Josh's husband, right?"

"I do, yes."

"We did a project together a few years ago. There was a big fancy lunch when the project wrapped and we were just making small talk. I mentioned I was looking for ways to stay in shape but that I hated my gym, and Tony goes, 'My husband is involved in this LGBT sports league.' Now, up to that time, I didn't even know Tony was gay and I don't know how he knew I'm gay, but either way, I told him to give me the information. He did me one better and invited me over to his and Josh's house for dinner. And Josh, well, he and I just clicked in a weird way. Not in a sexy way. He's like the brother I never had. We've been friends ever since. So I joined his baseball team."

"Plus, you use the league to meet men."

Ty shrugged. "Sure, that's a benefit." When Ian squirmed a little, Ty asked, "Does that bother you?" Then he lowered his voice. "You jealous?"

"I… maybe. You're really hot."

Ty laughed. "I like you, Ian."

"Because I stroked your ego?"

"I'd like you to stroke some other things. And I'd like to stroke some things of yours."

Ian's eyes went wide. He was still nervous, Ty supposed, and showing a lot of evidence that he was an anxious mess on the inside. Ball was in Ian's court, Ty figured. Ty had made his intentions clear.

"So, what about you?" Ty asked, hoping to allay some of the concern that seemed to have sprouted up in Ian. "Why did you join? Don't tell me it's because you expected each game to end in an orgy."

Ian laughed, which was nice. His whole face changed when he smiled or laughed. He looked much brighter, and even handsomer. Ty decided right then to figure out how to make Ian laugh more often.

"Josh used potential hookups as his argument for why I should join, but honestly? I just moved back to New York after fifteen years away. I don't really know anyone save for a handful of people who are either former colleagues or people I went to high school with. I just wanted to meet people generally. At first I thought the baseball league sounded a little, uh, out of my league, so to speak." He paused to let Ty acknowledge that, so Ty smiled and nodded. "But the more I thought about it, the more I figured, well, here is a large group of gay people. These are my people. There's none of that same awkwardness while you figure out if the crowd is friendly or hostile. So I thought, sure, maybe I could find someone to hook up with, but more likely, I'll make friends. Right?"

"Yeah. And to be fair, tales of my exploits are a little exaggerated. I'm not actually as big of a slut as I pretend to be. I do like to flirt, though."

"But you have had sex with other league members."

"Sure, a few. This is a social group. I'm just being sociable."

Ian nodded and took a sip of his beer. "So is that what you're doing with me? Just being sociable?"

"If you like."

"I don't mind the extra attention," Ian said.

"So how do you know Josh?" Ty asked, fishing for a conversation topic. "High school, right?"

"Yeah. We both went to Stuyvesant. That's the public school for overachievers."

"I know."

"Well, anyway, as you may have guessed, I was a nervous kid in high school. I found my people in high school, but I had a hard time making friends. Then one day, right around the time I started coming out to my friends, this awkward kid with big glasses handed me a flyer and told me to come to a meeting of the Gay-Straight Alliance. That was Josh."

Ty laughed. "I'd pay good money to see that yearbook picture."

Ian laughed too. "Yeah. He grew out of the awkwardness for the most part. But he was always Josh, so he'd of course taken over the GSA and bossed us all around even more than he does now. I had already moved out of New York by the time he met Tony, but Josh and I never dated or anything either. We never had that kind of relationship." Ian looked off at something in the distance. "It was nice to have an ally back then. I had a rough adolescence."

Ty lifted his beer glass in a toast. "Didn't we all."

Ian raised an eyebrow. "Really? I was the quiet guy in the corner nobody noticed until I was on the baseball field. You're so handsome and outgoing, I'm sure you did fine in high school."

Ty shrugged, not wanting to get into it. "I had my problems too. I didn't always have all this." He waved his hand over himself.

"Sure."

Ty grinned. "Are you enjoying being back in New York, at least?"

"Eh." Ian shook his head. "It's fine. I like this hotel. I mean, the owners are deeply misguided about the best ways to run a business, but I like the challenge of fixing it. When I'm done, this will be a place with rooms tourists fight over."

"I couldn't do it. Go to a business like that every day, I mean. I freelance because I hated how cutthroat working for a big company could be."

"Did you work for a big advertising firm or something?"

"Publishing company, when I first got out of college. I worked in the art department. Hated every minute. I'm much happier now that I keep my own hours and have some discretion over which projects I take."

Ian leaned forward and smiled. "That's interesting. And see? We're actually getting to know each other."

"Who would have thought?" Ty leaned close too. "I do really like you. I want to have fun, but this is not just a conquest. Just so you know." Ty meant it. The more time he spent with Ian, the more he liked the man.

"Okay. Thanks, I think."

Ty looked at Ian's face, met his eyes, and let his gaze trail down Ian's long nose to his pouty lips. His lips looked pale and soft. Ty imagined them swollen and bruised after a lot of kissing, or trailing kisses down the center of his chest to his....

Ty laughed at himself softly. "I want to kiss you, but I don't want everyone to see. Because then it will become a thing."

"Better save it, then," Ian said. He lowered his eyelids.

Dear Lord. Ian could kill Ty with a look like that. Ty's skin got all tingly just imagining how Ian would look in bed, what it would feel like to slide up against him. And with that, Ty was hard, uncomfortably so, though his uniform concealed his erection.

"Uh, give me a sec," Ty said. "Sit tight. I gotta go use the little boys' room."

Ian nodded, so Ty slid off the stool and went to the men's room at the back of the bar. He examined his reflection. He cursed his genes; his pale face had gone beet-red and the skin on his body was flushed and blotchy with arousal. He splashed cold water on his face, spent a minute thinking very unsexy thoughts, and then relieved himself. He was feeling relatively back to normal when the door opened and Ian strolled in.

"Before I lose my nerve," Ian said.

Ian backed Ty against the wall between the urinals and cupped his face in his hands. It took Ty a moment to get his bearings. Then Ian kissed Ty.

And *pow*! All of that arousal came back with a vengeance. The moment Ian's body came into proximity with Ty's, Ty's whole being went on red alert. He pushed forward a little, pressing his lips against Ian's delightfully soft ones and licking into his mouth while at the same time grasping at Ian's waist and pulling their hips together. He couldn't feel much between the layers of uniform, but he imagined Ian was just as hard as he was. Ian groaned and thrust his tongue into Ty's mouth, which gratified Ty.

Shit, this was hot.

Ty ran his hands up Ian's back, pressing his palms into Ian's hot skin through his T-shirt. He grasped at Ian's shoulder blades to keep Ian in place so he could keep exploring that mouth. Ian tasted of beer, sure, but he had that masculine metallic taste too, and really, Ty could do this all night.

But then Ian pulled away slightly. He was panting as he did it. "Sorry, needed to breathe."

"Not a problem. That was a hell of a kiss."

Ian nodded, still out of breath. "I thought it might be."

"So take me home. Tell the little voices in your head to take the night off and just have a night of crazy fun sexy times with me. I have no doubt that we'd be great together."

"Ha." Ian was all flushed too, though with arousal or embarrassment, it was hard to say. "You think we're sexually compatible? I don't even know if you're—"

"I'm a switch hitter, baby. I'll be anything you want. Top, bottom, upside down, anything. As long as you're there, I'll be good."

Ian laughed. "Okay. I… okay. Let's go, then."

Chapter 4

THEY GOT a cab because the thought of having to wait for the subway made Ian want to crawl out of his skin.

He'd already run through all the scenarios in his head. He couldn't go to Brooklyn because he had to work in the morning. Ty seemed to work indeterminate hours and said it was no big deal when he got home the next day. So obviously Ian's place was the best, but for the fact that he still wasn't entirely unpacked and he hadn't planned for company when he'd left that morning and he'd probably left the bed unmade and….

"Slow down there, tiger," Ty said in the cab, putting his big hand on Ian's knee. "I don't know what's going on in that head of yours, but I can pretty much see a hamster on a wheel behind your eyes. Whatever you're fretting about is no big deal."

"How can you know that?"

"Well, I assume you're fretting about me." Ty moved away and leaned against the seat. He set his hands behind his head, looking as relaxed as one could be in the back of a cab. "I ain't nothing to fret about. I'm easy, remember?"

"You know that your accent gets more pronounced when you've had some booze?"

Ty grinned. "Some people find the Texas sexy."

Ian raised an eyebrow, trying to convey that he was not one of those people, even though he totally was. "All right, Tex. Where are you from, exactly?"

"Just outside Dallas. Not even the cool part of Texas." Ty laughed softly. "Soon as I could, I ran to New York City. My little backwoods hometown is no place for a slutty gay boy."

Ian laughed. "Didn't you just tell me you weren't as slutty as your reputation would have it?"

"Well, sure, but I'm still pretty easy."

"Uh-huh. Of course you are."

"That sounds like a dare."

The words were almost comical in Ty's slow drawl. *That sahnds lahk a da-yer.* Ian leaned a little closer, hoping some of Ty's confidence would rub off on him. He wasn't at all sure he'd made the right decision; his heart was racing, his pulse was pounding, and he was a little dizzy with anticipation.

God, when was the last time he'd had sex? About a year ago with Jean-Pierre, probably. That had been one of Ian's less advisable decisions, getting involved with a fancy French man while in Paris on business. Oh, he'd liked Jean-Pierre plenty, and the man was gorgeous and smelled like cigars and magic, but he was also quite liberal when it came to his definition of "relationship." And one thankfully curable STI later, Ian had been done with all that.

Was it any wonder this situation made him anxious?

But he fought through it and leaned closer to Ty, a man he wanted badly, with a longing deep in his chest. He put a hand on Ty's thigh.

"That's more like it, babe," Ty said with a smirk. "You finally loosening up?"

"No. Am I faking it successfully?"

Ty barked out a laugh. "Sure you are."

Ian took a deep breath. "You may have picked up on the fact that I have a generalized anxiety disorder."

"I had a hunch."

"Most of the time I'm fine, but doing things outside of my admittedly narrow comfort zone can send me away on the first direct train to Crazytown. So I apologize in advance if I do something insane."

"Like OCD?"

"No, it's not that severe. I really am fine most of the time. But this?" Ian gestured between them with his finger. "This makes me a little nervous."

Ty nodded. "I appreciate your honesty. I hope I don't do anything to justify your pending nervous breakdown."

Something about the flippant way Ty said that went a long way toward disarming Ian, or at least pushing the anxiety aside. "Thanks, Ty."

The cabbie had spent the entirety of the cab ride speaking into his hands-free earpiece in some language that seemed to include words that all rolled into each other. Arabic, maybe, or Farsi, but Ian didn't know. That was good, because the cabbie was completely oblivious to anything going on in the backseat. He was so oblivious, in fact, that he blew right past the turn onto Ian's street.

"Hey," Ian shouted at the cabbie. "Eighty-Fourth."

"You say Eighty-Six!" said the cabbie.

"I live on Eighty-Fourth."

A fairly dramatic U-turn on Broadway and a jerky drive down Eighty-Fourth Street later and Ian was standing in the lobby of his building with Ty, pausing to wonder if he should get his mail while he was in the lobby. Then he realized he was being ridiculous, so he grabbed Ty's hand, waved at Armand the doorman, and pulled Ty to the elevator.

Once the elevator door closed, Ian laid a hell of a kiss on Ty. Ty grunted and put his hands on Ian's arms, and then grabbed him and pushed him against the wall. The bar that ran around the perimeter of the elevator pressed into Ian's back, but he didn't care. He thrust his fingers into Ty's fiery red hair and kissed and kissed him.

The elevator doors dinged, pulling Ian out of his lust-fueled haze. He fished his keys out of his gym bag as he led Ty down the hall. He hurried to unlock his door so that he could go back to kissing Ty as soon as possible.

Once inside, Ty and Ian dropped their bags just inside the door. Ty put his hands on Ian's face before pulling him in for another kiss. The kiss was hot, scorching, amazing, all smooth lips and tongues tasting. The texture was remarkable, the roughness of Ty's tongue and the stubble on his face mixed with the smoothness of his lips, and the sensation of having Ty near him sent Ian's blood rushing through his body.

"I'm sure this is a nice place you got," Ty mumbled into Ian's lips.

"Bedroom's to the left."

"Mmm. Lead me?"

It wasn't until they were crashing over the threshold to Ian's bedroom, less a few clothes, that Ian realized with a start, "I don't have any condoms here."

That seemed to bring up Ty short. He jerked away slightly. "Oh. Well, okay. Doesn't mean we can't do other things."

"I'm sorry. I wasn't expecting—"

"It's fine. Anal is not the be-all, end-all. I have a few other tricks up my sleeve."

Ian couldn't believe he'd arrived at this moment. Ty was so present and sexy and they were really going to do this. Ian tried to keep his demeanor relaxed, but his heart was pounding. From nerves or arousal, it was hard to say.

He focused on a spot on Ty's chest, bared now because he'd tossed his team T-shirt somewhere in the hallway outside the bedroom. Ty had a fair amount of fiery red hair there that was like a fuzzy orange cloud. Ian reached over to touch it, wanting to know what it felt like.

"It's okay, you know," Ty said, putting his hand over Ian's and holding it near his heart, which was pounding beneath Ian's palm. "I know you're nervous. It's okay to be nervous. I'm a little nervous too. But I'm also really excited because you're hot and I like you and I've got a hard-on like you wouldn't believe because it's been, like, two weeks since I've gotten naked with anyone, and my hand, while an attentive and patient lover, is not quite the same thing."

Despite everything, Ian laughed.

"There it is," Ty said with a grin.

"Two whole weeks you've gone without sex? Poor baby."

"I know. I don't know how to even cope with that."

Ian liked the breezy, jokey Ty, so he leaned in and kissed him, and as their lips slid together and Ian tangled his fingers in all that crazy red chest hair, Ian fell into it, forgetting why he was nervous and enjoying being in the presence of an attractive man whom he wanted badly. Ty slid his hand around Ian's waist to his ass and gave it a little squeeze.

"I'll tell ya," Ty said, breaking off the kiss to nibble on Ian's neck, "I gotta get out of the jock situation downstairs or I'm gonna break my dick."

Ian laughed again, and each burst of laughter that broke out of him relaxed him more. As he relaxed, he grew more confident, more willing to take an active role, happier and less nervous about taking what he wanted. He slid his hand down Ty's chest and hooked his fingers into the waist of Ty's pants. "Here," he said, feeling bold. "Let me help you with that."

In one quick motion, Ian pulled Ty's uniform pants and jock strap down to his knees, and Ty groaned. Ian knelt on the floor and took a moment to admire Ty's cock. That same fiery red hair, denser and a little darker, framed a nice, quite substantial cock. Ian salivated a little as he looked at it. He reached over and put a hand around the base.

Ty grunted and thrust his hips forward. "Don't tease me, man. I've been hard since the cab."

So Ian, feeling more brave than he usually did, licked the tip. Ty let out a frustrated moan.

Laughing again, Ian stood and pulled off his own pants and underwear. It took some deft maneuvering, but he made quick work of the rest of his clothes, kicking his sneakers aside and sliding off his socks too.

Ty followed suit and freed his ankles from the tangle of pants. Then the two of them stood there, each taking in the other.

"That's... wow," Ty said. "Definitely naturally blond, then."

"I don't think this dishwater color comes in a bottle."

Ty smiled. "I like it anyway. Come here."

Ty kissed Ian hard and brought their bodies together. He hooked his hands around Ian's sides and pulled until their hips touched. They were close enough in height that their cocks brushed together, and then, with a little thrusting on Ty's part, they pressed against each other. Ian dug his fingers into Ty's shoulders and groaned, loving that sensation of finally getting some texture and friction on his now aching cock. Ian's head spun.

"Bed," Ty mumbled against Ian's lips.

So they tumbled onto the bed, tangling their limbs together and rolling around, grabbing whatever flesh they could reach. Ian's nerves disappeared as he stopped thinking and arousal took hold and made his blood rush and his skin scream. Suddenly nothing much mattered but Ty and getting some good friction against his dick.

"I want to come," Ian mumbled.

"I'm on it," said Ty, who reached between them and wrapped his hand around both of their cocks.

Ian arched off the bed, moaning as he finally got what he wanted. Ty's hand was warm and rough, and he kept brushing his thumb over the head of Ian's cock, and it was delicious. Some combination of sweat and precum was helping lubricate things, and Ian didn't want to think about that too hard, nor the mess he'd have to clean up later, even though that thought was hovering around him. No, he just wanted to get off, he wanted to taste and smell and feel Ty, and he wanted Ty to get off too.

"There it is," Ty murmured, thrusting against Ian and squeezing. Ian wriggled his hand between them and started stroking too, tried to ramp things up and get there faster while also wanting it to last. He bit his lip.

"Man, that's.... Christ, I'm gonna come," Ty said.

"Do it. Come all over me."

"I...."

And then Ty sighed and vibrated and came against Ian's hand. His face when that happened was a picture of ecstasy, his brow furrowing before his whole body relaxed. Ian thrust his hips up, kissed Ty, and then the orgasm seemed to burst out of him. He came hot and sticky between them, just as Ty had. His mind went completely, gloriously blank.

He didn't think about the mess until a good five minutes later.

TY WASN'T quite sure what he had here.

He could see Ian struggle not to get too wiggy, acting at being casual even though the way he turned red indicated he wasn't. He kept running to the bathroom and coming back, and he wiped them both off with a wet washcloth and still didn't seem satisfied. When he made his third trip down the hall and back, Ty settled against the headboard and said, "Whoa, there, sailor, slow it down."

"I know. I'm sorry. I just started picturing jizz on my comforter and what if it made a stain and then I'd have to take it to the dry cleaner but I could never explain it. I'd just be all 'I have no idea how that got there,' but of course they would know. And that little Chinese woman who works the counter there, she already kind of has my number, and—"

"Ian?"

"What?"

"Will you sit on this bed?"

"Oh. Yeah. Sorry."

Not OCD. A generalized anxiety disorder. It sounded like a lot of hooey, but for the fact that Ian clearly had a hard time relaxing. That much was obvious. And he really did buzz sometimes like the Chihuahua Josh had once compared him to. As he sat on the bed, he even shook a little, like Chihuahuas did in their resting states.

When Ian settled, sort of, Ty put his arm around his shoulders. He pulled Ian close. Ian came willingly and put his hand on Ty's belly.

"God, I love this hair," Ian said. He played with the fuzzy hair on Ty's chest.

"Aw, thanks, baby." Distractions helped calm him down, then. Ty reasoned it was probably a bad idea to leave Ian alone too long. "You're pretty great, you know? I think I saw the secrets of the universe just now."

"That's an exaggeration."

"Dude, take a compliment. I like you. I think we're pretty hot together." Ty hoped this talk quieted whatever nonsense was racing through poor Ian's head. Because Ian was clearly coming unglued.

"Thanks," Ian said.

They didn't talk for a few minutes, just sat together in companionable silence as Ty held Ian and Ian traced lines around Ty's chest. Ty looked down and watched Ian's long, graceful fingers dance around with his chest hair. It wasn't that Ty was self-conscious, per se, but he'd never seen the big deal about being a redhead. If anything, it caused a lot of weird angst. There hadn't been a redhead on either side of Ty's family in a couple of generations, and Ty's father had joked with his mother about it so much that Ty had spent a portion of his childhood convinced his mother really *had* had that affair with the milkman. That it turned out Ty's paternal great-grandmother had once been a fiery redhead didn't do much to quash Ty's worry that he was a disappointment to his father.

Ty had, of course, turned out not just to have flaming red hair but also to be a flaming faggot, and that Ty's father definitely would not have appreciated, had he lived. As it was, he'd died when Ty was in college.

But happier things. Ty looked down at Ian, who seemed frankly fascinated by all the hair.

"You're kind of a bear," Ian said.

"Sure," said Ty.

Ian tugged on a handful of Ty's pubic hair.

Ian was mostly devoid of hair. What he had was nearly invisible. The guy was so blond, and he was so pale, the hair mostly blended in with his skin. Ty liked it and liked the surprising texture of Ian's body, which looked smooth but had rough patches. And Ian, once he'd let go of the nerves, had proven to have a great deal of potential in the lover department. Ty intended to continue coaxing Ian away from those nerves. For one thing, he wanted the chance to fuck Ian, who had a nice round little ass. Ty could easily picture his cock sliding in and out between those cheeks....

Ty coughed.

"What?" Ian asked.

"I was having lascivious thoughts. Alas, the disadvantage to being over thirty is that my body does not want to cooperate."

"What kind of lascivious thoughts?" There was a delightfully provocative edge to Ian's voice.

Ty laughed. "I'd like to fuck you. Not tonight, but eventually. Is that even in your wheelhouse? Can we make something like that happen?"

"Yeah," Ian said. "I'm not a virgin. I like to top too."

"Okay. Just checking. If you get wiggy over a little frottage, I just wondered what else might ping your crazy places."

That clearly pissed Ian off. He jerked out of Ty's arms and sat back a little.

"Hey, sorry," Ty said. "No offense. I was just trying to figure out where the boundaries are. I didn't mean to piss you off. I'm not even mad or judgmental. I want to have sex with you still. Again. More. A lot."

Ian sighed and rubbed his forehead. "Sorry, I guess I'm feeling defensive."

"Don't. You have nothing to feel self-conscious about. You're great. I promise I'm not just saying that."

"Great, sure. Also neurotic."

"We all are in some way."

Ian took a deep breath. "So, um, you want to stick around? Maybe try that again when we've sufficiently recovered?"

"Oh, babe. I thought you'd boot me to the curb. Can I stay?"

"You can stay as long as you want."

"Good." Ty kissed Ian's nose. He wanted to stay. He certainly wasn't done here yet.

Chapter 5

IAN LOOKED around the practice field. Nate sat on the grass, stretching out his calves. Behind him, Carlos and Mason were tossing a ball back and forth. Mason was clearly better at throwing; each of his pitches made a satisfying *thwok* sound as it hit Carlos's glove. Carlos wasn't quite as deft. He could throw the ball pretty well and had an easy grace, but he didn't have the same reliable precision, and a few of his throws went wide. Mason had to stretch to catch those.

Nate stood and did a few different stretches, but he looked stiff.

"It might help to run," Ian said.

"Yeah, thanks. Want to do a lap with me? Jogging, though. I don't run that fast."

"Sure," said Ian.

So Nate led his new teammate in a lap around the Prospect Park ball fields. Ian wasn't particularly interested in talking, but he didn't know the best route around the fields, either, so Nate kept having to tell him to turn or pivot to avoid obstacles. Ian stumbled a couple of times but kept a steadier pace than Nate, who was a bit out of breath at the halfway mark.

Ian was a little tight too, but as they ran, his muscles loosened up. Ian spared a glance for Carlos and Mason, still playing catch while they waited for an uncharacteristically late Scott. Scott wasn't even actually late yet, but everyone had figured out to get to the practices fifteen minutes early to avoid his wrath.

"So you and Ty, huh?" Nate asked when they were about halfway around the perimeter.

"Ugh, is the word out everywhere already?"

"I saw you guys flirting at the bar on Tuesday, and then you left together, so I figured…." Nate made a rolling motion with his hand, likely to indicate he figured the inevitable had happened.

"I think it might be a short-lived thing. We're not that compatible. And Ty is kind of a…." Ian held up his hand for Nate to fill in the blank.

"Man whore?" Nate supplied, a bit out of breath.

Ian laughed in a breathless, choked way. "Sure. I mean, I'm not even in New York long-term, so whatever. We had a good time. I don't know that anything will come of it."

They jogged a little farther; then Nate said conversationally, "There's a hot couple every season. I'd been expecting ours to be Carlos and Aiden."

"Aiden?"

"Third baseman for the Queens. Carlos has a wicked crush on him." Nate let out a shaky breath before inhaling again sharply. "Aiden hasn't made a move yet, but we're playing the Queens this week, and he's convinced something is going to happen. I was like, 'Are we in high school again?' It's one of *those* crushes, you know?"

Ian couldn't get a read on how Nate really felt about this situation. "Ty said you and Carlos played Little League together?"

"Yeah." Nate panted a bit. "We've been friends since we were knee-high, you know? He's like family."

"That's cool."

"Yeah. He's a little pissy with me now. Aiden's kind of a dick, if you ask me, and I told Carlos that. Probably I shouldn't have." Nate panted again. Ian slowed down his pace. Once Nate caught his breath again, he said, "I mean, not to be immature about it, but I don't really see what's so great about him. His neck is too wide for his head, so he just looks like a big brick. His hair is always a disaster, like he doesn't own a comb. I mean, I guess he's all-right-looking if you squint."

So Nate was jealous, in other words.

"There's a rock there, look out," Nate said. Then he immediately took a step too hard and stumbled.

When he recovered, Ian said, "Uh, you okay?"

"Yeah. Mind wandered and I wasn't paying attention."

"I know how that goes," Ian said, out of breath himself now.

Up ahead, Scott strolled onto the field. He gestured as if all of his team members would come running, and given that Nate and Ian were on a trajectory straight to Scott, perhaps there was something to that. They reached the ball field where the Hipsters had assembled to practice just as Scott started pushing everyone into lines for calisthenics.

The warm-up exercises went about the way they always went, with about half the team able to keep up with Scott's demands and the other half struggling while Scott pretended not to see that. That was one thing Ian would give Scott. He was tough, but he never belittled the players who couldn't do his insane workout. "Somewhere deep in his black soul, Scott understands that we're all there to have fun," Ty had said. From what Ian could tell, Scott didn't have a sense of humor to speak of, and he had a way of talking that made him sound condescending even when he was complimenting you, but deep down he was a good guy.

They got ready to practice. Scott appointed Nate pitcher, so he walked to the mound. He tossed a ball in the air and caught it a few times. Ty was up first in the batting practice order. He had a cocky grin on his face.

"All right, Tyler," Scott said. "You keep slicing the ball to the left. You gotta try to hit it dead-on. Nate here is a good pitcher and will throw a fastball right at you to start. Don't tilt the bat so far in your stance. Yeah, that's it. Straighten it out."

Ty nodded, grunted, and dug the ball of his left foot a little deeper into the sand at home plate. Nate paused, perhaps waiting to see if Ty would revert to his old stance. After a long pause, Nate threw the ball.

Ty hit it. It sailed through the air in a beautiful arc and then came down again. Right into Nate's glove.

"You hit it straight that time," said Scott.

Ty grumbled something nonsensical and then said, "Sure."

"Next."

Nate went through the whole batting order, lobbing easy pitches and getting everyone's confidence up. Carlos came up to bat and took a couple of swings while he waited for Nate to wind up.

On the mound, Nate stared out into space.

"Nate, dude, look alive," said Scott.

Nate nodded and wound up. He threw the ball toward Carlos, who whiffed right over it.

"Carlos! Pay attention!" barked Scott. "Again, Nate."

The interpersonal relationships of his teammates interested Ian insofar as these were new people he was becoming friendly with, but he sensed there was more drama in the Nate-Carlos-Aiden triangle than he really wanted to get near. But Ian liked Nate and thought he'd be a fun guy to hang around with. Not in a romantic way—Ian had enough on his hands with Ty—but as a friend. Ian could probably use more friends. Maybe his mother was right. Damn it.

Carlos whiffed another pitch. "Again, Nate," said Scott.

Nate threw the ball again, and Carlos managed to connect with it. The ball hit his bat with a satisfying *klok*, and it sailed right over Nate's head and into the outfield.

"Finally, Carlos," Scott said. "Next!"

After practice, as Nate iced his arm, Ian walked up to him. "Hey," he said.

"Hi," said Nate.

"Look, I just wanted to thank you. I mean all of you, the whole team, for making me feel welcome. You guys were pretty well established, so you didn't have to take on a new guy."

Nate shrugged. "You're welcome, but we do need you. Someone has to play third base."

Ian laughed. "Well, anyway, thanks. And now Ty is making weird faces at me, so I guess I better go."

Across the field, Ty seemed to be miming something. He grinned and then pointed toward one of the park exits.

"Good luck," said Nate.

TWICE MEANT it was a thing, didn't it?

Ty unlocked the door to his apartment as Ian lingered behind him. They still hadn't had dinner, which meant that the postworkout fatigue hit Ty pretty hard, but so did a wave of lust. Ian had unlocked something in him or created some kind of Pavlovian response. Now whenever Ian was in range, Ty's whole body became aware of it; Ian aroused him and made him sweaty and hard, and he frankly couldn't wait to fuck Ian, but one thing at a time.

"Hey, just so you know, I have a shiny new box of condoms and a bottle of good lube in my room," Ty said after he closed the door. "It's some kind of hippie organic nonsense, but the last guy I dated swore by it."

Ian laughed, but it was a shaky laugh, like he was struggling with nerves again.

"Or, hey, we don't have to fuck. It was just a suggestion."

Ian reached over and put his hand on Ty's forearm. "No, I want to. It's just…." He pointed his index finger at his ear and made a circular motion, the universal signal for "crazy."

"You're not crazy," Ty said. "Look, even I am not cool as a cucumber all of the time."

Ian smiled. "You don't say. You mean that little hissy fit you threw when you missed three of Nate's pitches in a row was totally relaxed?"

Oh, right. "Well, sure."

Ian laughed. "Okay."

But this was good, making Ian laugh. Ty liked Ian laughing. It meant Ian was not nervous. Or that he wasn't completely consumed by his agitated thoughts. He wasn't chattering like a rabid Chihuahua, either, so that was something.

"But maybe we could eat first?" Ian said.

Ty let out a breath. "Yeah, okay. You want to just have something delivered?"

"That's fine. I have a change of clothes in my bag, so I could put on something besides my sweats, but…."

"I'd rather see you take the sweats off entirely."

"I figured."

Ian seemed to be in a good mood. Ty hadn't even hesitated before suggesting they walk back to his place after the game. Ty rented the ground floor in an ancient brownstone, so his apartment was small, but it was a nice enough place. The building itself was gorgeous, if poorly maintained. Quintessential Brooklyn, basically.

He gave Ian a quickie tour before they ended up in the kitchen, where Ty fished his collection of delivery menus out from the drawer where he kept them.

"I'm starving," Ian said.

"I was going to make a lewd joke, but…."

"Tell me."

That made Ty grin. "Well, babe. I've got something for you to snack on."

"Chips?"

Ty laughed. "You're something else, you know that?"

Ian put the delivery menus down on the table. "Like I said, I do want to have sex with you. I like to bottom, even. I want to do it for you. I just have to work up to it. You know."

"Well, for the record, I have a dry cleaner that is never judgmental, so if we get anything on the duvet, it's all good."

Ian laughed and put his hands over his eyes. Ty could see his face going red. "God. I feel like such an idiot."

"It's all right, Ian, really."

Ian leaned over and kissed Ty. Ty was happy that didn't send Ian into paroxysms of anxiety. He liked kissing Ian a great deal, loved the way Ian tasted, how he felt under Ty's hands.

But they debated food instead of taking it further.

"Pizza?"

"Thai?"

"Sushi?"

They ultimately agreed on an Asian fusion place nearby. Ian ordered enough food to feed five people. Ty was impressed. Although he had worked up an appetite at practice too, he was far more interested in getting Ian naked. Food could have waited. But if Ian needed to stall for time, that was fine.

This situation was a little strange, though. Were they becoming friends and not just lovers?

Later, as he watched Ian deftly maneuver a pair of chopsticks over his dinner, he said, "Look, I don't want you to feel pressured. I'll just put it out there that I'd like to spend the night with you again."

Ian smiled. "I'll stay tonight. That fancy bottle of lube may have to wait, but I want to be with you."

"That's all I can ask for. How's your dinner?"

"Really good. Could stand to be a little spicier."

Ty grinned. "Oh, baby. I'll give you spicy."

Ian's smile turned wry and knowing. "Is that a double entendre?"

"You bet."

They spent most of the rest of the meal grinning at each other like idiots.

They finished dinner and Ty cleaned up, trying to work out if he should make a move on Ian or if that would just make things awkward. He figured he should let Ian decide, but maybe in the meantime he'd propose they watch a movie or something. He slid the last of the leftovers into the refrigerator, then closed the door and turned around.

Ian was right there, crowding his personal space.

"Hi," Ty said, a little startled.

"Hi," said Ian with a smile.

"What are you—"

Ian stopped that thought by kissing Ty. Ian put his hands on Ty's waist and tugged him a little closer. Ian's mouth was warm and pleading, and it seemed like they were back in business. Ty put his hands on Ian's back and pulled him closer, until their bodies touched, until they pressed together.

"Ian," Ty whispered when their lips parted. Ian trailed kisses down Ty's chin and nibbled at the section of Ty's neck that was wired right to his dick. Ty let out a groan against his will and thrust his fingers into Ian's hair. "Oh, Ian, baby. Come to bed with me?"

"Yes," Ian whispered against Ty's neck.

"I want to... I want to fuck you. I want to be inside you. Will you let me?"

"Yes." It was a whisper again, but the response was instant, no hesitation or fear.

Ty wondered what had made him change his mind but decided not to question it. Instead, he took a step back, grabbed Ian's hand, and tugged him out of the kitchen and into the bedroom.

They stood at the foot of the bed, kissing and undressing each other. As Ty peeled off Ian's shirt, he ran his hands over the skin he'd exposed. He loved all of Ian's beautiful skin, the invisible body hair, the softness and roughness and all of the textures that made up this fascinating, compelling man before him.

When they'd tossed aside all their clothes, when they pressed their bodies together, fully naked, Ty kissed Ian. He licked into Ian's mouth, tasting the lingering spice from dinner and a sweetness unique to Ian. As Ty pulled Ian close, heat rose in Ty's body, warmth spreading outward, his body tingling with the proximity. Ian's cock was hard and pushed against Ty's hip, which made Ty's blood rush.

"Lie down with me," Ty said.

Ian nodded and let Ty lead him to the bed. They lay down together and Ty kissed him again. He pulled Ian's knee up so that Ian's leg wrapped around Ty's hip. Thrusting forward, he pressed their cocks together. Ian dug his fingers into Ty's shoulders and threw his head back as he cried out. Ty dove, licking up Ian's throat, kissing his jaw, nibbling at his bottom lip, and finally kissing him again. Ian opened his mouth and let Ty in, tangled their tongues together, and put his fingers through Ty's hair.

"I want you," Ian said breathlessly as he wrapped himself around Ty. "Make me stop thinking. Fuck me until it's just you and me and I can shut out the world. Make me scream, make me come."

"Yes. Oh, baby, yes."

Ty didn't want to move from where he had settled into Ian's arms, but he knew he had to in order to make this work. He kissed Ian again while reaching for the drawer. Then he reached too far and nearly fell off the bed.

He had to pull away from Ian to keep them both from toppling over the side. Ian burst into laughter.

Ty laughed too, despite his embarrassment. His laughter was joyous, though. He was with Ian and he was having fun. And what the hell good was sex if it wasn't fun?

He pulled open his drawer and took out lube and a couple of condoms. Ian scooted over to the middle of the bed, still laughing. Ty climbed over him and kissed him hard, settling between his legs. Ty reached between them and wrapped his hand around both their cocks. Ian grunted and arched his back, pressing his hips against Ty's.

God, Ian was beautiful, from his long nose to his perfect chin to the long column of his neck. He was gorgeous from his soft shoulders to his flat pecs to the slightly-less-invisible hair at his groin.

"You're gonna make me come too fast," Ian said on a sigh.

So Ty backed off. He sat back on his heels and looked at Ian splayed out on the bed. He was gorgeous that way too, but he'd be even more so with his perfect round ass facing Ty. Ty patted Ian's hip. "Roll over, baby."

Ian did it quickly, seemingly eager for it. He propped himself up on his knees and elbows and lifted his hips so his butt stuck up. Unable to resist, Ty moved forward, running his palms over the globes of Ian's backside, savoring the softness of Ian's skin. Then he leaned forward and pressed his face against Ian's ass. Ian whispered something Ty couldn't hear, but it might have been "yes," or "please," and Ty was happy to indulge him. He licked between Ian's cheeks. Then he pressed his tongue against the entrance to Ian's body.

Ian groaned and pressed back against Ty's tongue.

Ian's smells and textures were more intense here, more intoxicating. Ian's body relaxed against Ty's onslaught, softening and opening up. Ian heaved and sighed, so Ty kept doing it, the sounds Ian was making flooding Ty's system, kicking up his heartbeat and his arousal. He wanted to make Ian come right then, but he also wanted to feel his cock slide between those amazing asscheeks, so he backed up again.

Ian let out a heavy sigh.

"I'm not done with you yet," Ty said.

"God," said Ian.

"My name is Ty, actually, but I understand the confusion. Happens all the time."

Ian laughed. The sound was like the most beautiful music.

Ty grabbed the lube. He poured some down the crack of Ian's ass, and Ian squirmed a little against the cool liquid. Ty kissed Ian's lower back as he rubbed the entrance to Ian's body. "Relax," he murmured against Ian's skin.

Ian let out a breath and let go of whatever tension he'd been clutching. His body yielded to Ty enough for Ty to press a finger inside.

Ty prepared Ian, kissing his back and whispering encouragements. Ian grunted and groaned and hummed as Ty worked. Anticipation mounted the more relaxed Ian became, the more his body opened up to Ty, and Ty's heart rate was off the charts. He couldn't wait much longer to get inside Ian.

He leaned back and stroked himself, though he didn't need much as he was already painfully hard. He rolled on a condom. He leaned forward and caressed Ian's hip. Then he poured a generous amount of lube on his fingers and smeared it on his erection.

"Ty," Ian moaned.

Ty rose and moved forward. He paused behind Ian for a moment before he pressed forward.

Ian was tight. He was hot and tight, and he squeezed Ty's cock as Ty slowly sank into his body. Ty took his time, letting Ian adjust to him, making sure Ian was comfortable and felt safe.

"More," Ian groaned. Ty knew he was doing this right.

Of course, it felt great to Ty too. Perfect. Ian's body was perfect. The way they fit together was perfect. The sounds and textures of Ian were perfect. Ty moaned as he gradually went harder and faster, thrusting in and out, ramping up everything between them. Ian pushed back, meeting Ty's thrusts as Ty picked up speed.

It was fast and beautiful as Ty let loose, fucking Ian hard, making him moan. Ty broke out in sweat and his skin tingled the closer he got to losing it.

Ian threw his head back. "So good," he said. "But I wish… I want…."

"What… what do you want?"

"To kiss you. I want… I want you close."

Reluctantly, Ty pulled out. "Roll back over, babe."

Ian lay on his back and spread his legs. Ty leaned forward and hooked his elbows under Ian's knees. He positioned his cock at Ian's entrance and very slowly pushed back inside. Ian moaned and put his arms around Ty's neck, pulling him down for a kiss.

It was warm and intimate. Ian wrapped his body around Ty's again, and being inside Ian and surrounded by him was almost too much. The friction against Ty's cock was pulling pleasure and arousal through his body. Ian hugged him close and whispered nonsense near his ear. Ty's blood rushed and his heart pounded.

"Come with me," Ty said, wrapping his hand around Ian's cock and starting to stroke.

"Yes," said Ian, arching into Ty.

"Come with me. Look at me."

Ian looked up at Ty and their gazes met. They were connected everywhere, it felt like.

And then everything went off the charts. Ty stroked Ian's cock until Ian grunted and sighed and started to shake. Then he was coming against Ty's hand, spurting between their bodies, clutching at Ty's shoulders as he lost his mind. It was one of the most amazing things Ty had ever seen.

Watching Ian's ecstasy was too much for Ty. As Ian's body squeezed Ty's cock, Ty tripped over the ledge and came hard, so intensely he saw nothing for a moment, could only feel the intensity of his coupling with Ian. He came inside Ian, pulling Ian close and whispering his name.

They lay panting and tangled up together for several moments, not speaking, holding each other.

Out of breath, Ian said, "That was intense."

Ty laughed and rolled onto his side, taking Ian with him. "It was amazing. It was beautiful. *You're* beautiful."

Ian nuzzled against Ty's chest. "Mmm."

They lay like that until Ty started getting itchy. He started to pull away.

"No," Ian murmured.

"I gotta clean us up, baby. I'm all sticky and sweaty. But I promise to come right back."

He kissed Ian and got out of bed. When he returned a few minutes later, Ian had slid under the covers. "Come here," he said softly.

Ty was happy to get into bed with Ian. He pulled Ian into his arms, and they settled into the pillows. "Regrets?" Ty asked.

"None."

"I'm glad. That was really awesome."

"I'm sleepy," Ian said with a yawn.

"So sleep." Ty was feeling pretty sleepy himself. "I'll be right there with you."

Ian sighed against Ty and his breathing slowed, so Ty closed his eyes and relaxed, content to hold Ian. He drifted off to sleep.

Chapter 6

TY'S FINGERS were stained Technicolor with paint and ink, something he found mildly bothersome but not enough to do anything about it. He stared at his canvas with the ineffable feeling that something was not quite right with the picture, but he was unable to put a finger on what it was. Everything was to spec, everyone's limbs were in the right place, the colors were what the client had asked for. But the painting was flat. Ty didn't believe the passion for each other the two figures were supposed to be conveying.

Not a lot of designers did actual paint-on-canvas paintings for book covers anymore, and though Ty knew all the digital tricks, for certain covers, he much preferred the real thing to Photoshop or Illustrator.

Spread on the canvas before him was a classic romance novel clutch cover, with a woman in a billowy red ball gown that was sliding off her pale, delicate shoulders grasping a burly man—this one had a lot of dark chest hair, which was one of Ty's additions and not in the client spec sheet—in a white shirt and black breeches. The breeches were probably apocryphal, but so was the dress, and historical accuracy didn't matter so much as how attractive the people in the painting were.

It was the facial expressions that weren't working. The woman in the painting looked like she wasn't really feeling it, although she was crazy, because the man Ty had painted was seriously hot. In fact, he looked a little like Ian, but bulkier and with dark hair. What woman wouldn't swoon? What man wouldn't?

And that was when Ty put the paintbrush down. If the people in his painting had suddenly developed feelings and opinions of their own, he was getting high from the paint fumes or something.

He hopped in the shower to hose off all the paint. When he got out, he saw he had a missed call on his phone from Josh.

He pulled on jeans and a T-shirt and returned the call with great reluctance.

"You're going to yell at me, aren't you?" Ty asked, wandering back into the spare bedroom he used as a studio and staring at the painting some more. Now it was bothering him. What the hell was wrong and how could he fix it? And why was there still paint under his fingernails?

"Now, why would you say that?"

"Because I've slept with Ian a few times now, and I'm guessing that pisses you off for some reason."

"I could be calling because of any number of reasons. Maybe it's about the Hipsters. It could be about work. Maybe I want to ask you to dinner next week."

"Are you actually calling about any of those reasons?"

"Well, no. Although now that I think about it, maybe Tony and I should have a dinner party. He just invented a new recipe for this lemon chicken thing. It's really good."

"So give me the lecture."

Josh let out a sigh, blowing air into the receiver. "Look, here's the thing with Ian."

"Here we go."

"He never stays in one place very long."

"He has to move a lot for his job, I know." Ty left the studio, figuring he could come back to the painting later. "I thought that was sort of ideal. No commitment, right?"

Josh was silent for a beat before he said, "Sure, except that I suspect that both of you are getting involved."

"Josh—"

"I'm not trying to meddle. But I just came home from lunch with him, and he talked so much about you that I just thought maybe you should be aware. And I know you better than you think I do, so I know you're not as promiscuous as your reputation would imply."

"Or, you could just let me have my moment and enjoy whatever it is that is going on with me and Ian, and stop butting in."

"I would never—"

"And stop saying that you never meddle, because you always meddle."

Josh gasped as if this accusation appalled him, but then he said, "Okay. Look, here's the thing. Part of me thinks the two of you are actually kind of perfect together. I realize I pointed you at each other too, so I feel responsible. Maybe it'll be awesome. But you both also have so much baggage that I could see it going horribly wrong, and I don't want either of you to get hurt."

Ty didn't like hearing any of that. He felt emotionally unprepared to deal with it.

"Ty?" Josh asked, making Ty realize he'd been silent too long.

"I'll take that under advisement."

"Fine. Uh. I *am* having this dinner party thing. Tony overheard me talking and agreed wholeheartedly. Didn't you, sweetie?"

Ty enjoyed the mental image of Tony, Josh's big Italian husband, being called sweetie. Ty could hear the murmur of Tony's deep voice in the background.

"I'll talk to you later, Ty."

Ty got off the phone and plopped in front of his television. He grunted. He was determined to enjoy this thing with Ian and wouldn't let Josh impose emotional angst on him. It was just fun. That was all it should be.

IAN WATCHED the field from his vantage point at third base. The Queens team was okay but not great, and they certainly didn't have the same discipline that the Hipsters had. In fact, the Queens kind of lived up to their names; the catcher had one of the most epic manicures Ian had ever seen, the first baseman was wearing lipstick, and the players currently sitting on the bench behind the home plate fence that served as a dugout were all horsing around. Also, apparently colorful silk scarves were part of their uniform, because each of them had one around his neck.

That included Aiden, who had earned starry-eyed looks from Carlos and the evil eye from Nate. Ian reminded his curiosity that he had no desire to get in the middle of their drama.

The batter up now was a guy named Hector, who lifted the bat above his head. His stance looked professional. Nate wound up and pitched, and Hector hit it handily. Mason whisper-shouted, "He used to play in the minors."

It figured. A sports league like this one would invite those players who couldn't be out in their professional lives but still wanted to play baseball. Not that this league was anything like professional caliber. The game against Hell's Kitchen had proved that. It had been sloppy at times, too many fumbled catches and runs allowed for it to have been a pro game. Will might have been a competitive son of a bitch, but competitive spirit didn't always translate into skill.

Ty stood at second, staring at home plate. He looked relaxed and sexy, and it struck Ian again that he was an interesting contrast to Ian's own overheated resting state. Ian often thought lately it might be too good to be true, that Ty was probably hanging on to some deep, dark neuroses that had yet to manifest themselves.

Ian wondered what he was doing here.

Hector hit the ball into left field and took off around the bases. Carlos fielded the ball and moved to throw it to Ty, but Hector breezed right past him, so Carlos pivoted and threw the ball at Ian. Ian tried to catch it, but it got past him, and Hector kept running. Ian managed to get ahold of the ball and threw it home, but not before Hector was safe.

Ian wasn't an especially good baseball player, basically, and never had been. Sure, he'd played in high school, but for an academically minded school. Most of his classmates had no idea the school even had a sports program. So, yeah, he'd done all right on that team, but they routinely got creamed by the other high school teams in the city.

Now wasn't much better. If his place on the team hadn't been voluntary, he could imagine being picked last to play.

A guy named Pete hit the next ball, and it soared right into Ty's glove, ending the inning.

It was a lot of names to keep track of, a lot of social time that, while not required, was mostly expected. The social time was actually the point; he'd joined to meet people, hadn't he?

He dragged himself to the Hipsters' bench and sat down hard. Scott slapped his back. Probably that was meant to be a "buck up!" gesture, but Ian felt bad for letting the other team score. In fact, his heart rate was already up a little higher than it should have been, and inside, he was panicking.

Low stakes, he tried to remind himself. This was the sort of league that gave everyone participation ribbons at the end of the season as if they were all in kindergarten. There was no reason to get worked up over a play he biffed that everyone had already moved past. And yet.

Ty walked over and looked at Ian with narrowed eyes. "Are you flipping out about something?"

Ian shook his head.

"That's interesting, because you're getting all flushed."

"I totally could have caught that."

Ty shrugged. "Who cares?"

"I care. I shouldn't have let Hector score."

Ty put a hand on Ian's shoulder. "Sure, maybe you could have caught that." The Texas accent was thick now, a sure sign that Ty was trying to talk Ian away from the cliff. Ian tried for a deep breath, but it sounded a little ragged. Ty went on, "Maybe Carlos threw it too wide. Doesn't matter. You know what the consequences are of missing that ball? Nothing. Zip, zero, nada. Nobody cares. You won't get benched or punished. No one will judge you. Everyone on this field has missed a play they should have made, and sure, maybe we'll spend a little bit of time beating ourselves up over it, but in the end, it doesn't matter at all. Whether the Queens win or we do, we'll all go to Barnstorm after and get good and blitzed, and probably Carlos and Aiden will finally hook up because God knows I'm sick of watching them make eyes at each other, and then it's next week and we're off to the next game. It's all just for fun. So don't sweat your missed ball."

Ian looked up at Ty's face. It was totally relaxed still. In fact, he had a small smile playing on his lips.

Ian felt his blood pressure sinking back to normal.

"Thanks," Ian said.

"*De nada*. You're up third this inning. You ready?"

"Sure, fine."

Despite the bad play, the Hipsters eked out a one-run win over the Queens. When the game ended, everyone hugged each other. Half the Hipsters wound up with scarves tied around their necks or arms. They walked en masse over to the bar, everyone laughing and enjoying themselves.

So why was Ian feeling so out of sorts?

Maybe he wasn't cut out for a noncompetitive competitive sports league.

Ty walked beside him on the way to the bar. And that was another thing. They were acting awfully couple-y, given the fact that the substance of their relationship was just that they'd slept together a few times and seemed to like each other's company. What did Ian even know about Ty? He didn't really know what Ty did for a living or if he had siblings or if he was a cat or a dog person.

Ty put a hand on the small of Ian's back. "Stop freaking out."

Ian let out a breath. "Yeah. I'm trying."

But maybe this wasn't what Ian wanted either, this relationship. He sighed.

"Let's get a beer," Ty said, turning onto Avenue B.

Chapter 7

THE EMPLOYEE cafeteria at the New Amsterdam Hotel was pretty grody. The floor looked like it hadn't been cleaned in about ten years, with suitable amounts of mysterious brown gunk caked into the corners, and the folding tables looked like they'd been bought secondhand from a prison or elementary school. Ian hated eating there—he usually just breezed in and got whatever food was available before heading back upstairs to the administrative offices and eating at his desk—but today he thought it might be nice to get a closer look at the kingdom he was supposed to restore to glory.

The employees eating lunch were allegedly in uniform, but the staff had a funny notion of what a uniform consisted of. The blazers worn by the front-desk staff weren't even the same shade of navy blue, and some had red trim while others had white. That was an easy thing to fix, at least. Easier to fix than the years of neglect or the leaky ceiling or the odd moldy smell that no one could figure out how to obliterate on sixteen.

It was going to be an uphill battle to get this place whipped into shape, though Ian was determined to do it.

He sat at the end of one of the tables and nibbled on his sandwich as he watched everyone interact. The mood in the cafeteria was relaxed and fun in a way life in this hotel rarely was, and Ian enjoyed soaking that up. The employees got along, which was more than could have been said for the place Ian had saved in San Francisco or that hole-in-the-wall inn in Paris.

When he'd sated his appetite, he dumped his sandwich crusts in the trash and walked out into the lobby. A few people milled around the registration desk. Ian would have preferred to shut the whole place down and do a rapid renovation, but management wouldn't stand for that, so instead they closed two floors at a time for renovations—the hotel had thirty-six floors in all—and filled the rest as well as they could. The vacancy rate in the hotel was so high that the whole place was basically bleeding money, but Ian couldn't convince the ownership of that.

A heavyset man checking in was berating the poor girl behind the desk—Ian was still learning everyone's name, a challenge given that the hotel had more than two hundred employees—and she glanced at Ian as he approached.

The man was wearing a yellow polo shirt so bright that it probably could have been seen from space. It had the effect of making the man look tired and sallow. He also looked like an asshole, his face red from rage.

"Hi, can I help you?" Ian asked.

He had a little brass name tag that said he worked in management, although generally he tried to stay low-key. Still, he wasn't the best in the business for nothing, and certainly he had a gift for dealing with problem customers, or so he'd been told.

"I asked for a park view room," the man said. "Instead, this lady here gave me a room on the other side of the building with a view into the building next door. It's just a brick wall, basically. I'm not paying through my nose to get a view of a brick wall."

"Let me just take a look." Ian walked behind the desk and peered over the girl—her name tag said Meg. The registration information stared back at him. The man had booked the room on one of the discount travel sites and was actually paying about half what Ian thought the minimum room rate should be, given the hotel's great location. "We can't guarantee park view rooms," Ian said as he reached over and made a few keystrokes, "but happily there is a vacancy, so we can move you into one of those rooms if you like. There will be an extra charge of fifty dollars per night for the room, though."

"Fifty dollars! For this shitty hotel? You've got to be kidding me!"

"The only park view room available is one of our premium rooms on the concierge floor." This was a lie; the hotel was half empty, which said a great deal about its general state of disrepair. If even bargain hunter tourists didn't want to stay there…. "The concierge floor has free snacks available in the lounge and wine in the evenings. It's very nice and worth the extra money. So if you'd like the upgrade, I can do that, and really fifty extra dollars a night is bargain. Those rooms usually go for three times what you'd be paying per night total. But I'm doing this for you because you're such a loyal customer."

The man nodded. "Well, all right, then. Eh, Janine. We got an upgrade."

A woman with a huge Louis Vuitton handbag walked over. She had on Louboutins too, if the red soles on her very high-heeled shoes were genuine. Either she bought very convincing knockoffs or yellow polo shirt could totally afford the room upgrade.

Ian hated customers like this, but he smiled and recruited a bellhop to help them change rooms. The bellhop probably wouldn't get a tip, which was a damn shame.

Ian went back up the administrative offices, feeling like he'd done what he could for the day in terms of customer service triumphs.

Of course, hell was waiting for him back in his office. "There's a leak in a bathroom on twenty-three again," his assistant informed him. "And we have a lot of unsold rooms this coming weekend. Jason wants to do some kind of promotional thing, but honestly, it seems like a cheesy idea."

"What is it?"

And thus Ian got pulled into a troubling discussion of half-assed advertising plans, and he spent a good part of the afternoon putting out fires in the hotel. He loved the work, he did, but the stress levels weren't great for his anxiety. He wondered how he could manage to deal with a bad customer without breaking a sweat but got quickly overwhelmed when he was back in his office. Sometimes his anxiety had no rhyme or reason.

After an impromptu meeting with his assistant, Ian was finally by himself at his desk. Uneasiness sat in his chest like a rock he'd swallowed. He wondered how to dislodge it. He could take a coffee break. The nice indie coffee shop on the corner made a salted caramel latte that had become one of Ian's most treasured guilty pleasures. He felt less guilty about it now, even, since he got a hell of a workout at least twice a week from playing baseball, of all things. Thinking about baseball made him think of Ty, who was a riddle he wasn't quite prepared to puzzle out yet.

Resolved, Ian went back downstairs and waved at the desk agents as he breezed outside.

The thing was, Ian felt like he was terrible at baseball and had trouble keeping up with the better players, people like Carlos and Mason and their left fielder, Shane, who all looked professional out on the field. Josh and Ty kept saying it didn't matter, that it wasn't a contest, that there were no literal trophies at the end of the season. Well, the team that won the playoffs got their name on a tiny brass plate that was screwed onto a plaque at Barnstorm and a round of drinks on the house, but that was the extent of the fanfare. So, really, Ian should push all the bullshit aside and just have fun. Why was that so hard?

Because he hated failure. It was why he worked his ass off at this job. Baseball was a risk in a lot of ways. It was Ian trying something he wasn't especially good at and setting himself up to fail. He actively hated trying things he couldn't figure out how to conquer, and baseball was suddenly one of those things in his life.

Ty was the other. What business did they have in a relationship together?

Ian ordered his frothy, sugary latte and thought about Ty as the barista took her sweet time making it. What did they really have to offer each other? Ian had a bag full of neuroses, and Ty owned his promiscuity like a favorite shirt. Not to mention, Ian hated New York and planned to leave as soon as he finished his assignment at the New Amsterdam. This… thing… between them had an expiration date. What the hell was the point, then? It wasn't like they were going to fall in love and live happily ever after.

Shit, was that even what Ian wanted? Was it possible? He thought of his own parents, who had been living in that same damn brownstone in Park Slope since the late seventies, when the neighborhood was a shithole and it cost a few pennies to buy a gorgeous Victorian home. Now that Ian's father had finally defected, those same houses were going for millions, so Ian's mother was staying put until she was unable to maintain it, even though it was full of what Ian could only imagine were memories of fights and misery with Ian's father.

The man had been a professional prick, never understanding his son or making anything like an attempt to do so. Where his father was butch and blue-collar, Ian was academically minded and a little fey. He'd been painfully pretty as a teenager, and thankfully age had made the edges a little less soft, but he had no delusions that he'd ever be a super masculine guy. He'd been fragile. He'd had a lot of allergies as a kid, most of which he had grown out of, but he'd also had the prone-to-escalation anxiety most of his life. He'd had his first panic attack at school when he was eleven, and when the principal had called home, Ian's father had told Ian to man up and not be so ridiculous.

Ian's father had never been physically abusive, but he knew how to tear down a person with a few words. He'd done it to Ian through his most vulnerable years, when Ian was first realizing he was gay, and he'd done it to Ian's mother plenty, and really, the divorce was a blessing. If Ian never had to see the man again, it would be too soon. And in the meantime, his grand introduction to marriage had been an awful, manipulative mess.

So why the romantic streak? Why did he still sometimes find himself wishing he could have the happily ever after with the right guy?

Wasn't it a total waste of time to think about Ty that way?

The baseball league had been a terrible idea, he decided as he received his latte from the barista, but he'd committed to it and he wasn't a quitter. He didn't want to leave the team stranded without a third baseman, even though the backup pitcher, Travis, could do it in his sleep.

As Ian walked by the hotel, though, he realized he didn't want to break up with Ty just yet, that he enjoyed the man's company, and his vague potential future plans weren't really a reason to end things just yet. They weren't going to get married, they were just going to have some sexy fun.

Right?

TY WAS tired. He dragged himself to East River Park for that week's game feeling the sort of fatigue that could only come from several consecutive days of insomnia. He wasn't sure what was preventing him from sleeping exactly, if it was nerves or stress or what, but he didn't like it. He missed sleep.

Ian was already at the ball field when he arrived, smiling and chatting with Mason as they did warm-up stretches. That made Ty feel a little better. He was happy that he'd be spending time with Ian that evening, and maybe he could talk himself into Ian's bed, where they could have athletic, energy-draining sex, and then Ty would get a good night's sleep.

Or maybe that was too much to hope for. Ian had been standoffish the last few times they'd talked on the phone. Ty wasn't sure what he'd done to push Ian away, but he wanted to figure out how to undo it so they could continue to spend time together. Because he really liked Ian, liked spending time with him, and their connection helped ease something in him.

Ian grinned toothily when Ty approached, so maybe the distance was all in Ty's imagination. It wouldn't have surprised him much because everyone left him eventually, didn't they?

Oh, boy. Had he fallen down that rabbit hole again?

Fatigue and work pressure often contributed to his stress and broken self-esteem, and he wished he could let it roll off his back more, but sometimes it got the better of him. He had days when he didn't much care for himself and didn't want to leave the apartment and impose his black mood on the world. This had been one of those days, and he probably would have skipped the game altogether if he hadn't had to come into Manhattan anyway earlier to drop something off at a client's office—

which hadn't gone that well—or if the promise of seeing Ian hadn't lain before him.

"Hi," he said when he got to Ian and Mason.

"Hi," Ian said back brightly.

Ty wasn't sure of the protocol. Were they friends with benefits? Were they lovers? Were they in a relationship? Was it okay to touch Ian in public like this? Was it okay to hug him, to kiss him? Ty started to feel a little crazier for every second the moment stretched out, and then he just stood there, because he had no idea what to do.

Ian ran a hand down Ty's arm. "Are you okay?"

"Swell," Ty said, not wanting Ian to see how far off the deep end he had fallen that day. Ty hated these moods when they came over him, hated that he didn't have a good coping mechanism.

But maybe Ian could help him without knowing it. A hug didn't seem to be too far out of the question.

Ty reached for Ian. He wanted to keep it casual so that what he was doing wouldn't be clear either to Ian or to anyone who might be looking on, but suddenly he needed Ian's proximity, needed his warmth and his scent, and he thought maybe the rest of the evening would be okay if Ian just hugged him back.

Dear Lord, what the hell was wrong with him?

Ian gazed off into the distance as if he were tracking something on the other side of the field. He didn't seem to notice Ty.

"Geez, can't a guy get a hug?" Ty said.

Ian shrugged and then reached over and gave Ty the briefest of hugs, complete with a back pat. Was this how this was going to be? Hell, it wasn't like they needed to be closeted. Everyone on the goddamn team was a 'mo.

Ty had to be content with the brief touch, because Scott started barking out orders. They were playing the Mermaids that day too, which was just fucking perfect.

Rachel strolled over. Ty had known the woman for many years, and he liked her fine outside of the context of a baseball game, but she became a competitive crazy person once the game started. She was a tiny woman, a petite five feet tall, with a brown pixie cut and heavy dark-rimmed glasses.

"Hello, Tyler," she said with a sneer.

"Rachel. Nice to see you again."

"I figured I'd come be nice to you now because our team is about to wipe the floor with yours."

"Thanks. I appreciate that."

Rachel raised her eyebrows. "What? No snappy insult? I'm appalled, Ty. You were always good for a good pregame put-the-lady-in-her-place sort of barb."

"I'm tired today. Don't have enough energy to come up with anything especially biting. Next time, though, I've got your number."

She smiled. "Okay. And who is this cutie?" She turned to Ian.

"Oh. Rachel, this is our new third baseman, Ian. Ian, this is the spawn of Satan, Rachel."

"There it is," said Rachel.

Ian amiably shook her hand.

"Speaking of new players, have you met Marla? She's the tall one over there talking to Karsten by the backstop."

Ty followed Rachel's gesture and saw a tall woman with a wide stance. "She's got some… posture," Ty said.

Rachel shrugged. "Yes, well. She's a dainty princess in the body of a linebacker. And I mean that almost literally, if you get what I mean."

Ty took that to mean Marla had been born male. "All right. She any good?"

"Runs like the Flash and throws like Cy Young. We also have a new third baseman named Judy who hits like Babe Ruth. Like, out of the field every time she's at bat. She played college softball for Rice, I think."

Of course. "Well, damn," said Ty. "We should start recruiting women to the Hipsters next season."

Rachel grinned. "That's the secret to our success."

Someone called Rachel's name, so she gave Ty a fist bump and then ran across the field. Mason had also wandered off while Ty wasn't watching, so it was just him and Ian standing by the bench.

"Seriously, are you okay?" Ian asked.

"Why wouldn't I be okay?"

Ian let out a frustrated huff. "Well, I certainly have no earthly idea. That's why I asked."

"What the hell? Why the hostility?"

"Boys!" Scott shouted. "I have no time for trouble in paradise. We have a game to play."

Ian turned on his heel and stalked off.

Talk about having no earthly idea. Ty wasn't sure what had just happened, beyond that Ian was clearly pissed off about something. Ty didn't have time for passive-aggressive bullshit or men playing relationship games. He was too exhausted. He sat on the bench and rubbed his eyes with the heels of his hands.

"You okay, man?" asked Carlos.

"I'm fine!" shouted Ty.

"Geez, okay." Carlos held up his hands and backed off.

Ty had to get a grip on whatever was plaguing him soon or this would just spiral out of control. He still wasn't sure exactly what he'd done to piss off Ian, but he could calm down and be nicer to everyone else.

The game proceeded apace, although Ty had a terrible time focusing, too tired to concentrate and too thrown off by Ian's weird anger to think about much else.

The Mermaids, the only team that ever gave Will's Hell's Kitchen team a run for its money, pummeled the Hipsters, but that didn't surprise Ty much. The women's team didn't hit or throw as far as most of the Hipsters could generally, but they ran faster and were much more in tune with each other in the field. Rachel and the starting pitcher, Karsten, had a system going, and sometimes all it took was Aubrey at shortstop to shout something incomprehensible and all the women on the team moved in perfected coordinated formations. There were more 1-2-3 innings that game than any other Ty had played in a while. It was to the Mermaids' credit, though; they could stay in the league because they were fiercely competitive with the men. The Bronx Bombshells, the other all-female team, was not quite as good but still won enough games to feel they belonged.

So the game ended with the Hipsters getting their asses handed to them by the Mermaids, as predicted, but everyone hugged at home plate. Well, Rachel slugged Ty in the arm when they met in the line before she hugged him, but still.

Ty gathered his things and shoved them into his gym bag. He thought about just ducking out. He didn't have the energy or the will to spend time at the bar.

Ian approached him, though.

"I'm sorry about before," Ian said. "I had a rough day at work and I was confused about some things, and I took it out on you, and I'm sorry."

Relief washed over Ty, but it left a strange uneasiness in its wake. Still, he plastered on a smile. "Apology accepted. What were you confused about?"

"I'd rather not talk about it here." Ian gestured at all the people around them.

"Okay. So." God, Ty was wiped. He could barely make sentences. Three hours on his feet through all nine innings of a disheartening game had not done much to reinvigorate him. He rubbed his eyes. "I, um. I think I'm just gonna go home. I'm exhausted."

"Oh." Ian's disappointment was palpable. His face just fell. He recovered quickly, but Ty had definitely seen it, so that was something.

"I'll, uh, I'll see you at practice this weekend, okay?"

"Yeah, sure."

When Ian just stood there stubbornly wringing his hands, Ty hoisted his bag on his shoulder and turned to walk out of the park.

"Hey, Ty?" Ian shouted.

Ty turned around. Ian walked right up to him and planted a big fat kiss on his lips. It surprised Ty and caught him completely off guard. A lot of the Hipsters and Mermaids had drifted out of the park, but a fair number of people stood around chatting still.

So what the fuck was this? It wasn't that Ty was ungrateful, and he opened his mouth to accept the kiss and Ian's tongue and all of it. But after Ian had been so weird earlier, it was strange and not completely welcome, this kiss. Ty put his hands up, pressing them into Ian's pecs, intending to push Ian away. Instead, he deepened the kiss—suddenly his brain had switched over to working primarily on instinct—and curled his fingers into Ian's T-shirt.

Ty managed to pull himself away eventually. "Not that I'm not grateful for hot kisses, but what the hell is going on?"

Ian shook his head. "Honestly? No idea."

"Oh, good."

"I'll let you go home, but do you want to go out this week? Maybe to dinner Thursday? Prove that we have more in common than baseball and sex."

"Seriously?"

"Yeah. I guess I realized… well, we hardly know each other. Maybe we should fix that. Unless you don't want to."

Ty did want to, but he was definitely confused now. If anything, dinner could perhaps be a good opportunity to get to the bottom of whatever the hell all this was. "Sure, dinner Thursday."

"You know the city better than I do, so pick a place and let me know. Yeah?"

"Okay."

"I'll walk you to the subway."

"Eh, not necessary. I might just get a cab. If I have to walk all the way to the F train and then I have to transfer... God, I'm tired."

"You sure you're okay?"

There was that question again. "I just need a good night's sleep. I'll see you Thursday. Okay, Ian?"

"Okay."

Ty kissed Ian's cheek and then loped out of the park.

Chapter 8

DINNER ENDED up being at a restaurant in the West Village—about equidistant between their two apartments, Ian couldn't help but notice, perhaps to discourage an overnight afterward. The place had a pretty eclectic menu of mostly vegetarian Asian food, which was an interesting choice. Ty ate healthy most of the time, Ian had put that much together after a quick perusal of his refrigerator the last time he'd stayed over, but neither Ian nor Ty was a vegetarian. Still, Ian was game. If Ty wanted to defy his Texas roots by eating tofu, that was fine by Ian.

He looked over the menu as he waited for Ty, who was already ten minutes late. Ian was trying really hard not to freak out about that, even though the anxious part of him was convinced that he had gotten the night wrong. Or that Ty had forgotten. Or worse, that Ty was standing him up, that whatever foul thing had worked its way into Ty's psyche Tuesday night at the game was convincing Ty to go ahead and end this farce of a relationship. Really, why were they bothering? Ty probably didn't even like Ian much and this dinner was just a pretense to break up.

Ian put down the menu and rubbed his forehead. God, he was a mess. Probably Ty had just gotten stuck on a subway train with a sick passenger and Ian was working himself into a tizzy about nothing. There was no reason to panic. *There was no reason to panic.* Ian felt his heart rate kick up and tried repeating that line to himself, but the more he repeated it, the more he panicked. A cold sweat broke out over his body and his stomach started to churn. He picked up his water glass, but his hands were shaking so bad he didn't think he could actually sip any of it without spilling most of it down his shirt.

Ty walked into the restaurant right when his tardiness had reached the twenty-minute mark. He sat down across from Ian and looked harried. "I am *so*, so sorry. I got stuck at a client's office and then the A was running on the F or something so the subway was totally FUBARed, and…." Ty laughed softly and took a deep breath. "I hate that I kept you waiting. Someone like you is the sort who gets everywhere fifteen minutes early, so you've probably been sitting here close to an hour."

"It's okay," Ian said, though Ty was correct. Well, forty minutes, but still.

"It's not, but I appreciate your saying so." Ty picked up his menu. "Uh, how are you?"

"I'm hanging in there. Trouble at the client's?"

"Eh. So I, um, I design book covers? Among other things. I work freelance and do a little bit of everything. So I just did this book cover and brought the mock-up to the client today and they hate it. Too retro, they said. I thought that was part of the charm of the cover, but no, they want something radically different from what I gave them. It took me three weeks to do that cover, and now I have to go back to the drawing board. So, yeah, today was not a great day."

"That sucks. I'm sorry to hear that." Although, finally, Ian had a crumb of what Ty did for a living, what "design stuff" meant. Designing book covers was more specific, so that was something—Ian had no idea what that would entail or how well it paid, but he was impressed nonetheless. Ty probably had some artistic talents he kept well hidden. Or, hell, maybe everyone who knew Ty knew he was a designer and Ian was the interloper impostor and….

God, there he went again. What the hell was wrong with him?

Ian took a deep breath. He shoved his hands into his lap so Ty couldn't see how bad they were still shaking, but now that Ty had slid off his jacket and settled into his chair, Ian's mouth seemed suddenly devoid of all saliva. Ty had on a tight black T-shirt that nicely showed off his pecs and upper arms, and his hair looked damp—probably from the light rain falling outside—and he had about two days of beard growth that looked like fiery bronze dust across his jaw. His dark blue eyes looked down at the menu, and he traced circles around the restaurant's logo on the embossed leather cover.

"So," Ty said. "How was your day? Better than mine, I hope."

"Yeah. It was fine. We have some terrible people staying at the hotel who distracted a lot of my attention. They kept complaining about the construction noise two floors above where they were staying. I thought, you know, it's the middle of the afternoon in New York City, so if the noise is really that unbearable, they could go outside. But whatever, I had to find them a new room so that they could, I don't know, sit there for five minutes before going to Times Square."

"I thought you worked on hotel remodeling?"

"Not quite. I mean, I'm hired as a consultant, so I work on all parts of the guest experience, getting the hotels up to code, hiring better employees, and yes, sometimes dealing with customers. I don't like to, but management at this hotel is so inept that they're going to get sued one of these days. So I'm helping out until I can find a manager worth hiring."

"Interesting," Ty said, but he still seemed a little baffled.

Ian smiled. He looked down at the menu. He'd almost settled on a noodle dish with imitation chicken, although he wondered what that was made of. Why not just call a spade a spade… or in this case, call tofu tofu.

Ty opened his menu. "I like this place. I recommend the glass noodles. That's my favorite thing on the menu. But really, it's all good. They make an egg dish that's sort of a hybrid of an omelet and crepe but not really. You can put whatever the hell you want in it."

"Okay," Ian said.

Ian hated that there was so much up in the air, that they'd failed to communicate so thoroughly that neither could make sense of what was going on in the other man's head.

When he'd decided what he wanted, and once Ty had as well, Ian put the menu to the side of the table and mentally ordered his hands to stay still long enough that he could sip his water and get some moisture back in his mouth.

"Can I ask you a question?" he asked, though nerves raged. The panicky feeling from earlier came back. It wasn't quite a full-on panic attack, but it had a few symptoms and warning signs. His pulse was thready, his stomach was churning again, and he looked at Ty, really looked at him. Ian tried to figure out what he wanted from this.

That he was attracted to Ty went without question. Ty was the most physically appealing man Ian had met in quite some time. The Texas accent was smooth and deep, like a lazy river passing through a desert. Ty had long fingers and slim wrists and a narrow nose and a scar on his chin from some long-forgotten childhood injury, probably.

But what else was going on here? What did they even know about each other? Ian mentally calculated everything. Ty lived alone in Brooklyn. He was from Texas. He did freelance design work. His father had died when he was in college. He was versatile in bed and flirty with everyone and acted shameless but by his own admission hadn't behaved nearly as badly as he wanted people to believe.

"What did you want to know?" Ty said.

Ian liked Ty the man pretty well. Ty was funny and charming and liked needling Ian and making him laugh. That should have gone a long way. Why wasn't it enough?

"This is, like, a date, right?" It wasn't the question Ian really wanted answered, but it was as good a prelude as he could come up with, particularly since he wanted to put off asking the big question until he had a better notion of how to phrase it.

"Sure," Ty said. "We are two men who are interested in each other sitting at a froufrou Asian restaurant in a fairly gay section of the city. There's candlelight and white tablecloths and everything. I changed clothes before I came to the city today and agonized over which pair of distressed jeans made my ass look the best. So, yeah, that seems like a date." Ty smiled, but it didn't go to his eyes. Ian tried to read his expression. Nervousness? Uneasiness? Did Ty even want to be there?

Stop, Ian told himself. *Don't jump to conclusions*. He needed to find out what the situation really was before his mind went off half-cocked and he said or did something that jeopardized this whole thing. Because as Ian saw it, he had two options: break up with Ty for… reasons he wasn't even sure of himself. Or confess that he was starting to develop real feelings despite his best intentions and see if Ty was game to explore them for at least a little while longer.

"What happened the other night?" Ian asked.

Ty's eyes went wide. "Well, honey, I was kind of hoping you could tell me that."

A tiny waitress appeared then and took their orders. Ty did indeed order the glass noodles with egg and tofu—no imitation meat for this man, just the genuine soggy article—and Ian decided to venture toward whatever mystery lingered in the imitation chicken noodle dish.

Ian said, "Okay, so, let me tell you something." God, he was nervous. Why was he so nervous? Oh, because he wanted Ty. He wanted Ty to make him laugh and to keep him company.

The problem with New York was that it was so fucking lonely. Ian lived in a building that was at least several stops on the subway from everyone he knew, and even though there were probably twenty-some other units in his building, he didn't know any of his neighbors. His mother lived on the other side of the city, more than an hour away by subway on a good day. So many people just put their heads down and got on with their lives. Ian had come here and lived in his little box of an apartment and went to the hotel every day and then went home again at night. He mourned the life he could have had if he just stayed put in one place long enough to put down a few roots. Other cities had been friendly, or at least helped concoct the illusion of friendship. Other cities were not so expensive, so dirty, so complicated, so isolating. Other cities didn't have long nights when Ian could only sit at home and ache and wonder why his life had turned out this way. Other cities didn't have childhood memories of disappointing his father or getting picked on for being a skinny gay kid imprinted on them. Other cities didn't have the threads of every part of Ian's past he wanted to forget and leave behind indelibly stitched into their fabric.

Ty looked at him expectantly.

"I move a lot," Ian said. "Sometimes I'll only be at a job a few months before moving on to the next one. Since I started consulting, I've never stayed in a place longer than two years. At first I wanted to travel, to see the world. I've worked for hotels in four countries and a dozen American cities."

"Must be lonely, never putting down roots anywhere."

Funny how Ty could reach in and grab Ian's thoughts. "It wasn't, not at first. I got my start working for a company run by this guy I interned for in college. He had a firm, so I was working with a company of guys who traveled with me. I was always kind of a loner anyway, so if anything, working this way helped me make more friends. I got to meet so many people through my work. A lot of those people are still in touch with me, and we talk on the phone or e-mail frequently enough. But the thing was, honestly?"

Ian paused. Ty waited, his expression inscrutable as he gazed at the table.

"This is hard for me to say," Ian said.

Ty looked up then, and his eyebrows curved in a way that conveyed sympathy. "So tell me. Whatever it is, I won't judge."

"You realize that if we start divulging secrets to each other, we'll start developing more intimacy between us. We might find ourselves in a real relationship."

"Would that be so bad?" Ty's face didn't give away anything.

Ian frowned and considered. "It's just...." Ian took a sip of water again, still working out what he wanted to say. "Look, the thing is, I've been running for a long time. I grew up in Brooklyn, where I had a perfectly shitty adolescence, and as soon as I could, I lit out of here and never wanted to come back. My mom still lives in Brooklyn, so I came home for holidays, and every time, it was awful and I dreaded it. There's just... it's so much. My past. My family. And now I'm here again and not really having an easy time of it because I can't figure out how to get over myself and just be in this city again without letting all the old bullshit close in around me. So when Josh suggested the damn baseball league, I thought, well, I've never done that before. I'll give it a shot. And when I met you, I thought, hey, here's some fun. But I'm finding that the more time we spend together, the more panicky I feel, okay?"

Ty tilted his head and pursed his lips. "Panicky how?"

"I'm not so great at baseball. It's not that I'm competitive and ambitious, though I am those things, but I hate not being able to control the outcome of something, and baseball is so unpredictable. I can't make myself more coordinated. I can't hit every ball pitched at me. I can't catch every ball tossed at me. I can't always run fast enough to make it on base before the out." Ian let out a breath. "God, I sound like a crazy person."

"Keep going," Ty said.

"So I'm finding baseball really unnerving, enough so that I want to quit some days. And then there's you."

"What's your beef with me?" Ty sat back and crossed his arms over his chest, a gesture Ian recognized as a way to make himself look intimidating, but it was more like a shield going up. Ty was protecting himself.

"It's not with you specifically. It's just that I wasn't looking for a relationship, and when you joked that first time we met about being the team slut, I thought, hell, he's perfect. We'll have a wicked affair and some great sex, if I could have gotten over myself faster, of course, and it would have just been fun. But instead, I'm finding that I really like you and I want to spend more time with you."

Ty let go of the rigid stance. "Why is that a bad thing?"

"Because I'm probably going to skip town as soon as this job is over. And, well, I wasn't sure how you felt about me."

A passing waiter dumped a bowl of fried noodles and a little metal contraption full of sauces on the table. Ty picked up a fried noodle and fiddled with it for a moment before popping it in his mouth.

"Man, I thought you had my number," Ty said. "But you *do* think I'm a slut and I'm not looking for anything wholesome and monogamous after all."

"Are you?"

"Not precisely, but I'm open to anything." Ty picked up and ate another noodle. "You telling me all this as a way to ask if I'm interested in having a relationship with you? Like, more serious than fuck buddies?"

Ian nodded.

Before Ty could answer, there was a jingling sound coming from under the table. "Shit," Ty said. He squirmed in his chair and the sound intensified—Ian recognized it as a pop song he vaguely knew—and then Ty produced his phone. "I gotta…." He answered the phone.

TY PROBABLY could have ignored the call. It was just Carlos, presumably calling about a baseball-related matter. But the conversation had gotten a little intense, so Ty reached for the parachute. He wanted a moment to figure out how to respond to everything Ian had just said.

"Hey, man, how's it going?" he said.

Ian shot him a look like he found the way Ty spoke deeply unsettling.

"Oh, I just wondered if I could borrow your extra glove at practice this weekend," said Carlos. "Mine finally gave up the ghost after the game the other night."

"Yeah, sure. But doesn't someone else have one? I'm surprised you called me."

"Well, I remembered you had one. Also, I did call Nate first, but he was super weird about it, so I told him to forget about it. Do you know what *that's* about?"

Ty had a hunch, but he didn't want to get in the middle of whatever craziness was happening between Carlos and Nate. "Not a clue. But yeah, I'll bring it for you. Text me an hour before so I don't forget."

"No problem. Thanks, Ty."

Ty was almost sad when Carlos said good-bye. Not that it was socially acceptable to take a damn cell phone call in the middle of a restaurant while he was on a date. It was a nice place too, and people at other tables were staring at him now. When he looked back at Ian, Ian was staring at his water glass and tracing the rim with the tip of his finger.

"Sorry about that," Ty said.

Ian shrugged.

The pause the call created hadn't really given Ty enough time to regroup. He took a deep breath. "So Tuesday night, that was… well, that was not me at my best. I've been having a rough go of things with a few of my freelance clients, and I haven't been sleeping well, and it kind of created a perfect storm of tired crankiness. I was unforgivably rude, and I apologize for that. I was having a terrible time even making sense of the game, let alone anything you said to me, so if I reacted badly to something that happened, I am very sorry."

Ian nodded. "Well, sure. You're forgiven. If that was really all."

"Yeah. That was all. I was just really tired. I get these bouts of insomnia sometimes, where I just can't sleep for a few days on end. I've seen doctors and the whole nine and no one can figure it out. I don't like to take sleeping pills or medication for it because I react badly to most of them. So, yeah, that was really it."

Ian picked up a fork and put it back down. He fiddled with his napkin. He took a sip of water. "See, because I worried maybe you didn't like me much after all."

"What? No. That wasn't it at all."

"I mean, I wouldn't blame you. I'm neurotic and anxious a lot of the time. I have some issues, as you may have gathered by that crazy speech I just gave you. So I thought, even if you were just interested in sex, I might have been too much bother and you were working out how best to break up with me without sending me off the side of a bridge."

Ty felt like he'd been punched. He let out a breath. "No. That wasn't it at all." Then he laughed because this whole situation was just so ridiculous. "That really wasn't the case. Hell, I was worried you invited me to dinner tonight to break up with me."

"No." Ian squirmed. "I mean, I wasn't really clear on what I was going to say when you got here, but I… no. I don't want to break up."

"Okay. Good."

Ty was saved again by the waitress coming with their food. She made a production of laying out their dishes too. It gave Ty time to look at Ian across the table. Ian was focused on the waitress putting the food down and asked her a couple of questions about ingredients. While the waitress distracted Ian, Ty studied him. Ian was sexy as hell. He had really intense hazel eyes too, and when the waitress finally finished, he turned the full force of his gaze on the noodle dish laid before him. He picked up his chopsticks and poked at a piece of imitation chicken while the waitress gave the same fussy treatment to Ty's dish.

Ian had a round face, but it was still masculine. His hair was just a little too long, and it curled around his ears and at the base of his neck. Ty wanted to play with those little curls, wanted to yank on them and watch them curl back in on themselves. He wanted to run his hands through the hair on Ian's head and down the sparse blond hair of his chest. Under the striped shirt Ian had on, Ty knew Ian had a solid body, a bit on the thin side maybe, but strong in its way. He'd lost a little weight since the baseball season had started too, which Ty wasn't sure he was completely on board with.

What did Ty want out of this relationship with Ian? Did he want sex? Did he want a friend? Did he want another baseball buddy? He wasn't entirely sure, but he did know he didn't want to end whatever it was.

When the waitress left, Ian picked up a piece of fake chicken with his chopsticks and held it up to his face. "Here goes," he said. He took a moment to taste and chew it; then his Adam's apple bobbed as he swallowed. "Not bad. Guess what it tastes like?"

"Chicken?"

Ian grinned, which was nice to see. "Actually, really peppery tofu. It's weird, but I like it."

Ty nodded and spun his fork in his noodles to pick up a few. He'd never quite gotten the hang of chopsticks, particularly for noodles, and a date was hardly the time to experiment, lest he end up with noodles decorating his shirt.

"Look," he said. He tried to keep his tone even, but his own nervousness about the situation was starting to burble up. What was he really worried about? Well, he'd been worried for two days that Ian didn't want him. Because really, once Ian got to know him, he probably wouldn't be as into him. But the truth was that he was starting to really like Ian. He was attracted, yes, of course he was. He had eyes and Ian was hot with just enough softness around the edges to make him look interesting instead of generically handsome. "I'd like to keep seeing you. I can't make any promises, but it seems to me that we're pretty good together."

Ian nodded. "Good. That's all I really wanted for now."

"And hey, maybe if we keep going on these date things, we'll actually get to know each other as people instead of pieces of meat."

Ian laughed. "Yeah. Crazy, right?"

"Hey, don't mock it. I ain't got a lot of experience with this whole committed relationship situation. Dating? That's so strange to me."

"You prefer to fuck your way through the Rainbow League instead?"

Ian's tone had just enough edge that Ty wasn't sure if he was joking or not. And here they'd been making progress. God, this was hard. Trying for a joke, Ty said, "Well, baby, when there's that much fine flesh on display, it's hard to keep your hands off."

Ian rolled his eyes, so hopefully he took that as the joke it was intended to be. "You're a lot of bluster, aren't you?"

Ty shrugged.

Ian ate a bit of broccoli and said, "So, is that what we are in now? A committed relationship?"

"Maybe that wasn't the greatest phrase to use. I just meant that maybe we keep seeing each other for a while as if we're a real couple and everything, and just see where it goes. Maybe aside from our great mutual love of baseball we don't have that much in common." He winked to show he was definitely joking that time.

Ian laughed. "Right. You love baseball so much that you don't watch it on TV, and I love it so much that I'm thinking about quitting the team because I suck at it so hard."

"Yup, that's about the sum of it."

Ian sighed. "Okay. We'll see where it goes. That seems reasonable."

Ty nodded, feeling pretty pleased with that resolution. "Great. So... wanna come back to my place tonight?"

Ian smiled. "Let's go to mine, if that's okay. Gotta be at the New Amsterdam bright and early in the morning. Did you know it takes more than an hour to get there from Brooklyn?"

"Really? What the hell trains are you taking?"

"I just know that from my mom's place in Park Slope, it's kind of an epic journey. F train to that fake transfer to the 4. Whatever station that is, the one near Bloomingdale's. It's supposed to be a free transfer, but the damn turnstile still charges me half the time anyway."

"Dude, you can transfer from the F to the 6 at Broadway-Lafayette."

"Since when?"

"Since two years ago. Get with it." Ty made a face that was meant to convey that he was still just kidding. "They renovated part of the station and added a stairway so you just go up the escalator from the uptown F platform and the uptown 6 is right there."

Ian sighed and sat back in his chair. "I grew up in Brooklyn, and somehow living in the city again after so many years away is total culture shock. It's not at all like I remember it."

"Well, sure. The city was the last exit before hell when we were kids in the eighties, wasn't it?"

"It had started to turn around by the time I was old enough to ride the subway by myself, but it was definitely nothing like this. The trains are all different, none of the landmarks are where I remember them being, most of the stores and restaurants I frequented the last time I lived here are long gone. It's like a completely different city now." Ian rubbed his forehead. "I'm still adjusting, I guess."

Ty smiled. "Yeah, I hear you. But okay, your place. I can do that. I gotta get up early anyway if I'm gonna redo this commission."

"Have you done a lot of book covers?"

Ty wasn't ready to talk about his art yet. He was going to have to work up to that. Because he could picture a guy like Ian taking one look at the last few paintings and bolting. He didn't even want to admit he did a lot of romance novel covers, nor that they were his favorites to do. Sure, he could throw blocky lettering and some kind of motif on a cover and call it a day—that seemed to be the trend for a lot of literary fiction lately, at any rate—but the clutch paintings were so much fun to do.

"I've done a few, yes. And covers you'd have seen too." He rattled off a few of the covers he'd done for mainstream best sellers.

Ian looked impressed. "Oh, I read a couple of those. Do you read them before you design the covers?"

"No. Usually I just get a description of the book and a few of the themes or important images. Then I go back and forth with the editor and the art director a couple of times. I send sketches and mock-ups until we agree on a concept, and then I'm off to the races. I do some covers the old-fashioned way with paint or drawings, which is why sometimes I end up bringing physical copies to the client."

"That's really cool."

Ty shrugged. Hell, he did what he could to keep himself in paint and canvas, although he hadn't painted anything original in a long time. He was too busy with other design stuff these days.

Ty managed to change the subject to something else, and they talked about innocuous things like weird people Ian had seen in the city since he'd moved back and restaurants where they'd both eaten and Broadway plays they might like to see. Ty was proud of himself for suggesting they go to one of the plays together.

He didn't want to let it get awkward. He wanted everything between them to be okay. It was a strange thing to realize, because he hadn't known he even liked Ian this much, but he supposed that was his answer. He wanted everything with Ian to be great. He worried it wasn't.

They argued over the check at the end of the night, both of them offering to pay, until Ty finally just insisted they go dutch, and then they were in a cab uptown. When they crashed through Ian's door twenty minutes later, Ty felt on firmer footing. This, he knew how to do. The rest was uncharted territory.

Chapter 9

NATE STARED across the lawn, looking for Carlos but trying not to be obvious about it. Carlos's sister Lourdes was holding court in front of a gaggle of girlfriends. Somehow Nate had gotten himself invited to her odd coed baby shower, which had turned into an excuse for her huge Puerto Rican family to gather in one place for a few hours on a Sunday afternoon. In this case, they were under a canopy someone had erected in the middle of Van Cortlandt Park in the Bronx. As was Lourdes's wont, there were more than a hundred people in attendance.

Nate snuck over to the snack table. He grabbed a toothpick and stabbed a few pieces of chorizo. He kept an eye trained on Carlos, who was at the moment having his cheeks molested by a *tia* wearing too much bright pink lipstick. Nate could see her lip prints on Carlos's cheek from the other side of the canopy.

"Hello, Nathan," said a low female voice to his right.

He turned toward Carlos's sister Marisol. "Hey, girl," he said. "Fancy meeting you here at your sister's wackadoodle baby shower."

Marisol rolled her eyes. Nate grinned. She'd always been his favorite of Carlos's three sisters. "Ugh, this party, I can't even. You know how this even started? I just wanted to throw her a nice traditional baby shower. A few of her female friends could all gather at Tia Maria's house, where we'd play some dumb party games and then open presents. But nooo. First Lourdes was all, 'Oh, we have to invite Carlos!' and then it turned into a whole thing."

"Lourdes is aware that Carlos is not a woman, right?"

"Barely. I explained to her that it would be ridiculous to have one man at a baby shower and it would probably make Carlos uncomfortable, but instead of uninviting him, which is probably what he'd want, she invited all the men in the whole fucking family, present company included." Marisol waved her hand. "Anyway, really it was an excuse to throw a bigger party. Mama was beside herself. And here we are."

"Indeed. Well, thanks for inviting me. Good excuse to eat Mama Lulu's tres leches cake."

Marisol crossed her arms over her chest and raised an eyebrow, shooting him a look that only a sassy Puerto Rican girl from the Bronx could make. Nate would have smiled if the look didn't make him fear he was about to get a fist to the nose. "Don't eat too much of that."

"Too late. Have you had this chorizo? It's really good, especially with whatever that yellow sauce is."

Marisol let her arms drop and peered at the table. "Eh. It'll go straight to my ass."

"If you say so, skinny girl."

She picked up a toothpick and stabbed the tiniest piece of chorizo on the plate. She bypassed the sauce and popped it in her mouth. "So apparently Carlos has a terrible crush on some guy in the Rainbow League. He's got a totally Anglo name."

"Aiden."

The disdain that dripped out of his mouth was not entirely intentional, and Marisol looked up in alarm when he spoke. "So we don't care much for Aiden, I take it."

Nate sighed. "He's an okay guy, I guess. Good-looking in a bland, brunet way. Not the sharpest pencil in the box."

Marisol hovered over the food like she really wanted to sample something else. She stuck her toothpick into a tiny piece of cheese. "So you're jealous. I see how it is now."

"What do you see?"

"I see, Nathan, that you are in love with my big brother, but you are a huge wuss and never made a move. Now your chance is slipping right through your fingers, but instead of going up to Carlos and saying, 'Dude, we should go out,' you just sit back and stew about it. Like always. You're so predictable."

"Pretty sure Carlos would end our friendship if I said, 'Dude, we should go out.'" Nate affected his best surfer-boy California accent to show it was more the phraseology than the actual statement that Carlos would react poorly to, although he suspected that Carlos didn't especially want to go out with him, either. Carlos had never thrown one scrap of interest Nate's way, in fact. "Anyway, it's not like that. Carlos is my friend."

"A friend you want to bone. And believe me, since that's my brother we're talking about, it pains me to say that."

Nate groaned. "Maybe I find him attractive, but really, it's not like that. I don't love him that way. I love him like a brother."

"Look, no one is rooting for you as much as I am. I have thought for years that the two of you would make a good couple. I'm surprised, actually, that you haven't already gotten hitched and moved to Westchester and adopted African orphans."

"Not in the cards."

"I wouldn't be so sure about that. Unless, of course, you keep letting the Aidens of the world win. Because Carlos is a smart guy about a lot of things, but he's a complete idiot where his love life is concerned. So if you never say anything, he's going to continue to go out with men who aren't you, and one of these days, one of them will stick. Then what will you do?"

"Nothing. Find my own man."

Marisol sniffed. She popped a chip in her mouth. "That new man won't be Carlos."

Lourdes came over to the snack table then, with Carlos in tow. He smiled at Nate, and Nate felt his heart melt just a little.

Dammit.

"Mari, I need you," Lourdes said as she grabbed Marisol's hand. She gave Carlos a little push as if she were swapping one sibling for the other. The women took off toward the other side of the canopy.

"Oh, hey, did this salsa come from a jar or is this Tio Feliz's?" asked Carlos.

"Tio Feliz," said Nate. "That's your aunt and uncle's Fiestaware it's sitting in, if I'm not mistaken."

Carlos grabbed a chip and scooped a healthy serving of salsa. He ate it with relish. "Man, that's good. Feliz always uses chipotle peppers instead of jalapeños. It's nice and smoky."

"I can't help but notice that this spread is kind of a confluence of various Latin cuisines," Nate observed.

Carlos shrugged. "Honey, I'm third-generation American. Now that my generation is procreating, everything is mixed together. Plus, don't tell anyone, but Tia Lola is actually Mexican."

"¡Escándalo!"

Carlos laughed. "I know. But come on, this is not a surprise. You've been to hundreds of these parties over the years. Hell, Lourdes invited you because you're basically family, and there is not one Latino hair on your head, is there, white boy?"

"Not a one."

"So nobody cares. Family is family." Carlos looked around the spread. "Is there any of Mama's cake left?"

"A little, but it's kind of soggy because it's been sitting around for an hour."

"Irrelevant." Carlos found the prize. He cut a huge slice and spooned some of the leftover sauce on top. Then he grabbed a plastic fork and took a bite. The look on his face was one of pure ecstasy, and Nate found himself uncomfortably aroused by it. "That's the stuff," Carlos moaned.

"Keep it in your pants, big guy," Nate said.

"Ha."

Carlos kept eating while making funny faces at Nate. Nate laughed despite himself.

"So what did you get Lourdes?" Carlos asked as he polished off the last of the cake. "I had a hell of a time finding a gift."

"A onesie and some bottles and bibs and things that were in her registry."

"The registry, duh. Why didn't I think of that? See, I'm no good at this girl stuff. Remember her wedding?"

Nate did. Carlos had agonized for weeks about what to get Lourdes and her husband on the occasion of their marriage, and Nate had pointed out that they'd registered at a half-dozen stores in the city. Hell, Carlos lived across the street from a Pottery Barn. He had no excuse.

But Carlos had always been a terrible gift giver. He'd wait until the last minute and sometimes just bought whatever he ran into on his way to a party, as happened the year he'd given Nate a couple of random used books he'd gotten from a street vendor in the Village. Not that Nate hadn't appreciated the gift—he'd ended up reading and enjoying both books, in fact—but it was pretty clear that Carlos hadn't given it a lot of thought.

"I went to that fancy baby store near Union Square," Carlos said. "It was completely overwhelming. So many little outfits and shoes and toys that are only good for certain age groups and everything is pastel. Ugh. I wound up picking out some board books about farm animals, because this kid's gonna live in the Bronx, so that's, like, exotic. And I bought a little pink dress. So it better really be a girl!" Carlos laughed.

There had been a time when it had been this easy, when Nate and Carlos could just hang out and talk about whatever. Nate had known the whole Ruiz clan for most of his life, so he knew a lot of the family stories, and he felt totally welcome at a family gathering like this one.

It was one of many reasons he thought he and Carlos should be together.

Marisol was right; he was a coward and it was his own fault for never making a move. But Carlos, well, Carlos had never given any indication that he was interested in Nate as anything more than just a buddy, and honestly, after all these years, Nate couldn't bring himself to do anything that would fuck up the easy, casual relationship he had with Carlos and his sisters and their whole family. They'd operated in a certain way for so long, and the romantic feelings were relatively new, so it stood to reason they'd pass and Nate would get over it.

"Looks like they're getting ready to do something over there," Carlos said.

Indeed, all the women had gathered in the middle of the canopy, and some of the men were putting out chairs. Lourdes's long-suffering husband carried presents over to Lourdes by the armful as she arranged herself on a folding chair as if she were the Queen of Van Cortlandt Park. And, Nate supposed, for the next half hour or so, she basically would be.

"Well, let's watch this horror show," Carlos said.

"Lead the way."

SOMEHOW SCOTT got his hands on of one of those guns that could measure the speed something traveled, so he was able to verify that, at his peak, Nate could throw an eighty-six-mile-per-hour fastball. Ian probably could have told everyone that given how much his hand smarted after twenty minutes of practicing ball handling with the Hipsters' pitcher. Ball handling, Ian had learned, was Scott's fancy and kind of obscene-sounding way of describing what was basically a game of catch.

Ian shook out his catching hand as he walked back to the bench. He looked for Ty, who was at that moment deep in conversation with Josh and Mason.

It felt like something with Ty had been resolved, although there was still a strain between them. They enjoyed each other's company. They still held each other at arm's length.

Ian suspected his hand was going to bruise or something from catching all those pitches. If anything, it showed that Ian was making a little bit of progress. His reflexes seemed faster, his instincts honed. Perhaps he wasn't quite professional grade—hell, he wasn't anywhere near that—but he wasn't embarrassing himself either.

"You catch the game last night?" Nate asked. Carlos converged on the bench as well.

"Which game?" Ian asked.

Carlos and Nate exchanged a look. "Um, there's only one baseball team," said Carlos.

Ian was at a loss. He wanted to point out that New York City had two major league baseball teams. But, of course, Carlos and Nate knew that because they were both baseball fans. And they were from... the Bronx, right? Was that true? "Yankees?" Ian tried.

"Yes." Nate narrowed his eyes. "Please don't tell me you're a Mets fan."

"No offense to the Mets, but that's a losing proposition if there ever was one," said Carlos.

"I'm not really... I don't follow pro baseball."

Nate and Carlos both gasped. "How can you not?" asked Nate.

"I dunno. I just don't. I hardly watch television."

Nate and Carlos both devolved into a parody of shock, clutching their invisible pearls and throwing their arms in the air. It looked like a skit they'd practiced just for this moment. Ian wondered about these two. From what Ty had said, they'd been friends since childhood and spent a lot of time together but weren't dating. Probably that kind of long-term friendship meant they had a lot of shorthand, that they had acts and skits they could recite from memory with just a short prompt or a facial expression.

"God, you and Ty are made for each other," Carlos said. "Ty wouldn't know a major league game either, even if a pitch went wild and hit him in the head."

"Or if the entire Mets' lineup were blowing him," said Nate with an eye roll.

Somehow professional sports had never even come up with Ty. Ian couldn't remember them ever having a conversation about baseball that wasn't about the mechanics of playing. Even their conversations about the Rainbow League were mostly gossip about the players. "It's possible to like the game without following the pros."

Carlos shook his head and looked deeply skeptical. "Uh, sure."

Nate smiled. "Look, Carlos and I grew up not too far from Yankee Stadium. We've been going to games with Carlos's uncle since we were this tall." Nate held his hand up at hip level. "He's got season tickets. Still buys seats for us every year."

"I mean, I'll watch a game," said Ian. "If it's on at a bar."

Nate laughed. "Oh, sure. Everybody loves sports when there's alcohol involved."

"Guys! Stop horsing around!" yelled Scott. "Two laps around the ball fields."

Running had never been Ian's favorite physical activity, but the more the more he did it, the easier it got. He struggled at first, but it got better as his body warmed up. He started off running alongside Carlos and Nate, but as they devolved into breathlessly talking about the previous night's Yankees game, he passed them, putting an increasing amount of effort in until he was running with most of his power and had pulled a fair distance ahead of the other two. His heart pumped harder, sweat poured off his body, and he started to feel a little light-headed. It was… freeing, in a way he couldn't explain. As he rounded the backstop and headed into his second lap, he threw out his arms and just let himself feel the sensation of the air against his skin, the pumping of his heart, and the pounding of his feet against the dirt.

By the time practice wrapped, Ian felt tired but also oddly euphoric. Part of him wanted to keep running, to recapture that feeling.

It was probably born of adrenaline and the fact that he hadn't eaten enough that day, but it was also a little bit like really vigorous sex. He wanted that sensation back. When Ty walked up to him as practice was ending, Ian knew he had to make a quick decision. He suddenly knew exactly what he wanted.

"Your place," Ian said, barely able to speak through his panting. "Let's go to your place."

Ty tilted his head. "Uh-huh. You don't want to eat something first or…."

Ian grabbed the front of Ty's shirt in his fist and pulled Ty close. "I want to fuck," he whispered. "Right now."

Ty's eyes went wide. "Christ. Okay. Yes."

Getting to Ty's place involved something of a hike through Prospect Park and then several more blocks farther north after that. Ian set a fast pace, power walking there, and Ty struggled to keep up.

"What the hell, man?" Ty said, jogging to keep pace. "What's the hurry?"

"I feel… I feel incredible right now. I mean, that was great, right? The practice?"

"Are you on something?" Ty frowned. "I don't really think that dropping balls and getting yelled at by Scott for two hours is the best time I've ever had."

Ian didn't know how to explain what he was feeling. "Probably I'm experiencing some kind of weird chemical imbalance, but I don't care. I feel great! I started feeling a little manic during my last lap around the ball field. I mean, I'm most likely losing my mind. But I want to keep that feeling going."

"With sex?"

"Hard sex. Rough sex. The sort of sex that leaves a mess of ripped clothes and broken dishes on the floor. The sort of sex that rips the sheets off the bed. Messy, dirty, athletic sex."

Ty stopped walking. "Jesus fucking Christ," he said on a light breath.

"I know. I want to… can we? I mean, are you not in the mood?"

Ty reached out and put a hand against a tree. He leaned there for a moment, catching his breath. He shot Ian a warm half smile. "Oh, baby. I'm always in the mood."

"Am I crazy? Am I about to have a seizure or something?" Because, really, this was completely unlike Ian. He hated when things were messy. But he was high, or something, and he didn't want to let go of this feeling.

Ty resumed walking. "Well, I can't guarantee that you have not lost your mind, but frankly, I'm okay with it. You want to fuck? Let's fuck."

Ian grabbed Ty's hand and pulled him as they walked, hoping that would help Ty keep pace. Ty laughed as Ian pulled him along.

"You remember the way to my apartment?" Ty asked.

"Yes, yes. Park Place, right?"

"Yup. Three blocks up from Grand Army Plaza. You want me to meet you there?"

"No. Just… walk faster. Let's go."

TY'S BACK hit the wall and the impact forced the wind out of his chest for a second, but he gasped his way back to breathing sort of normally until Ian's mouth crashed down against his. He grabbed at Ian's back, ripped his T-shirt off over his head between kisses, and pressed his palms against Ian's chest. Ian toed off his shoes and thrust his hips against Ty's, slamming him farther into the wall. A painting hung just to the right of his head that he was in danger of knocking off the wall, but… eh, he'd never liked that painting much anyway.

They banged through Ty's living room until Ian threw Ty at another wall. This wall banging was going to bruise, but Ty didn't give a shit. He curled his fingers into the skin of Ian's chest and the fine hair there brushed against his palms. He was already totally and completely aroused, hard to the point of aching, wanting Ian like he hadn't wanted anything in a while. He wanted Ian inside him, wanted Ian to fuck him hard, to piston in and out, to make his body hurt. Somehow he'd gotten caught up in whatever crazy thing was going on with Ian. He kissed Ian, tasted his saliva, licked into his mouth. Ian snaked his tongue out and slid it roughly across Ty's lower lip. Ian was also hard, his erection pushing against Ty's hip, nudging him insistently, making its presence known.

Ty hooked his fingers into the waist of Ian's warm-up pants. He realized with a certain amount of delight that they were pull-away pants, that Ian had slid them on over his shorts when they'd left the park. Ty tugged and the snaps came undone with a series of satisfying metallic clicks, the front pulling away from Ian's body and hanging open like an invitation. Ian's cock was tenting his shorts in a fairly amazing way.

"I didn't," Ian said, leaning over and nipping at Ty's neck. "I didn't, um, with the whole jock thing today, because Scott said...."

"Fuck it. Who cares?" Ty asked. He shoved his hand into Ian's shorts and was satisfied when he was able to wrap his hand around Ian's hot, hard cock. Dear Lord, that was something amazing right there, big and smooth and warm against Ty's palm.

Ty grabbed the waistband of the shorts-and-underwear situation and pulled it down, sinking to his knees in front of Ian. Ian's cock bobbed free, seeming to hang in the air for a moment. Ty didn't even hesitate. He engulfed the whole thing in his mouth.

Ian was a little larger than average, but he fit quite nicely in Ty's mouth, fit even better down Ty's throat when he relaxed it. Ian groaned loud enough to anger the neighbors, but Ty figured the neighbors would just have to put up with it. He sucked on Ian's beautiful cock, ran his tongue over the smooth skin, felt every vein against his tongue. God, this was hot, sucking on Ian, making him moan and grunt and thrust forward. He loved it when Ian slunk his hands into his hair, when he brushed and scratched his fingers against Ty's scalp. He wanted to make Ian keep moaning, to make the man scream, to make him come over and over. Ty wanted Ian to work through his aggression on Ty's body.

"Fuck," Ian panted. "Fuck, I really want to fuck you. I want in your tight ass bad. I want to make you feel everything you're making me feel right now."

Ty reluctantly pulled away. "Bedroom."

Ian nodded. Ty walked into his room while Ian followed behind him, shedding the rest of his clothes. "Get naked," Ian said forcefully.

That was easy enough. Ty had already kicked off his shoes and socks and lost his shirt in the living room. He pulled off his sweatpants and underwear in one fell swoop and stood before Ian, hard and wanting and needing to get fucked. He wanted to feel Ian moving inside him, wanted to feel that perfect combination of pain and pleasure, wanted to rub his cock against Ian and find some release for the insane arousal pulsing through his body.

Ian walked up to Ty, grabbed his face, and laid one hell of a kiss on him. It was all lips and teeth, licking and biting, and it sent waves of pleasure and warmth through Ty, making him feel hot and tingly everywhere.

Ty groaned. He moved toward the bed while reluctantly pulling away from the kiss. He fell onto the mattress and pulled Ian with him so that they landed with a huff of breath and a grunt and a tangle of limbs. Ian laughed softly and ran his hands over Ty's face, over his shoulders, down his belly, to his cock. He wrapped his hand around Ty's aching dick and started stroking long and slow and, *fuck*, that felt good. Ian crawled up the bed a little and eyed the drawer on the side of Ty's bed.

"Yes, do it," Ty said, gesturing toward the drawer. "I don't need a lot of foreplay and romance. Just fucking. God, I want you inside me."

"That's what I want to hear," Ian said. He reached for the drawer and pulled out lube and a condom.

Ty took the lube from him and uncapped the bottle. Ian raised an eyebrow as he tore the wrapper off the condom.

Ty was blessed with long arms and long fingers. He poured the lube on himself and then plunged a finger deeply inside, feeling the burn of that but also totally ready for it. He wanted more but knew better than to rush. Ian rolled on the condom and stroked himself a couple of times before Ty handed over the lube and thrust a second finger into himself.

"That's...." Ian shook his head. "That's so hot, I think my brain shorted out. I'm dizzy."

Ty used his other hand to stroke his own cock. Might as well give Ian a show.

"Christ," Ian said. "You are one sexy motherfucker, Red. I want to put my cock where your fingers are. I want to fuck you until you scream."

Ty groaned. "I want you to fuck me. I want you to come inside me."

Ian moved forward. He slapped Ty's hands out of the way and then reached forward himself. He thrust three fingers inside Ty in one fast movement, and Ty groaned with the surprise of it, with the pain. That felt amazing. It felt like he needed more. It felt like he was about to get his mind blown.

"Front? Back? Top? You got a preference?" Ian asked while thrusting his fingers in and out of Ty.

"Like this," Ty said, pulling his legs up, using his hands to hold his knees to his chest.

"Yes. Yes, like that. You are so fucking sexy. I can't wait any longer." Ian pulled his fingers out. Ty spread his legs farther apart to make room. Ian approached, putting one hand on the bed beside Ty's shoulder and holding his cock with the other. "You ready?"

"I was ready five minutes ago, baby."

"Mmm."

Ian dipped his head and kissed Ty, diverting Ty's attention for a moment to just the meeting of their lips and the soft slide of them against each other. The kiss was sweet as well as sexy, affectionate but also full of promise. This wasn't *just* fucking, the kiss said. Ty understood that. He and Ian were building toward something, and he had a sense of that now as they shared a kiss that wasn't quite as insane as before.

But then Ty felt Ian at his entrance, the blunt head of his cock pushing forward, pushing inside Ty. And all bets were off.

Ian went slowly, working up to thrusting into him. Ty lifted one of his hands to run his palm over Ian's head, the texture of his hair rubbing against his hand. He ran that hand down Ian's face, felt the roughness of his invisible blond stubble, felt down his throat and over Ian's Adam's apple, and down his chest. Ian kept pressing forward, moaning as he did it, stretching Ty to the point where Ian was impossibly big but also amazing. It hurt—it was a sweet, searing pain, but it was so fucking good too, both literally and figuratively filling something inside Ty.

He felt like he was on the edge of something really intense. He felt like something big was about to happen.

Ian rocked his hips and slid into Ty until he was fully seated.

"Okay?" Ian asked.

"Move."

Ian nodded and pulled out slightly. Then he slammed back in. Both of them groaned.

Ian worked at it for a few moments, thrusting experimentally, pulling out, pushing in, trying to find the pace. It wasn't enough. There wasn't enough speed or force to get Ty to the place he most wanted to go.

"More," he groaned. "More, faster. I'm not breakable. Fuck me, Ian. If you want to fuck me, do it. Do it right."

"Hell yeah."

Then Ian totally let loose. He thrust with increasing intensity and speed, moving his hips quickly and pushing into Ty hard. Ty was slick and wet with sweat, groaning and grunting and grasping at Ian as if his life depended on it. He arched up to meet Ian's thrusts. He pulled on Ian's hair and tugged on Ian's nipples and wrapped a hand around his own cock to get to that place faster.

"Oh, that's good," Ian grunted. "So good, baby. You're so tight. So fucking sexy. I'm not gonna last…."

Ian kept going. The pace was frantic. His expression was fraught.

"Touch me," Ty said, lifting his hand. "Make me come."

Ian nodded and wrapped his hand around Ty's cock. He stroked it at the same crazy pace he was pushing on Ty's body, and everything in Ty seemed to speed up and rush forward. Ty grabbed Ian's shoulders and dug in his fingers. This was insane and hard and fast and perfect and then *wham*! The orgasm slammed through Ty, the sensation starting at his toes and rising through his legs and then just exploding out of him. He came in long streams over his chest, crying out as he did, arching his back, clutching at Ian and urging him to keep going.

"I'm… shit, I'm coming," Ian said, bowing forward and clutching at Ty. He pulled Ty's nearly limp body into his arms and then thrust one last time before he went totally still. He groaned and Ty imagined he could feel Ian's cock vibrating inside him.

They kissed as Ian came down, tender and sweet.

"That was… that was exactly what I needed," Ian said.

"I'm glad," said Ty. "That was pretty fucking awesome."

Ian settled against Ty's chest. "Glad we decided to make a go of this."

"Me too."

"I'm hungry."

"Me too."

"Can't move quite yet."

"Me too."

Ian laughed. He kissed Ty's chest. "Maybe we just lie here a few more minutes."

"Sounds good."

Chapter 10

IN THE aftermath, Ian let himself sink into Ty's mattress. Ty had gotten out of bed to clean up and call for pizza, but Ian had decided to languish. His body felt loose and fluid, and he still had a bit of that postworkout euphoria. But it was nice to just lie in Ty's big bed, which was covered in jersey cotton sheets and a big blue-and-white-striped comforter. It was soft, and while not quite luxurious, it was spacious and extremely comfortable.

Ty walked back into the room as Ian was deciding whether he should wake up or let sleep claim him. Ty was still stark naked and looked incredible, all tan and muscles and fiery red hair.

"Hey, Texas," Ian said sleepily.

Ty lowered his eyelids and shot Ian a sly grin. "Hey, yourself, cowboy. Pizza's on the way."

"You gonna greet the pizza boy looking like that?"

"You think I should invite him to join us?"

Ian pretended to consider. "Nah, I want you all to myself. Also, he's probably some teenage boy with bad acne. We don't need that."

"No." Ty sat on the bed. "I like the idea of you wanting me to yourself. Like you're claiming me."

"I am. I planted a flag and everything."

Ty laughed. "You have a weird sense of humor, you know that?"

"Uh, thanks?"

Ty leaned down and kissed Ian thoroughly, slipping his tongue into Ian's mouth before pulling away again. "Can I ask you something?" Ty said.

"Sure."

"The anxiety thing. You feeling it now?"

Actually, Ian hadn't felt anxious all day. No anxiety at all. Not at practice, not with Ty. "Nope. I feel awesome. It's possible there's something to the idea that exercise helps relieve stress. Maybe that's what's happening. I have some kind of natural high."

"Because Scott is a bully who made you run laps?"

"And also because I had great sex with you." Ian struggled a little to sit up. His limbs still felt a little gelatinous. "Take the compliment, Ty. Because that really was incredible."

"I'm glad, baby. And hell, you need to relieve more stress, you know where to find me."

"I didn't hurt you? I got kind of rough."

"Nope. I mean, you know, I'll be sore tomorrow, but it was great. That'll be like a reminder of you every time I sit down."

Ian laughed. "I can't tell if that's a compliment or not."

Ty kissed Ian. It was quick and hard and very nice. Ian wanted to pull Ty back into bed with him, but Ty backed away and stood back up. "I'd better find some shorts so I don't traumatize the pizza guy."

"Are you anxious?" Ian asked, because suddenly Ty seemed antsy, fidgeting around his room as he looked for his shorts.

"Nope. I feel great too."

But Ian didn't quite believe him.

WHEN THE intercom buzzed, Ty left Ian in bed and went to answer it. On the way, he passed the closed door of his studio and thought briefly about what might happen if he showed Ian his art. Would Ian like it? Would he judge?

Well, there was no time now if he had to get dinner.

The pizza guy turned out to be a skinny twentysomething guy with a seventies-era mustache who was cute if one liked 'em pale and emaciated. Ty found himself amused that the guy was almost good-looking enough to invite inside. But he paid him instead and sent him on his way.

Ian emerged from the bedroom wearing his white briefs. He rubbed his eyes, stretching his torso as he did so, showing off a lot of toned body, pale skin, and his fuzzy invisible hair. The blond got a little darker at his armpits and just above his cock.

Ian yawned and sat next to Ty on the couch. "Sexy pizza guy?"

"Skinny guy with a hipster mustache."

Ian wrinkled his nose. "Ugh. Is this what Brooklyn has become since I've been gone?"

"'Fraid so." Ty opened the pizza box. He considered getting up to get plates, but the roll of paper towels he'd left on the coffee table the previous night would get the job done. He grabbed a paper towel, passed the roll to Ian, and grabbed a slice of pizza.

"At least you didn't get some hippie vegetarian pizza," Ian said.

"I'm not actually a vegetarian. I just like to eat healthy. But every now and then you have to splurge. Pizza is one of my vices."

Ian raised an eyebrow. "If pizza is a vice, I don't want to live."

"Well, you know. I have other vices. Reality TV. Red licorice. Anal sex."

"One of these things is not like the other," Ian sang.

"So I eat healthy. So sue me. I want to maintain my girlish figure."

"I like your figure just fine."

Ty grinned. "Yes, well. Don't think it's easy to maintain all this." He gestured toward himself.

Ian laughed and took a slice from the box.

What Ian had just said reverberated in Ty's head as he ate. *Is this what Brooklyn has become since I've been gone?* Ty wondered if maybe one of Ian's problems was that he was already predisposed to dislike the city. They hadn't really discussed the particulars of Ian's childhood or even whether Ian liked where he was living now, but Ty had definitely picked up on some deeply uncomfortable vibes when they'd walked through Park Slope to go to the bar after practice. Hadn't Ian grown up in Park Slope? Some bad memories were probably embedded in those streets. Ty wasn't sure that he was ready to go fishing for those—and, really, he respected Ian's privacy and didn't want to know—but maybe Ty could turn this around.

"You don't like New York much, do you?"

Ian shrugged. "It's fine. Not what I remember."

That was a perfect nonanswer. "Look, I'm a Texas boy, and this city welcomed me with open arms when I arrived. I left a lot behind to come here, but New York snagged me and made me never want to go back. I love this city and can't imagine living anywhere else."

"That's great. I'm happy for you."

"You could make me sound less deluded."

Ian sighed. "Look, it's… different when you grew up here. This city might have welcomed you, but it wasn't very kind to me. More to the point, I'm not sure I like how it's changed. Sure, there's less crime now than there was when I was a kid, but it's also expensive and crowded and pretentious and smelly and dirty and terrible in a lot of ways."

"Sure, but nowhere is perfect."

Ian rolled his eyes.

"I accept your challenge," Ty said.

"What challenge? I didn't issue a challenge."

"You hate New York. You're stuck here, though, for the next, what? Year? Two?"

"Yeah."

"I'm going to prove to you that this city is awesome and a place worth hanging around. At least until your job ends."

"Right. How are you going to do that?"

Ty polished off his slice of pizza and leaned back on the couch. "Oh, I have tricks up my sleeve."

Ian tilted his head. He shifted his gaze up, like he was thinking about it. "Okay. I give you until the end of the Rainbow League season."

"Yeah?"

"Yeah. When does it end?"

"Early October."

"Okay, then. That gives you all summer, basically, to prove to me that New York doesn't suck."

"That's hardly a tall order. I mean, take this pizza right here." Ty took another slice. "I know it's not, like, Totonno's or Lombardi's or whoever's, but it's a hole-in-the-wall, tackily decorated, standard Brooklyn pizza joint where a slice still costs the same as a ride on the subway. This stuff is my ambrosia. They don't make pizza like this anywhere else in the world. Only New York City. Right?"

"I kinda prefer Chicago style."

Ty gasped. "Blasphemy! No. I will make a New Yorker out of you. By the end of this summer, you will be talking with the old accent you must have had as a kid and sound just like the guy who took my pizza order just now. You will be parading around town in an 'I heart New York' T-shirt. You will love this city again, the kind of love you must feel deep in your bones."

"If I don't?"

Ty shrugged. "If you don't, you finish your job and move on to the next one. But if you do?"

"This is an odd bet. What does either of us win?"

Ty decided to go out on a limb. "Maybe we get each other."

Ian stared at Ty for a long moment. "What do you mean?"

"Look, if you still hate the city and I lose this nonbet, then you leave. But if I win the nonbet and you end up loving the city again, maybe you'll stay here a little longer. We have more sex like we just had. Then I win. Or, really, we both win."

"Er, okay." Ian looked unconvinced.

"Hey, whatever. It's not a bet so much as a mission. And I think I can prove to you that this city is a great place to live. So there it is."

"You're crazy, but you are certainly welcome to try to convince me. I'll warn you that it will be an uphill battle."

"That's just fine, baby. I like a challenge."

Chapter 11

OPERATION: IAN Hearts NY began with Ty doing something he wasn't sure he wanted to do: he asked Mason for Yankees tickets.

"Christ on a stick," Mason said. "Do you know how many people ask me for tickets every week? I'm not best friends with the ticket people. I haven't played there in five years."

"Yeah, but… look." Ty explained the mission.

Mason groaned over the phone but said he'd see what he could do.

It wasn't even that Ty wanted to see the Yankees specifically, it was more that he thought it might be a fun way to apply their knowledge of the sport learned from too many practices with Scott shouting at them. Plus, this Yankee Stadium had been built while Ian was away, and it was symbolic of the new city in a way—cleaner than its predecessor and not so blue and dingy on the inside. Ty could still count on one hand the number of professional baseball games he'd seen in person, but he certainly remembered how much he disliked the old Yankee Stadium.

At the Rainbow League game Tuesday, Ian kept shooting him looks, and then finally, when they were waiting to go up to bat in the sixth, he said, "This isn't going to be one of those dumb out-of-towner tours of the city, right?"

Ty had spent the better part of the last two days brainstorming what he was going to do with Ian to really prove that Ian belonged in the city. He wasn't sure what was motivating him so much, but motivated he was. "No. I know better than that. A trip to the top of the Empire State Building or buying a foam crown at the Statue of Liberty are not the ways to prove to a disillusioned man that New York is the greatest city in the world. This will be a more subtle siege."

"Okay. 'Cause I did all that shit when I was a kid."

It had crossed Ty's mind that it might be fun to have a dumb tourist day. Ty had spent his first month in New York just gawking at everything. He'd come to the city at eighteen, an art school kid with too much Texas in his voice and an underdeveloped, skinny body. He'd had a hard time making friends at first. He'd spent a fair amount of his time between classes just wandering around the city. He had gone to the top of the

Empire State Building—he went to the top of the World Trade Center too—and he took the Liberty Island Ferry and he saw Rockefeller Center at Christmas and he rushed Broadway shows and he saw the Naked Cowboy in Times Square and he went to the big museums and Central Park and he loved every minute of it. He went home for the summer after his first two semesters in New York and he couldn't wait to go back.

But he saw the doubt in Ian's eyes, so he knew he had to come up with a better plan, and that would be a plan born of having lived in the city long enough to know the hidden parts, to know what was special about it and what was worth going out of his way to see, but it also came with a non-native's starry-eyedness. He still loved this city down to his bones, and he was determined to make Ian see that it was a place worth staying.

He really liked Ian, was what this meant.

Ian went up to bat. He'd been hitting better lately; Scott kept a log of their hits and runs so he could quickly calculate everyone's batting averages. Ty could not have given two shits about any of it; he was just happy to play. But it seemed to matter to Ian, who had seen his average go up as the season progressed.

Tonight they were playing the other all-female team, the Bronx Bombshells, who were much less competitive than the Mermaids. Ty liked these ladies; they didn't seem to care much about who won or lost the game, so everyone seemed to be having fun. One woman was literally braiding the hair of another over on their bench. The Hipsters had a decent lead, but that was only because Scott kept yelling at them to pay attention and at least try.

Ty sat on the bench and watched Ian at bat. He had a pretty good stance, probably from the muscle memory of having played in high school. He held the bat aloft and swirled it in the air over his head before resting into his stance. The first pitch went wide and was called a ball. The second one did the same. Ian didn't even swing for those. So he was learning. The third pitch went right over the plate and, consequently, connected with Ian's bat and went sailing toward left field. The Bombshells' left fielder was barely paying attention, spacily staring up into the sky, and so she missed the ball by a couple of yards. She ran after it and tossed it toward second, but not before Ian was safe there. Ty clapped.

"Cute of you to clap for your boyfriend," said Mason.

"He's not my boyfriend."

"Um, let's review. He's a guy you go out with sometimes, right? And don't tell me you're not sleeping with each other, because the two of you have the body language whenever you're near each other of two guys who are about to rip each other's clothes off."

Ty rolled his eyes. "Yes, I'm sleeping with him, and yes, we've gone out a couple of times aside from the postgame drinks. Okay?"

"Sounds like a boyfriend thing to me."

Ty shrugged. "Whatever. So *maybe* he's kind of my boyfriend." Ty didn't want to let on too much just yet. The relationship still felt too new.

Ty glanced at Josh, who was at bat then. He fouled out.

"Right," said Mason. "And you have this crazy convince-Ian-to-stay-in-New-York mission because he's maybe kind of your boyfriend?"

"Ty!" Scott barked.

Ty shrugged and walked up to the plate. That was the thing about a low-stakes amateur athletic league, particularly when your team was winning. It didn't much matter what you talked about between innings. Actually, since the whole league was basically an excuse to be social, most of the guys discussed their love lives between at bats.

So Ty was distracted when he got to the plate. It felt strange to call Ian his boyfriend, but the clues all pointed in that direction. Ty had barely even flirted with another guy since meeting Ian. There certainly wasn't anyone else in the league that season he would rather have been fucking. So there was that.

And maybe this whole endeavor with the Prove to Ian that New York Doesn't Suck Project was a byproduct of some desire to have Ian by his side on a more permanent basis. Because Ty was pretty sure he did want that. Or he at least wanted to see if that was where this was going.

He totally biffed the first pitch. He swung too late and the ball missed his bat as it flew into the catcher's glove.

"Strike," called the umpire.

Focus, Ty, he told himself, although his focus was totally shot with Ian standing across the field. Ian had a bit of a lead on second base, angling toward third, but his attention was on home plate and Ty, waiting for Ty to hit the ball so he could run.

Or watching Ty for other reasons.

He whiffed over the second pitch too, swinging way too late to even have a prayer of connecting with it. Into the catcher's mitt it went again.

"Shit," he muttered.

Suddenly it mattered. Ty had never cared if he struck out or hit the ball or got a home run or what. He was just there to horse around and have fun. But he lifted his bat and held it toward the pitcher, and he felt like it mattered. Ian was watching him, and he wanted to impress Ian. He tried to focus on just the pitcher, a petite woman with really jacked-up arms, which he suspected she needed to throw the ball with that much force. He watched the ball carefully as she wrapped her hand around it and then pulled it close to her body. She wound up and pitched, so he moved the bat, knowing he would hit it this time and—

"Foul ball!"

He cursed again.

The catcher tossed the ball back toward the pitcher. Ty took a deep breath and tried to focus again. The pitcher wound, pitched.... Ty moved his bat....

"Strike!"

Ty wanted to make a scene. He wanted to throw the bat on the ground and shout in frustration and stomp around. Instead, he took a deep breath and walked off the field. He handed his bat to Mason.

He wondered if one of Will's or Josh's schemes was competitiveness in the form of trying to impress one's teammates.

He sat on the bench feeling frustrated and a little sad that he hadn't been able to pull that off.

Mason, of course, hit a home run, batting in both Ian and Josh.

Ian trotted over and sat next to Ty, all smiles. "Hey, bummer about your at bat, but how great was Mason?"

"You did well too. That was a great hit."

"Thanks."

Ty knew that Ian wasn't terribly confident in his ability to play baseball as well as some of the other guys on the team, so he probably needed some validation. Seeing Ian now did take the edge off some of the disappointment Ty felt in not doing well that inning. In fact, seeing Ian that happy did a tremendous amount to lift Ty's spirits.

Ty leaned over and kissed Ian's cheek.

"What was that for?" Ian asked.

"You deserved it."

Ian kept on grinning.

AT THE after-party, Ian was happy to celebrate a victory, even one that had been fairly easy. The game had just been fun. The women from the Bombshells were good sports about losing, and they bought everyone on the Hipsters a round of shots. So Ian was pretty well in his cups, talking to the Bombshells' first baseman—basewoman?—about a hotel she'd stayed at in Paris when he felt a pair of strong arms wrap around him from behind.

"Your boyfriend?" the woman—her name was Martha—asked.

"This is Ty," Ian said.

"I know. His reputation precedes him. Fair warning."

"I know all about Ty's reputation," Ian said.

"I am not a *total* slut," Ty said. "I could be faithful if I wanted to be."

"We're just dating anyway," said Ian.

Ty rested his head on Ian's shoulder. Ian wondered if what he'd just said was even true.

"I'm dating a woman from the Mermaids. You know Leah?"

"I know Leah," Ty said. "She hits better than most of the men on the Hipsters. Even Mason."

"Oh, that's right." Martha laughed. "You accused her of using performance-enhancing drugs last season."

"As a joke." Ty backed away from Ian. Ian missed his touch. Ty said, "I was kidding. But Leah has no sense of humor." He rolled his eyes.

Ian still couldn't remember which woman from the Mermaids was which. Being in the league meant he had to learn a lot of names, and really, aside from his own teammates, he couldn't remember most of them. But Martha he liked; she seemed to get his sense of humor, and she had also grown up in New York, gone away, and come back. She was from Queens originally—"Not even cool Queens, like Astoria. I grew up in Forest Hills," she'd explained—and she had gone off to Massachusetts for college, gotten snagged in Boston for a while afterward, fallen in love with New England, but wound up back in New York after a bad breakup and a new job offer.

"Sounds familiar," Ian had said.

Now they stood there with Ty making jokes about PEDs and how clearly the petite Asian woman who served as the Bombshells' catcher was on some sort of steroid. Martha laughed, presumably because that woman probably weighed ninety pounds soaking wet.

"Actually," Martha said, "the SoHo team got in trouble a few years ago because a couple of the guys were getting high before, during, or after games. I can't remember which."

"Probably all three," said Ty.

"Yeah, probably. I always thought it was dumb to consider pot a performance-enhancing drug. If anything, the opposite is true," said

Martha. "Like, what were they worried would happen? The players would space out on the field and then wander off when they got the munchies?"

The joke wasn't as funny as Ty and Martha seemed to find it, but both of them laughed uproariously just the same.

"Let me get you guys another drink," Martha said. "What's in your cups?"

"Gin," Ian said. "Tom the bartender made me some kind of gin cocktail. It's got, um, juice in it."

Martha giggled. "With my mind on my money and my money on my mind."

"What?" Ian asked.

"Snoop Dogg? 'Gin and Juice'? No?" Martha shrugged. "All right. An Ian special. What're you drinking, Ty?"

"The summer ale."

"Be right back."

Ty walked next to Ian and put an arm around him once Martha was gone. It was nice, but Ian recognized it for what it was—Ty being a little bit possessive. He enjoyed the attention, but he doubted himself a little. He wanted to make the most of something that felt good, but the temporary nature of their relationship nagged at him.

But Ian put his arm around Ty's torso and gave him a little squeeze.

"Good game today," Ian said.

"I stunk like a ten-dollar hooker after a long night," Ty said, all Texas that time, his accent rolling off his tongue. "Maybe Scott's right and I need more batting practice."

"Since when do you care?" Ian asked.

"I don't, I just…." Ty pulled away.

Martha came back then. She had three cups in her hands, which she carefully placed on a nearby table before distributing the drinks.

"So, Martha, let me pose a hypothetical question," Ian said.

"Sure."

"You grew up here, but how do you really feel about the city?"

"I like it more than Boston. My ex, she sort of… she *is* Boston in a lot of ways. Grew up in Dorchester, has this pretty amazing accent. Now any time I hear one on TV or in a movie, I think about her. 'Mahtha, you wanna come ovah to my place tonight? You can pahk on Boylston.'"

Ian giggled.

"I like New York fine. Especially now. I mean, I got a place in Brooklyn, in Fort Greene? It's pretty swanky. I moved in before the neighborhood got super trendy. I dated a girl who was a painting student at Pratt for a while and it was cute. It's not Queens, at least."

"Fair enough," Ian said.

"I'm working on convincing Ian that he's wrong to hate the city as much as he does," said Ty.

Martha gasped. "How can you hate it?"

"It's… I dunno. It's loud and crowded and smelly. My mother still lives in Park Slope, and—"

"You grew up in Park Slope?"

"Yeah, but it wasn't then like it is now. And now isn't really much of an improvement. Last time I went to see my mother, I got my foot trampled first by a small child and then by his mother when she ran over my toes with a stroller."

"Okay. I can see how that might predispose you to not like the city much. But it has things to recommend it too. Museums. Theater. Amateur baseball leagues." Martha smiled.

Ian shrugged.

"It's my summer project," Ty said.

"Well. To summer projects, then. And to New York City." She held up her glass.

Ian and Ty both clinked glasses with her.

Later, Ty and Ian walked to the subway together. Ty surprised Ian by taking his hand. Ian liked the press of their warm palms together, but he also was surprised by how affectionate and couple-y the gesture felt.

"Why, Texas," Ian said, "I think you might be starting to like me."

"Starting?"

Ian squeezed Ty's hand. "You do like me?"

"Little bit."

"I like you a little bit too."

"Even if I can't hit a baseball?"

"Baseballs are not the balls I'm most concerned with."

Ty laughed. He leaned over and gave Ian a quick peck on the lips. "Good thing."

Chapter 12

THE FIRST part of Ty's onslaught began on a Sunday morning. Ty showed up at Ian's building and made Armand call upstairs and instruct Ian to come down immediately wearing comfortable shoes.

Ian showed up fifteen minutes later—"I had just gotten out of the shower, Red," he said, exasperated—but Ty was undeterred.

"When was the last time you went to the Met?" Ty asked.

"This is your strategy? I thought we weren't doing dumb touristy things."

Ty shook his head. The Met was basically his favorite place in the city, and he would not stand for Ian denigrating it. "There's a pop art exhibit that I've been wanting to see. I won't waste too much of your time if you are not an art person. But I thought, okay, if I had a whole day in the city do anything I wanted, what would I do? I'd go see all the things I've been wanting to see for a while, and I'd bring a boy I like to make it a little more festive."

"Okay. What else do you have planned?"

"Nope. Not telling." Although now Ty wasn't being coy so much as he was nervous Ian was going to hate every moment of the day he had planned.

"All right," Ian said, sounding resigned. "Am I dressed okay for this mystery date?"

Ty looked him up and down. Ian was wearing a blue-and-white seersucker shirt tucked into a pair of dark jeans. He wore preppy but practical white sneakers on his feet. He looked like he was dressed to keep cool and comfortable, which was pretty perfect for what Ty had planned. "Yup, you look fine." Ty winked.

"Well. Lead the way."

Ty tugged on the edge of his T-shirt, which was casual but still pretty nice, a dark gray heather with a V-neck deep enough to show off his collarbones but not so deep that it was vulgar. He hiked up the hem of his own jeans and kicked the door open with the tip of one of his docksiders. Outside, the day was overcast and a little dingy-seeming, but he had faith the clouds would clear. "It's nice out. Not too hot," Ty said when they got outside. "You want to walk?"

"Sure?"

"Did you eat?"

"No. Some dude turned up at my place and made me leave before I could."

"How rude of him." Ty nudged Ian with his shoulder. "Well, do you want a quick breakfast or something more involved?"

"What did you have in mind?"

"Well, there's this really cute little coffee shop on Eighty-First that has good pastries if you want to do something quick. Otherwise, there's a restaurant near the natural history museum that does a good, hearty brunch."

"Let's eat a big meal. I want, like, pancakes and bacon and eggs and the whole nine yards."

"Whole nine it is. This place is pretty good. Opened last year. It's a little pricey, but there are bottomless mimosas."

"How did you find out about it?"

That was a pretty valid question, given that Ty lived in Brooklyn. He was something of a connoisseur of brunch, and frankly, the quieter places in his neighborhood were a far better deal, both in terms of price and the quality of the food. But.... "Well, if you must know, there was a guy I was seeing who lived a few blocks from here."

"Ah."

"He moved to Scarsdale about six months ago, so, you know, *long distance*. That never works out."

"Isn't Scarsdale only, like, forty minutes out of the city by train?"

Ty waved his hand dismissively. "But the *suburbs*."

Brunch was tasty and abundant. They chatted about nothing and ate until they felt like they were bursting, and Ty, at least, got a little tipsy from the mimosas the wait staff was kind enough to keep pouring. By the time they stumbled out of the restaurant, Ty felt pretty good about the potential for this date.

"Let's cut through the park," Ty said as they walked up Seventy-Seventh. They had to get from the West Side to the East Side to go to the Met, and the wide sprawl of Central Park was in their way.

Ty knew of two ways through the park: one along the road that started at Seventy-Ninth Street, the other a less direct route via the walking paths that went around the lake. Easy peasy, but for the fact that

Ty had done the latter route only once before and didn't remember it very well. But no matter. It would be scenic and romantic, and it wasn't like they were in a hurry.

Ian followed along as Ty made a series of turns down different paths, asking twice if Ty knew where he was going but otherwise just making snarky comments about joggers and pretentious-looking dogs.

"Okay," Ty said. "If we keep going straight, we run into the lake, but I think if we go left, there's a path that kind of winds around it."

"You think?"

"Come on, Ian. Where is your sense of adventure! And see, there's another token New Yorker experience for you. A museum, brunch, getting lost in Central Park."

Ian frowned. "I'd really rather we didn't get lost."

"Honey, this is Central Park. It's not that big, and every inch is landscaped and manicured within an inch of its life. It's hardly the wilderness. Plus we both have phones with GPS. What's the worst thing that could happen?"

Perhaps Ian was on to something, though, because a couple of turns later, they were in a woody area. Low, gentle hills made some of the walking paths look like they suddenly went vertical, and large rocks blocked some of the footholds. No other people seemed to be around. A tiny sign indicated they had stumbled into the Ramble.

"Hey," Ty said, pointing to the sign, "isn't this where all the men came in the seventies to have sex with each other?"

"I think so, yeah."

"Well, ha, there's your adventure. A secluded area, surrounded by trees, hidden from the rest of the park. A sexy man hiding in the bushes. You stumble in here by accident and hear moaning, and at first you think someone is being grievously injured, but then you realize those are moans of pleasure. You step closer, you peer through the leaves, and there's a tall, rough-looking man joyfully plowing into a big, beefy, hairy guy, both lost to the joy of coming together that way. You step on a twig, and they both turn to look. The rough guy sees you and smiles. He crooks his finger." Ty crooked his finger at Ian.

But Ian wasn't buying what Ty was selling. "Ugh, no. Can you imagine?"

"Uh, yes. Was I just speaking in Swahili? Did you not hear that sexy fantasy I just cooked up? You don't think it's kind of romantic, being lost in the woods together?"

"No. First of all, it's dirty."

Ty laughed. "Okay, Miss Priss."

"Second of all, I don't see what's romantic about being stuck so deep in the closet that the only way to get your dick sucked is to find strangers in a grody part of the park to do it."

"Well, when you put it that way—"

"I mean, I know they didn't know about AIDS in the seventies, but there were other diseases, and I just can't imagine being so desperate for sex that I'd have to sneak out and just stick my cock in whatever willing hole I could find, never mind if he was attractive or sad or homeless or what."

"Okay, geez. I just thought it was a fun fantasy."

Ian suddenly picked up the pace, walking forward quickly. Ty had to jog to catch up.

"There has to be a way out of here," Ian said. His breath was coming fast suddenly.

"Hey, whoa, slow down. I'm sorry, I was just horsing around. There's no hurry. We have all day. None of the stuff I planned has to get done at any particular time."

"I know, but... we're really lost, and I...."

Ian was panting now, like he was having trouble breathing.

"Ian, wait. Stop walking. Slow down. Are you okay?"

Ian was not okay. He put one hand out on a nearby tree as if he needed it to support his weight. He put his other hand to his throat, where he undid one of the buttons on his shirt.

"Attack...," Ian wheezed. "Panic... attack."

"Oh, no. Shh, it's okay, I'll find a way out of here. Deep breaths, okay? We'll figure this out."

Ty had never seen anyone have a panic attack before. Ian had gone pale but for the blotchy flush crawling up his neck. It was clear he was having trouble catching his breath. Ty wasn't sure if it was okay to touch him or if that would make it worse. He put out a hand tentatively, but Ian slapped it away. Ty sighed and whipped out his phone and found their location on the map.

"Okay, if we hang a right up here, that should put us back down by the lake," Ty said. The map didn't show all of the paths, so he had to make some guesses, but he figured that as long as they headed east, they'd be okay. "Maybe the path will be more open up ahead."

Ian nodded.

Ty led him shakily forward, and a few turns later, they came to a more open area. Ty saw the bridge over the narrow part of the lake up ahead. A photographer was there, herding a guy in a tux and a woman in a wedding gown into position.

Ty put Ian on a bench and sat beside him. "Are you okay?"

Ian nodded, though he was still taking in great gasps of air.

"I didn't mean to make you panic. I really thought, even when we were lost, that it was just the Ramble. A few yards in any direction and we'd be out. I mean, it's Central Park, not the Catskills, you know?"

Ian took a deep breath. He was panting now instead of gasping, which seemed to be a good sign. "That's so... rational. But there's... nothing rational... about a panic attack."

Hard to argue with that. "There's a hot dog vendor over there. You want me to get you some water or something?"

"Yeah, that... yeah."

Ty went and came back with two bottles of water and a big pretzel. "One gold-plated bottle of water, sir." He handed one of the bottles to Ian.

"Gold plated?" Ian's voice still had a wheezy quality, but the worst of it seemed to have abated.

"For what he charged for fucking water, it better be gold plated."

Ian nodded and opened the bottle. Ty tore off part of the pretzel and popped it in his mouth.

"How are you still hungry?" Ian asked, which seemed like a good sign.

"Dunno. I just saw the pretzels and thought they looked good. Sometimes hot dog cart pretzels are all dried up and wrinkled and hard enough to break glass, but these looked fresh. You want some? It's nice and chewy."

"Okay."

So they split the pretzel and drank water and watched the wedding photographer bark orders at the poor couple on the bridge. Ian's breathing gradually settled back to normal.

"That happen a lot?" Ty asked. "The panic attacks?"

"Not... a lot. Maybe once a month or so. I took medication for it for a while, but it had some weird side effects I didn't like, so I stopped. The anxiety, most of the time it's manageable. I can tell when I'm starting to panic and I can pull myself out of the situation and talk myself off the ledge, you know? And it's not like I'm not a functioning member of society. I do pretty well for myself."

"You do. You're great, Ian." Ty smiled and rubbed Ian's knee.

"Thanks. I saw a doctor for a while. We tried a lot of things. There's not a lot you can do for anxiety besides learning healthy ways to cope with it. I do cope well for the most part. This is my life and I've accepted it. These days I only call my doctor when it's really bad, which is rare." Ian took a deep breath and a sip of water. "Just sometimes, I get overwhelmed. Back there, when we were lost, it felt like all those trees were closing on me, and I didn't know the way out. It was like getting stuck in a briar patch or something, and just… I lost it. I'm sorry."

"Don't apologize. I should have planned the route better."

"I'm better now. We can keep walking."

"You sure?"

"Yeah."

Ty nodded and looked at his phone. "Well, if we go over this way, it looks like there's a path that goes through those trees, and then we can follow the East Drive up toward the museum."

"Okay. Lead the way."

"Are you sure?"

"Yeah. Just don't get us lost again."

IAN DIDN'T know what to make of pop art. He didn't know much about art generally, beyond "That looks nice." He sometimes had to pick out art or paint colors for a hotel, but he knew that kind of work was beyond what he could do competently, so he usually hired designers or consultants. He had final sign-off, but he didn't put himself in a position where he had to make important decisions about decoration.

So the pop art thing was strange to Ian, who didn't know what to make of the bright colors. It looked like advertisements or comic books, not art, per se. He stood next to Ty staring at a painting that basically just looked like a comic book panel blown up gigantic.

"That's the point," Ty said when Ian voiced his opinion. "Lichtenstein's whole deal is parody. He's criticizing the way the subject is represented in comics by reproducing it here out of context."

"Okay." Ian still didn't really understand.

"I think what I appreciate about the pop artists of the sixties is that they weren't trying to do anything radically different. They were kind of just making fun of, say, more mundane forms of art. Like Andy Warhol and the soup cans."

So Ian didn't get it, but he enjoyed following Ty around the exhibit as he peered at the information cards next to each painting. Ty would pause and say something about the painting, most of which wouldn't make much sense to Ian, but Ty was so knowledgeable and enthusiastic about all of it that Ian's lack of comprehension didn't matter.

As they walked out of the exhibit, Ian said, "How do you know all this stuff?"

"I *did* go to art school."

"You did?"

Ty nodded. "Did I not tell you that?"

Ian paused in a little gift shop just outside the exhibit. He idly picked up a coffee table book and flipped through a few pages. "What was a boy from Texas doing at art school?"

Ian meant the question playfully, but Ty bristled as if he were offended. "Getting the hell out of Texas, that's what."

Ian put the book down and walked over to Ty. "Sorry, no offense intended. Just… you don't talk about it much, so it surprised me. You work in marketing, right? You do graphic arts? So I thought maybe that was what your interest in the exhibit was about. But clearly it goes much deeper than that. So I just wanted to know because I'm trying to get to know you. Okay?"

Ty nodded and frowned. "Yeah, sorry. But, yes. I have a bachelor's of fine arts from Parsons."

"See, that's really cool. I didn't know that."

"I always liked art."

Ian wanted to keep up the feeling he'd had in the exhibit, wanted to let more of Ty's enthusiasm rub off on him. "What else do you want to see in the museum?"

Ty shrugged. "I dunno. I mean, I'll go anywhere. What I like about it is that it's so big that no matter how many times you come, you always see something different."

"And how often do you come?"

"Eh, five or six times a year, probably. I'd come more if I lived closer. Sometimes it's all I can do to leave Brooklyn, you know? You settle into a routine and forget there's this whole huge city around you, so you get a bagel from that place on the corner where you always get bagels and go about your business—laundry and grocery shopping and whatever. And hell, I live spitting distance from the Brooklyn Museum, which also has some really great art if you're into that sort of thing, and I hardly ever go there either." Ty started walking, so Ian followed. "But that's kind of the point of this whole adventure. You are currently living in the greatest city in the world, but you're going to let whatever baggage from your childhood you're still holding on to ruin that. I want to show you how great this city is and experience some of it for myself too."

Ian was tempted to let Ty work whatever powers of persuasion he had. Today hadn't done much for proving that New York was this great place—the panic attack in the Ramble certainly had not been his finest moment—but Ty wanted to show him this so much, and he wanted to make Ty happy.

"Do you have a favorite painting?" Ian asked.

"Sure, lots."

"No, like, is there one piece of art in this museum that just… speaks to you. As an artist, maybe, or in any way. It doesn't have to be rational, it just has to be something you like."

Ty tilted his head and appeared to think about it. "I… yeah. Yeah, I have a favorite. It's going to take a little effort to find it because they just remodeled that wing and I don't remember exactly where it is."

"That's okay. I want you to show it to me."

"Okay." Ty nodded. "Yeah, okay. Come with me."

Ian followed Ty on a circuitous route through European Decorative Arts, which mostly seemed to be rooms full of fancy old furniture. Unlike the trip through Central Park, though, Ty seemed to know exactly where he was going.

They passed what seemed like hundreds of people milling around in the galleries. Single people maneuvered around families and couples. That gave Ian a moment of pause. He could imagine strolling through these galleries might be romantic for someone who liked art, and there suddenly seemed to be couples everywhere, holding hands and quietly explaining what they liked about each piece to their partners. A pair of fortyish men near the entrance to one of the rooms commented on the scrollwork on a four-poster bed, and Ian could tell by their body language that they were a couple. One of them kept touching the other on the small of his back.

Ty was now too far ahead for Ian to touch him, but he was tempted.

They paused for a moment in one of the medieval art galleries that seemed to be kind of a central hub. "They usually put the Christmas tree here," Ty said.

"Yeah, I know," Ian said, recognizing it. "My mother had Christmas cards with a photo of that tree printed on them. There were so many of them that she sent them out almost every year, so I saw them a lot as a kid."

"That's kind of cute."

"Sure."

"This way."

They walked past paintings of Jesus and altarpieces and huge granite tombs until they came to a grand, high-ceilinged atrium.

"I don't remember this," Ian said, surprised.

"When was the last time you were in this museum?"

Ian couldn't remember. "When I was a teenager, maybe."

"They've done a lot of renovations in the last decade. Some of this is still shiny new. The gallery I want to go to is in the American wing."

It did take some time to find what Ty was looking for. They passed a lot of paintings of men in white wigs—they couldn't all be George Washington, but to Ian, one middle-aged man in a curly white wig could have been the same as the guy in the next painting—and then they passed a lot of huge landscapes, and finally they arrived in a room that seemed to be mostly full-length portraits of men and women in Victorian or Edwardian garb.

"Here, I think, yeah…," Ty was saying. "Here."

They stood before a portrait of a woman in a black dress.

"I get that it's kind of an obvious choice," Ty said. "But I've always liked this painting. I think it does speak to me."

"What speaks to you, exactly?"

Ty looked at Ian. "Do you even know what we're looking at?"

"Not a clue."

Ty laughed. "Okay. John Singer Sargent is the painter. This is Madame X."

"Okay."

"The woman in the painting is striking but not exactly beautiful, right? Like, your eye is drawn to the creamy skin of her shoulders, or the long lines of her arms and her body. But if you look at her face, she's got that hawk nose and the snooty expression, which, to me, anyway, keeps her from being beautiful." Ty paused and tilted his head. "When Sargent showed this painting originally, one of the straps of the dress was off her shoulder. That scandalized the salon where it was being shown, so he changed the painting to put the strap on her shoulder instead. See on the side there where the bodice of the dress tilts a little bit?"

Ian nodded. "Moving the strap made it okay?"

"I know, right? I wondered about that. I suppose scandalous is in the eye of the beholder. Actually, if I remember correctly, the public reaction so shamed Sargent that he kept the painting in his studio for years, away from judgmental gazes."

Ian succumbed to the temptation and ran a hand down Ty's arm. Ian wanted to be one of those couples, he realized. He wanted to talk about art sotto voce to each other, and he wanted Ty's joy to wash over him. He didn't think that Ty could ever persuade him that New York was a place worth staying in, but he really wanted to let Ty try.

Ty smiled.

"You think the painter had an affair with the woman in the painting?" Ian asked, because it seemed logical. Why else paint a woman in such a so-called scandalous way?

But Ty shook his head. "No, probably not. She was married, for one thing. Also, Sargent was probably more into men. His male nude portraits are detailed and sensual, which I suppose isn't really proof of anything. Some scholars think he had affairs with men, some are certain he had a long affair with one of his female subjects. He was very secretive, though, so if he *was* gay, we'll probably never know about it." Ty looked back at the painting. "I went through a phase when I was in college during which I read the biographies of every artist who had a whiff of gay rumors about him. Most of the stuff I read was inconclusive or the book had been de-gayed to make it okay for the masses. I guess, I don't know. I wanted reassurance. I wanted proof that men like me had come before."

"Ty."

"They did, I know they did. It's kind of a stereotype to say that gay men are drawn to the arts, but I certainly was. Hell, my dad spent so much time telling me art school was a terrible idea because 'only fags go to art school,' but I couldn't think of anything else I'd rather do than paint and draw all day."

Ty's sentences had so much to unpack, and this hardly seemed like the right venue for it, so Ian let it go. He took Ty's hand instead.

Ty smiled and squeezed his hand back. "'Washington Crossing the Delaware' is nearby if you want to see it. That painting is a farce of historical accuracy, but it's kind of fun."

"Sure, Ty. Lead me wherever you want to go."

Chapter 13

IAN GOT stuck at a work function Tuesday night and had to miss the game. Ty missed having him around and found himself continually glancing toward third base, expecting to see Ian there and not Chad, who was subbing.

They were playing the Park Slope Strollers, which consisted only of gay dads. Ty thought that was pretty fun as far as gimmicks went, but it meant that most of their games had a bunch of kids sitting in the few bleachers that constituted the stands. Josh kept joking that if he and Tony went through with their plan to adopt a child—still in the discussion phase, thank goodness—he'd have to switch teams. "At least I'd get away from Scott," he'd joked.

If only.

Hell, Ty liked Scott because he helped them win, which they did pretty easily against the Strollers that day. Ty felt Ian's absence even more acutely at the bar afterward. He sat with Mason and Nate, who both seemed similarly morose.

"We just won," Ty pointed out. "What's eating you guys?"

Mason shrugged. "Nothing specific."

"He had a date that went badly Sunday night," Nate said.

"Oh, really?"

"Can we not talk about this?" said Mason.

Nate crossed his arms over his chest. "I'm right, aren't I? You went out with that guy from the 'Mos. What the hell is his name? Danny?"

Mason nodded. "Yeah. Danny. He's really hot, but he's got a brick for brains."

"I could have told you that," Nate said. "Sure, his arms are like tree trunks and he can hit a ball to Brooklyn, but that's about all there is to that guy from what I can tell."

"I was hoping for more, but…." Mason shrugged. "I think I just have to stop dating these meatheads."

"It's a heavy burden, only being attracted to the brawny, stupid ones," said Ty.

He was joking, but the frown that crossed Mason's face indicated that Mason perhaps wasn't in on the joke.

"Speaking of dates," Nate said, "how was the big day with Ian on Sunday?"

"It could have gone better," Ty said. "I thought it would be romantic to walk across Central Park before we went to the Met, but I ended up getting us lost."

"It happens," said Nate. "I've lived in New York my whole life and I get lost in Central Park every damn time I go there."

"He also seems to not be much of an art person. Every time I started explaining why I liked something, his eyes kind of glazed over. So maybe the Met wasn't the way to go."

"I got you those tickets, by the way," Mason said. "July 18, like you wanted. Field level. I won't tell you what I had to do to get them."

"Or who you had to blow," Nate said.

Mason shrugged.

Ty didn't think Mason would actually perform a sex act to get Yankees tickets, but he imagined Mason probably had to sweet-talk someone out of the seats.

Mason laughed. "Since you're making that face, the tickets are a couple that were unsold but part of the tickets they usually reserve for friends of the media. Like, if you work for ESPN but are at the game to schmooze with someone you're trying to do business with and not to report on it, you sit in these seats. So there will probably be a lot of people around you conducting shady business deals while the game is on."

"That's fine," said Ty. "Do you think they'd object to a gay couple that doesn't know much about professional baseball?"

"Nah," said Mason. "Especially not since security started cracking down on guys who shout homophobic nonsense at the field. I mean, they can't stop you from calling one of the players a faggot if you only do it once, but they stop the guys with offensive signs and that kind of thing."

"That's nice of them?" Nate said, holding his hands up like he wasn't sure it was.

Mason shrugged. "Look, I was only on the team for a short time, but you're a Yankee for life basically, so after I came out publicly, some of the front office management decided to do some token gestures, especially since the taunting from the stadium had gotten really out of hand. Like, during one series, some guys in the bleachers made up a song about how every member of the Red Sox was committing some gay sex act. It was actually some clever songwriting. Not a lot of things rhyme with 'blow job.'"

Ty didn't know if he could laugh at that or not. It seemed safer not to. He knew that Mason let a lot of the bullshit that had been shouted at him over the years roll off his back, but it couldn't have been easy to hear all of it.

"I think the game will be fun," Ty said.

"If you get bored, that section of the stadium has whatever the stadium equivalent of table service is," said Mason. "There's a cute waiter who works most weeknights who will bring you beer. It costs three pieces of gold and your firstborn child, but it's usually cold."

"I hate concessions at sports venues in this city," said Ty, shaking his head. "Not sure that having to sell our souls for overpriced light beer is going to go far to convince Ian that New York is the city he should be living in."

Nate raised an eyebrow. "I thought you were just doing this as a lark. Are you actively trying to convince him to stay when his job ends?"

"Maybe," Ty said honestly. "At first I liked the challenge. Like, he's pretty bitter about his childhood, and he's tied a lot of that to the city, so convincing him this city is great is an uphill battle. At the same time, it seems… I don't know. Pointless to be in a relationship with a set expiration date. So I thought maybe I could convince him the city didn't suck so I could push that expiration date a little farther away."

"Because you like him," Nate said, tipping his pint glass toward Ty.

"Sure. What's not to like? We get along great both in and out of bed, we have fun together. What more could I want in a relationship?"

"What indeed," said Nate with a sigh.

"Let's review," said Mason, turning toward Nate. "You, Nathan, are pining after a man who is currently on the other side of this very bar flirting away with a guy from another team."

"I thought the Queens were playing on Wednesday this week," Ty said, taking in Carlos, who was leaning quite heavily on Aiden.

"They are. Aiden just showed up tonight all on his own." There was no small amount of bitterness in Nate's voice.

"You know," Mason said, "if you just walked up to that boy and told him how you felt, you wouldn't have to stew over here."

"He's not into me that way. Let him have his fun with Aiden."

"All right, dude." Mason looked over at Ty and drew a circle around his ear with his finger, indicating he thought Nate was crazy.

"Well, anyway. I do like Ian," Ty said. "I think even if he doesn't decide to stay, it'll be fun to spend the summer seeing all the sights, you know? Putting together this list of ideas for what we could do has been kind of fun, if nothing else. Reminds me why I moved here."

"Just… you know," Mason said, gesturing vaguely with his hand. "If he decides to leave…."

"That's at least a year away. So I might as well have fun in the meantime. Who knows? Hell, we might not even make it past the end of the Rainbow League season."

"Uh, have fun?" Mason tried.

IAN DIDN'T love visiting his childhood home, but he couldn't in good conscience not see his mother when they were in the same city. After all, it wasn't his mother who had ruined things for him. Ian didn't put together that his father was an asshole and also probably an alcoholic until he was out of the house, and by then he had no particular desire to return.

Ian's mother had always been his great defender. He wondered sometimes if that was at great cost to herself. If it was, she'd never said.

They sat now in the large eat-in kitchen on the first floor, which was perhaps a little worse for wear. They were eating turkey sandwiches and chatting about nothing in particular. Ian was already counting down the minutes until he could leave. Even with his father gone, something about the house felt suffocating.

"How is the baseball team going?" his mother asked.

"Fine." Ian sighed. "I've been seeing one of the men from my team. In a romantic way, I mean."

"Oh, really? You think he might motivate you to stay in New York?"

No. That was Ian's first thought. He didn't think anyone alive could move the sun and stars and anything else necessary to make him stay in the city permanently. "We're just dating. It's not serious."

It wasn't just the house. It was the panel of sidewalk down the street that he'd bled into the afternoon Tommy Blackwood had beaten him so badly he'd had to go to the hospital. It was the street corner just outside the Seventh Avenue F station where he'd been mugged on the way home from a late-night event at his high school. It was the man who still worked at the little bodega on Seventh Street who had called him a faggot when he went in to buy milk and eggs one evening as a favor to his mother. It was every kid who'd picked on him, called him names, punched him. It was best to leave it all behind. Why would he ever want to come back to this place?

"You're looking well, at any rate," Lorraine said.

She picked up and fiddled with the old metal napkin holder, a U-shaped antique that had been on the table for ages. The table had always graced this kitchen, a cheap particleboard situation covered in plastic meant to evoke the memory of wood. The same placemats made of woven cotton lay in front of each chair at the table, even though Lorraine lived alone now. The framed photo of Ian's grandmother serving the Thanksgiving turkey, taken in the fifties, still hung just behind Lorraine's head, a Norman Rockwell moment Ian had often thought was meant to emphasize just how unpicturesque his childhood had been.

"Thanks," Ian said. "I think it's the baseball. All the running and conditioning."

The only things gone had belonged to Ian's father. There was no leather jacket hanging over the hook near the front door. The bright green Jets blanket was no longer draped over the back of the sofa. The photos of his family had been taken down from the stairway that went up to the third floor. Lorraine had systematically removed all evidence of her ex-husband from the house. But she couldn't eradicate the memories.

"You look good too," Ian said.

Lorraine smiled. "I've been taking Pilates at this little studio on Ninth Street. I feel great."

"That's good."

He found he didn't have much to say to her, though the awkward silence was killing him. He wanted to have an easy rapport with her, but things had been so strained while his father had still been around that Ian felt like they were strangers now. He sighed. "Mom, I just—"

"I know, sweetie." She reached over and grabbed his hand. "I appreciate your coming all the way down here for lunch."

"It was no problem."

"It was. I know why you left New York, and I know why you don't want to stay. I wish you would because I missed you a great deal while you were away. But I understand. The only argument I can really make for staying here is that the city is different now. This neighborhood is like a different planet compared to what it was. Used to be you couldn't even cross Seventh Avenue, but now all the best restaurants are past it on Fifth. Used to be you couldn't go into Prospect Park after dark, but the worst thing I heard about recently was the neighbor's son getting a ticket for walking his dog off the leash at two in the morning. Used to be we lived here because this was what we could afford, and now all the other houses on this block are worth millions of dollars." She let go of Ian's hand and sat back in her chair. "Used to be a lot of things that aren't anymore. I get it, Ian, I do, but I wish you'd at least give this place a chance. Things are different now."

Ian nodded to concede the point, but he didn't see how it could be true. Not when this kitchen was the same as it had been in 1979, when his parents had bought the house. Not when the same copper pots hung on the rack near the sink. Not when the same olive green refrigerator hummed in the corner. Not when his childhood bedroom upstairs still had dinosaur sheets on the bed.

"I love you, Mom, I do, but I'm just here for a short time to do a job."

"Of course. I know." She took a sip of water. "Now finish your sandwich."

Chapter 14

THE SEATS at Yankee Stadium were good, but Ty was starting to regret the decision to bring Ian here.

Something about the baseball game was not Ty. But the museum—very much Ty—had not been Ian. It all made Ty nervous. What if he showed Ian his work, especially his book covers, and Ian laughed? What if he showed Ian one of his paintings and Ian thought it was terrible? Ty didn't think he'd be able to handle that.

So instead they sat just to the right of home plate. They drank overpriced beer and ate hot dogs and french fries. They tried to pay attention to the game, but that almost seemed beside the point. Mostly they talked.

"My dad thought I should go out for a sport," Ian said. "So I gave baseball a shot. I didn't seem to have the right body for any other sport. And I wasn't even that good, but when I was at Stuyvesant, none of the sports teams could really do much beyond putting on a uniform, so the fact that I could throw with decent accuracy and run pretty fast gave me a leg up over some of my teammates."

Ty nodded. "In Texas, as you may know, football is religion. My father was mighty disappointed when I didn't make the high school team. But I didn't have a prayer. I was an artsy kid who would rather watch football players than be one."

"So the design stuff. You did that in high school?"

"Naw, I painted. Did a little sculpture and drawing too, but I loved to paint. Still do." And there it was. Out in the open.

"Really? Is that why you love the museum so much? You're an artist?"

Ty shrugged. "Sure. I do all right. I mean, the money is in design these days, so that's what I do professionally. When I do paint for fun, I mostly just do it for myself."

"What do you paint?"

Ty shrugged, feeling uncomfortable now. "Oh, you know. Cityscapes, mostly. Or I'll take stock photos I like and tweak them a little to make them mine. They don't... I don't really show anybody. It's just for fun."

"Well, now I'm curious. I'd love to see your work."

Ty couldn't tell if Ian was just being polite or if he meant it.

Ian peered at the field, clearly trying to make sense of what was happening. "Hasn't this guy been at bat for, like, thirty pitches?"

"Not quite." So they were changing the subject. Ty gestured toward the scoreboard as a way to demonstrate what was going on. The numbers on the board indicated that the batter had been at home plate for five pitches, three of which had been ruled balls. One more pitch and something would happen either way.

The pitcher wound up. Ty tried to study the whole field, wondering if he could glean something from the way a professional team functioned that he could apply to his game in the Rainbow League. He wasn't entirely sure he could. He had a good working knowledge of the game, but the professional league had so many strange rules. In the Rainbow League, hitting the ball and running the bases seemed to be all that really mattered. There was no designated hitter. There were no rules about whether one could win on walk-off home runs. Games rarely ended in ties or had to go to extra innings.

"You don't really follow professional baseball, right?" Ian said.

"You're right, I don't. I find watching baseball on TV to be unspeakably boring. But can you see how it's more fun in person? We've got a hot guy bringing us beer. We've got seats close enough to the field to see that guy's ass." Ty gestured toward the Yankees' first baseman, who had a fantastic ass. "We're chatting and talking and taking advantage of this lovely summer night. It's pretty great, don't you think?"

"It's nice, yeah."

"Too touristy for you?"

Ian shrugged. "Not necessarily. I'm not that much of a snob. I mean, there are clearly a lot of tourists here, and a bunch in this section, but season ticket holders are their own species of New Yorker, you know? The rabid Yankees fan, they're a part of the city."

"New York is weird, though, because there are so many sports teams. There's no unifying team that everyone rallies around. Sports fans have so many teams and sports to choose from." Ty sighed. "See, in Dallas, we had the Cowboys. I mean, sure, there were the Rangers if you followed baseball, but sports in Texas is really all about football. *Friday Night Lights* and all that, you know? We lived in this little suburb just outside Dallas, where everyone in town went to see the high school game on Friday nights in the fall. Not even a question, that's what you did. But in New York, I don't know. Everything seems more diluted."

Ian nodded. "I mean, I never stayed in one place long enough to build up much team loyalty. I always thought the Yankees were kind of the gods of New York sports, if only because every boy in the city owns a Yankees cap."

"Sure."

Ian took a long pull from his beer. "My father loved the Yankees, but he loved all New York sports. He loved the Yankees and the Jets and the Knicks and the Rangers." He stared at the field. "Well, probably he still loves them, but we don't talk much anymore."

Ty wanted to ask, but he also knew better than to do so, because he knew all about how strained relationships between fathers and sons could operate.

"You want something else to eat?" Ty asked, mostly as a diversionary tactic.

"Eh. Maybe something sweet."

Ty grinned. "I bet the cute waiter would bring us sundaes in those little plastic baseball hats."

Ian laughed. "I appreciate your enthusiasm. Little plastic baseball hats, you say?"

"Have you really never been to a professional baseball game before? Because those kind of come standard. I will be very surprised if they don't have them at Yankee Stadium."

"Hey, go for it. I could totally go for some ice cream."

Ty considered going into the stadium to buy them, but he opted to wait for the waiter to come back. He leaned back in his seat. "So, are you having a good time at this quintessential New York experience?"

"Sure," said Ian. "If nothing else, I'm gonna get to do a lot of weird things this summer, aren't I?"

"Not weird. There's nothing weird about going to a baseball game. This is pretty mundane, I would say. Totally normal. Very New York City."

Ian rolled his eyes.

"Oh, here comes the waiter," said Ty.

IAN WAS enjoying himself, though he was reluctant to admit it. He liked just sitting with Ty, horsing around or shooting the shit or talking about whatever, and he was happy to have food and beer brought to him. As they ate hot fudge sundaes served in little plastic Yankees caps, he went back to watching the game, hoping to discern what was going on. Most of what he needed to know was on the giant electronic scoreboard, making it unnecessary to pay much attention to the game, but he gave it a go anyway.

The Yankees were up by three runs against the Orioles. The Orioles, from what Ian could tell, were not playing especially good baseball, with the pitcher letting the Yankees have too many runs and the infield handling the ball sloppily. Ian and Ty kept watching and then talking about what they saw in terms of what Scott would probably say. The mental image of Scott standing in the dugout and letting loose all his shouty glory on a professional team was a mental image that brought Ian no small amount of glee.

"I feel like a kid, kind of," Ty said.

"Because of the eating of ice cream out of tiny hats and the getting serious about sports the way only little boys can?"

"Sure," Ty said. "That's a lot of it. I dunno. This place is also sort of isolated from the rest of the city, you know? You can't even really see the skyline, only the rest of the stadium. And we're up in the Bronx, away from all the hustle of Midtown."

Ty got some hot fudge on his chin. Ian reached over to wipe it off with his thumb and only succeeded in smudging it more. "Um…," Ian said.

Ty grinned. "Do I have hot fudge all over my face?"

"Yeah, basically."

"You want to lick it off?"

Ian did. Wow, did he. He could imagine the rough texture of Ty's stubbly chin against his tongue. Ty had recently shaved off the chin strap but had otherwise not demonstrated a great aptitude for shaving, so he was still pretty scruffy. His red hair stood out like a fiery cloud against his jaw. Ian really wanted to lick it but couldn't quite bring himself to do it in the stadium.

Ty put his thumb in his ice cream, getting a bit of cream and hot fudge on it, and then he wiped it on Ian's nose. Then he leaned over and licked it off, making Ian giggle with embarrassment.

"Dude, nobody cares," Ty said.

It felt like a dare. Ian could suddenly feel the eyes of however many thousand people were in the stands trained right on them. He wondered if this was how couples on the Kiss Cam felt. Ty just sat there, blinking as if he were trying to be cute, with hot fudge smudged across his chin, begging to be licked. Ian got nervous, his heart rate and pulse kicking up as he looked at Ty and thought about all the people who could see them and what they might say or do. He did not believe for one second that nobody cared.

But the section they sat in wasn't quite full. The three guys in the seats just behind them had been having some kind of business meeting all evening, based on what Ian had overheard. A het couple at the end of their row had been mostly making out the whole game, so apparently PDAs were not off-limits in the stands. There were a smattering of other people too, but no kids and no one who had shouted anything offensive. Ian wasn't sure that he and Ty necessarily read as a gay couple, although now that Ty had licked ice cream off Ian's nose, they probably did.

So, because no one had really reacted to that, Ian steeled his courage and told his anxiety to shut up, and he leaned over the armrest and licked Ty's chin. It was indeed as rewarding as he'd thought, the skin rough against Ian's tongue, the fudge sweet and a little salty from Ty's sweat.

While he was over there, Ian gave Ty a quick peck on the lips. When Ian backed away, Ty pulled a napkin from his pocket and wiped his chin. He reached over and wiped off Ian's nose too. "Now," Ty said, "was that so hard?"

"I guess not."

"You gotta live, is what I'm saying. I get nervous too. Not quite like you do, but I have my own things that I get anxious about. You can't let it rule you, you know?"

Ian nodded, because he did know. He'd spent most of his adult life trying to get his anxiety to go away so that he could just live the life he wanted. "You're right. Let's just have fun," Ian said. "I can do that, I promise."

"Okay. Good."

They finished their sundaes. Ty took the little plastic hats with him on a trip into the stadium and returned a few minutes later with them rinsed off. "I mean, I'll buy you a real hat if you want one," he said.

"No, I like this one."

Ty laughed softly and then surprised Ian by leaning over and kissing his cheek. "Don't look now, but we seem to be making a memory. Or are you going to look back on this moment next year when you're in Prague or Toronto or Kalamazoo and think, 'That Ty sure did some dumb touristy shit with me. Good riddance!'"

"I can't imagine I'd ever think 'good riddance' where you are concerned."

Ty smiled. "Me neither."

"So, yeah, I think this will be filed away in the 'fond memories' folder. Okay?"

"Yeah. Definitely. Score one for Ty."

Ian rolled his eyes.

Chapter 15

TY'S FATHER was a hero.

Robert Arnold was something of a legend in the Dallas suburb where his family had settled. As a teenager, he'd been a football star, the quarterback who led his team to back-to-back state championships. Then he went to college, where he married his sweetheart. He was in the Army for a while, on active duty in Asia in the seventies and eighties, until he retired to be with his family. Then he went on to an illustrious career as a teacher and volunteer firefighter. All the while, he tried to be an upstanding example to his son. Little Tyler was supposed to grow up to be as big and strong as his father, to be just as heroic. Instead he was a delicate, artistic child who preferred reading and drawing to football or fighting. To say that Robert Arnold had been disappointed in his son was probably an understatement.

He wasn't a total failure as a father. Ty had indeed worshipped him, particularly when he was a teenager, wanting to do his father proud but never quite able to.

When the doctors handed down the cancer diagnosis to Robert Arnold, his whole family went into a tailspin. His death left a hole in Ty's life that he'd never been able to fill.

He wondered sometimes what his father would think of his life now, of his work successes and failures, of his involvement with the Rainbow League, of his homosexuality. He'd never told his father he was gay; he'd never known how. That, somehow, felt like the final blow. Ty would never be a great football player. He'd never do well in the Army and he'd never have a career where he saved people's lives. Instead, he'd channeled his interest in art into a successful career and he played ball with an amateur league. He lived in New York City. He'd made a life for himself that he could be proud of.

But would Robert Arnold be proud?

That Ty didn't know.

He wasn't explicitly worried about disappointing his father. Not anymore. He thought sometimes that his father probably would have been okay with a gay son. Robert Arnold had a bigoted streak, an old way of thinking about the world, but he'd been a compassionate man and an intelligent one, a man who probably would have found a way to come to terms with who his son really was. If only Ty had given him a chance. Instead, teenaged Ty had been so obsessed with proving to his father that he was worthy that he forgot to be himself.

Ty had regrets. Probably everyone did. If he had it to do over, he would have told his father. But he never got the opportunity, because Robert Arnold had died when Ty was nineteen.

But there was no sense lingering on the past. Instead, he'd focus on the future. Maybe something in his life now would help him come to terms with the sadness that came with thinking of his father and what a disappointment he must have been.

Ty was not especially fond of losing, but the Hipsters sure were playing bad ball against the West Village team that evening. He sat next to Ian on the bench while their teammates paraded up to the plate and failed to get on base. Ian seemed somewhat uninterested in the proceedings, instead focusing on relacing his cleats.

Ty knew he was part of the problem. His head was a mess. The anniversary of his father's death had been the day before, and he always felt strange around this time of year. On top of that, his feelings for Ian were clouding his judgment. The more plans he made to convince Ian that New York was a great city, the harder he fell, the more he wanted Ian to stay.

Ian, on the other hand, seemed more determined than ever to flee.

Case in point: "Did I tell you?" Ian said, apparently successful in knotting the laces on his shoes. "I finally got the management at the New Amsterdam to shut down the hotel for a couple of days so I can get the carpet and paint guys in there to get it all done in one fell swoop instead of over months as the manager had planned."

Ty sighed. "Thus shaving months off your stint at this hotel, eh?"

"Is that a problem?"

"Ty! You're up!" called Scott.

"Why would it be a problem?" Ty said as he got up to bat.

He'd managed to keep his tone glib, even though the issue here was that he liked Ian. He liked Ian enough to shuck the bravado and be a one-man man. He could see the two of them going to museums or taking goofy day trips or even just sitting around with each other doing nothing on weekends long into the future.

But Ian didn't seem to be in the same place. And that sucked, not to put too fine a point on it.

Ty picked up a bat and swung it a few times. When he went up to the plate, he wanted to pulverize the ball, to let his frustrations out on the field. The pitcher wound up and threw the ball, and Ty went for it, swinging hard and connecting with the ball. It flew toward left field, so Ty took off, his feet pounding against the dirt as he ran.

Ian went up to bat after Ty—a change from the usual order, but Scott liked to screw around "to keep everyone on their toes"—and managed a grounder to third base that advanced both of them. Ian seemed happily oblivious to the—well, not turmoil exactly, but something stormy for sure—going on inside Ty.

Josh successfully hit the ball into center field, so Ty decided to run for home. He was safe, but then Josh was tagged out at second, ending the inning.

On the way back to the bench to grab their gloves, Ian walked over and patted Ty's back. "Nice run, Red."

"Thanks."

"You feeling okay?"

"I'm fine. Great. I just made our loss slightly less embarrassing, so there's that."

"All right. I'll see you out on the field." Then he ran off.

NATE TOSSED a ball up in the air and caught it. Tonight's game against the West Village Idiots should have been a pretty easy one, but somehow the Hipsters were losing by two runs. Travis had started as pitcher, which was part of the problem. Nate was tired and his arm was a little sore after overdoing it at practice a couple of days before, so he'd opted to sit out the first few innings, but the game had quickly gotten away from Travis, who always pitched just slightly to his right. It meant he had a nasty habit of hitting right-handed batters. There hadn't been any serious injuries as a result of that, but it was probably only a matter of time.

But now Nate was back on the mound and he was determined to end this nonsense. He quickly assessed where each of the members of his infield were—and it was his infield, now that he was in command. A short player whose name Nate didn't know came up to bat, and Joe, the catcher, shot Nate a funny look before he pulled his mask down. He signaled for a fastball—that was pretty funny, considering Nate could only effectively execute two pitches—but Nate complied and lobbed the ball over the plate. Strike one.

Nate's other pitch was a knuckleball he'd learned from staring at footage of the pros doing it. He figured out how to get his fingers around the ball, how his hold on the ball affected the ball's momentum, and how the slower pitch was harder to throw with any accuracy. The Hipsters had gotten destroyed at a game last season at which Nate decided to debut the pitch, because almost all of his pitches had gone wild. But now Nate had more control, so when Joe gave him the signal, he threw the knuckleball. Clearly the batter hadn't seen that coming. Strike two.

Joe shook his head. Joe had been the catcher for the Hipsters for five seasons and had probably seen just about everything. He could tell if a batter was good just from his stance, and he had a series of signals that meant things like "This guy couldn't hit the broad side of a barn with a target painted on it," and "Definitely walk this guy because he'll hit it out of the park otherwise." Nate and Joe had worked together for a couple of seasons, so Nate knew all the signals. They were a good team. He wondered sometimes how they'd do if they were pros. That was, if Major League Baseball could figure out how to handle Joe's color-changing mohawk—hot pink this week—and Nate's decided proclivity for baseball player asses. Probably the other players on the team wouldn't appreciate Nate ogling. That was one of the many things he liked about the Rainbow League. Everyone ogled everybody else.

Joe shot Nate his signal for "Whatever the hell you feel like doing, bro," so Nate threw another fastball, and again, the batter couldn't figure out what to do with it, and it sailed right into Joe's mitt. Strike three. End of inning.

Nate jogged to the dugout bench. Carlos gave him a high five. "Shutout inning, man," Carlos said. "Not even a hit."

"I do know what I'm doing," said Nate.

"A thing of beauty. Right, guys?"

A few of their teammates were standing around while they sorted out the batting order. Mason and Ty murmured their congratulations on the nicely pitched inning.

"You up soon?" Nate asked Carlos.

"No, I hit last inning, remember?"

Nate shrugged. "It's all kind of a blur, actually."

"Mason, Ty, Ian, Shane, Zack, and then you are all up before me. So I'm guessing I'm not batting this inning."

"Fine, whatever. Just asking."

Carlos sighed and dipped his head. He leaned toward Nate. "Is this how it is now, Nate? Are we just fighting all the time? Because I have no idea what you're so pissed off about, but I wish you'd either get over it or talk to me."

Nate grunted. "You're right, I'm sorry. I'll get over it. It's not something you did." That was close enough to the truth.

"Ty had that poster a while back, remember it? The one hanging in his living room? It said 'Relax' across the top and then had a series of instructions. Like, 'One: Remove stick from ass.'"

"I see what you're saying." Nate narrowed his eyes. "I really am just being silly."

"Okay. Well. Don't make it a habit." Carlos reached over and patted Nate's arm, a gesture that felt both welcome and patronizing. "Seriously, that was a great inning."

"Thanks, man."

Carlos sat on the bench to watch their teammates bat, so Nate viewed the conversation as over. He took a deep breath and started fiddling with equipment. This thing with him and Carlos, it really was all in his imagination, and that was his own fucking fault for never saying anything. Part of him wanted to ask about Aiden, but part of him didn't want to know.

TY WAS acting strangely. Ian was sure something was wrong as they walked to Barnstorm after the game. They'd eked out a victory thanks to Nate keeping the Idiots' batters at bay once he took over on the mound, so everyone seemed to be in a celebratory mood. Everyone except Ty.

"So what's your next big plan for me?" Ian asked, trying to lighten the mood.

"Well. I just bought this book of Brooklyn walking tours. Each of them is about three miles, and the paths take you to various landmarks, and the book says a lot about the history of the place… it's kind of dorky, but I thought it might be fun. Unless you disagree?"

"No, that does sound fun."

"We can avoid Park Slope if you want. This one tour of Brooklyn Heights historical sights looked pretty good."

Ian nodded. He still wasn't sure what the point of this whole campaign was, but he was willing to go along with it. It wasn't so much that he had any particular desire to tour Brooklyn, but he wanted to spend time with Ty, and a day spent walking around with him could be pretty fun.

He had the sense now, though, that something was really bothering Ty, something he wasn't willing to talk about, but Ian couldn't figure out whether it was appropriate to ask. Did they have that kind of relationship? They'd been growing closer, yes, and Ian felt like he was getting to know Ty, but so much still seemed mysterious.

Was it worth it to explore the mysterious places if he was planning to leave?

They walked into the bar and Ty ordered Ian's drink for him. He knew which beer Ian preferred, knew which ones he didn't like. Ty knew about Ian's anxiety, had seen Ian at one of his worst moments recently. Ty knew Ian well enough to know that Ian wasn't too keen on spending extra time in Park Slope, but knew also that Ian would be game for a walk around Brooklyn.

Ian was an open book. Ty was a closed one.

"Are you all right?" Ian asked as they settled at a table near the jukebox. "You've seemed a little mopey today."

Ty sighed. "My father died twelve years ago yesterday. It's... it's silly to hang on to that anniversary, but he's been on my mind a lot today."

Ian remembered that Ty had mentioned his father had died when he'd been in college. "I'm so sorry. Do you want to talk about it?"

"Not really." Ty took a sip of his beer.

Ian reached over and put his hand over Ty's. He curled his fingers into Ty's palm.

"I mean," Ty said, "he had cancer. I was young and across the country in college, and when my parents called to tell me about the cancer, I didn't believe it could really take him out. Not a guy like my dad. He was so strong. Nothing ever got him down. But then I got that phone call." He shook his head. "Probably it still bothers me because I didn't get to say good-bye in person. Toward the end, I talked to him on the phone, but it wasn't quite the same."

"You must miss him a great deal."

"I do, yeah. Although sometimes I think I miss the relationship we could have had. I wonder a lot what he'd think of me now. I'm not... I'm not the sort of man he would have expected me to be."

Ian was thrilled that Ty was talking this much, though he wondered if Ty was just so rattled emotionally that he forgot to put his guard up. "What sort of man was that?" Ian asked softly.

"Like him. He was… he was a pillar of the community. Everyone loved him. He was just so… I don't know. Masculine isn't the right word. But he'd been in the Army; then he was a firefighter and a teacher. He should have been able to survive anything. Of course, the cancer was probably caused by some chemical he was exposed to, either overseas during his military days or when he was at a fire. So his job took him out anyway."

"You're a good man, Ty. I'm sure he'd be proud."

Ty shrugged. "I do all right. But I'm not heroic like that. In a lot of ways, I'm still that artsy kid I was in high school, who'd rather stay home to draw and paint than go to another football game. I left home to finally find a place where I could just be myself—and I did in New York City—but I'm not sure my father ever approved. I guess I don't really know that, though. I never got to ask him."

"Ty?"

Ty looked up and met Ian's gaze. Ian leaned over and put an arm around Ty, pulling him close to give him a hug. Ian said, "You're an artist, right? So you want the world to be beautiful. You found a place you love, a place you belong, here in New York City. I'm honored that you want to share it with me. I'm amazed that you see so much beauty in this city that I don't. You are a good man, Ty, and even if your father never got to know the adult you, he must be proud. He'd be a fool not to appreciate a son like you."

Ty leaned against Ian. "Thank you."

"I want you to show me what you see in this place that I don't. Because this city has lost its magic for me, but it hasn't for you. So show it to me."

"I will, Ian. I'll prove it to you."

"And if there's ever anything you need to tell me, ever anything you want to talk about, please just say it. If nothing else, we're friends, right?'

"Yeah. We are that."

Ian didn't want to push any of this further just yet, so he held Ty and rubbed his back. "Tell me some stories about your dad," he said.

Ty smiled as he sat back in his chair. He took Ian's hand and said, "Well, there was one time he took me to a Cowboys game…."

Chapter 16

THE ROUTE, as modified slightly by Ty, began in Manhattan at the foot of the Brooklyn Bridge.

The late-July sun was blaring down on Ian, so he slipped on his sunglasses as he walked to the designated meeting spot. Ty had sent him an incredibly detailed e-mail: they were to meet just outside City Hall Park, across the street from the Municipal Building, at a spot near the Brooklyn Bridge subway station. And indeed, Ty was casually leaning against a lamppost as Ian approached. Ty was wearing a white T-shirt half-tucked into a pair of khaki shorts, as well as his beat-up docksiders, a look that was super casual but also showed off his body nicely.

"All right, Texas," said Ian when he got there. "I'm ready for you. Do your worst."

Ty laughed and gave Ian an appraising look. "You look hot in sunglasses. You're all sexy and mysterious."

Ian didn't know what to do with the compliment, so he said, "It's sunny."

"That it is." Ty pulled a thin paperback from his pocket and flipped it open. "I made some changes to the itinerary, so the whole walk will be almost four miles in all. Think you can handle it?"

"I've been running," Ian said, posing a little in an attempt to show off his physique. He had on a pair of cropped khakis that he wasn't altogether sure he was pulling off—the girl at the store had assured him they looked cute, but he was pretty sure they mostly just telegraphed that he was gay—and a short-sleeved green-and-white-checked shirt that was trying its best to keep his body cool in the summer heat. Ty looked him over again.

"I think you've lost weight since I met you," Ty said.

"Yeah. A little. Blame Scott."

"Not that you were even anything like overweight before."

"Hell, I'm in the best shape of my life right now. Who knew playing baseball in an amateur league would do that?"

"It's mostly Scott. The all-star team in Chicago calls themselves the Bears, and it's, like, a triple entendre."

Ian laughed. "There's an all-star team?"

"Yeah. The Rainbow League has spread. Most of the major cities have some version of it, and then we have, like, a gay amateur World Series in October with each city's all-star team playing off against each other."

Some competitive part of Ian sat up and took notice of that. "How does one make the all-star team?"

Ty grinned. "In New York, Will has an evil network of scouts that report back to him about who the best players are. He puts together a twenty-man roster to send to the championships."

"Have you ever played on the all-star team?"

Ty pointed toward the street and they started walking. "Yeah, two years ago. I didn't make the team last year. I guess I ran too slow. Partied too hard after the games." He patted his stomach. "Anyway, the year I made the team, that was how Rachel from the Mermaids and I became friends, actually. I adore her, but she's fierce out on the field, if you haven't noticed."

"So who are the secret spies?"

"Who knows? Audience plants intended to look like the well-meaning husbands of players? Other players Will is blowing on the side? Not a clue."

They got to the foot of the bridge and were caught up in the swell of traffic. "This'll clear up by the first tower," Ty said, waving his hand toward the masses of people embarking on a trip across the bridge. "Most of the tourists just want to say they've been on the bridge, so they walk to the first tower to take pictures, then they turn around and come back. Heaven forbid they should accidentally wander into Brooklyn."

There were suddenly so many people that Ian worried he and Ty would get separated in the shuffle. He reached out for Ty's arm. Ty smiled and took his hand as they pressed through the throng. Ian thought perhaps he should be savoring the experience—despite his childhood in Brooklyn, he'd never walked across the Brooklyn Bridge before—but the people walking slowly and gawking at the sights were too distracting.

Ty was right, though; the crowd thinned after the first tower. They kept walking with Ty promising, "We'll stop at the Brooklyn-side tower so you can take blurry cell-phone photos of the Empire State Building," and it wasn't until they were about halfway between the towers that Ian realized they were still holding hands.

The view really was spectacular.

"I took a New York City history class in college," Ty said, "and also consulted the guidebook, so I'm an expert."

"Uh-huh."

Ty squeezed Ian's hand. "The bridge was built in the 1870s and '80s. The construction was done mostly by Irish immigrants who got the bends from going far underwater to dig out the sediment the bridge is resting on and then coming back too fast on the elevators, or something like that."

"That's... charming."

"The bridge designer got the bends too, and was confined to his house, so his wife came down to oversee the construction after that. She was the first person to walk across the bridge. That's pretty cool, right? A woman engineer in the 1880s?"

"That is pretty cool."

Ty smiled. "I always liked this bridge. There's something so gothic and dramatic about it. You compare it to a bridge like the George Washington, which is just, like, some exposed steel structure, and this one seems even more beautiful."

Ian stepped a little closer to Ty. "I love hearing you talk about art."

Ty blushed furiously. Ian supposed Ty being a redhead caused the natural flush of his skin, but there was something cute and bashful about the way Ty colored at the compliment. Ian found it endearing.

They paused at the Brooklyn tower. Ty got out his phone and maneuvered Ian over to a corner of the footpath that ran around the brick structure. "Smile!" he said as he held up his cell phone and took a selfie of the two of them with the East River and the Statue of Liberty in the background. Then he tilted the phone to get a better look at it without the glare of the sun.

"We look pretty cute together," Ty said.

Ian agreed. He didn't usually photograph well, but in this close-up, his skin looked good and he was smiling, and Ty, still a little flushed, was leaning against him, looking happy and adorable.

"I'll text you this," Ty said, fiddling with his phone. "It'll be like a postcard. Proof we were here."

They chatted as they walked the rest of the length of the bridge, mostly about what they saw: skyscrapers and other landmarks in the distance, the Manhattan Bridge just up the river, the bikers gliding by them on the bike path. When they got to the foot of the bridge, the streets were confusing, but Ty pulled out his book, made a couple of turns, and soon they were cutting across the park in front of Brooklyn Borough Hall and the courthouses, walking by a statue that Ty identified as being of Henry Ward Beecher. Ty seemed to know where he was going, so Ian followed.

They cut over to a side street that Ian didn't see the name of, but it was cute, mostly historical houses and churches.

"Oh, according to the book, that museum is here," said Ty.

"What museum?"

"The haunted house one."

Ian didn't find this particularly enlightening. "There's a haunted museum?"

"Oh. Yeah. I read a whole book about it last year. Or, actually, the book was by this historian who was posing a theory on the deaths of two men who were killed in the house in the 1870s, but the rumor is that their ghosts are haunting the house. Now the house is some kind of Victorian museum. The historian thought the two men were a gay couple, by the way."

"Interesting."

They paused when they got to the museum, but Ian didn't especially want to go in. Ty shrugged and kept walking.

Eventually they got to the Promenade on the East River.

"You want to sit for a few minutes?" Ty asked, gesturing toward a bench.

"Yeah, sure."

Despite the sunny weather, there weren't many people out. A few couples and a few single people strolled along the walkway, and one family with a mess of kids leaned against the railing, but the Promenade was quiet and open, the sun shining overhead, the East River meandering in front of them. From their bench, Ian could see the Brooklyn Bridge, the skyscrapers of Lower Manhattan, and the Statue of Liberty.

"What a view," he said.

Ty laughed. "See? The city's not all bad. This is pretty incredible, don't you think?"

"Yeah, okay. I will concede your point."

Because this part of the city was unlike any other part of the city. It was clean and quiet. Manhattan looked like a model made of blocks. The skyscrapers went right to the edge of the island, almost comically so, as if developers had just kept building until they abruptly ran out of room. A bright orange Staten Island Ferry chugged along in the distance.

It was odd to be just far enough outside Manhattan to see it from an outsider's perspective but still feel a part of it. For years Ian had gotten a lot of questions from curious people he'd met. He'd grown up in New York City? What had that been like? For Ian, it had been dreadful, and not just because his childhood had been less than idyllic. He'd grown up in Koch-era New York, when there was still plenty of crime and urban decay. The city seemed... shinier now. Not like itself. That seemed especially true now that he was looking at the sun bouncing off the glass façades of the Lower Manhattan skyscrapers, the new World Trade Center tower rising up taller than all of them.

Ian shook his head. "It doesn't even seem like the same city."

Ty reached over and rubbed Ian's thigh. "Have you never been here before?"

"Oh, once or twice when I was a kid. My mom brought me to see the Fourth of July fireworks here. They shot them off over the East River back in the day."

"The move to the Hudson wasn't that long ago. I heard they're moving them back next year. My first few years in New York, as long as you knew someone with roof access near this part of Brooklyn, you had a great view of the fireworks without the crowds cramping your style." Ty sighed. "I actually met a guy on a rooftop like that when I was in my early twenties. He lived on a different floor of the same building my friend lived in. I'm still not really that great at sussing out which guys are straight or gay, but this one just winked at me, and I was smitten. We were together the rest of the summer."

"Aw. That's kind of cute."

"The relationship didn't last, but I always thought that was kind of the magic of the city. There are so many people here, so many ways to meet them. My hometown is kind of closed off and insular. And, you know, I never met another gay person until I moved here, so that was nice too."

"Really? Surely there are gay people in Dallas."

"Oh, there are. I didn't know any of them. Or if I did, I didn't know they were gay. I mean, as far as I know, I'm still the only gay person my mother speaks to regularly. Every now and then she'll call and say something like, 'Tyler, I saw a man at the grocery store in a pink shirt. Do you think he's one of your people?'" Ty rolled his eyes. He'd beefed up his accent and spoke a little higher to imitate his mother. "I don't wear pink. Pink is not an indicator of gayness."

"You're pink enough as it is, I guess."

Ty smiled. "I never really figured out how to wear colors, as you've probably noticed. I think I prefer putting color on my canvases to on my body."

That was true. Ian had picked up on the fact that Ty mostly wore neutrals. The only notable exception was the Hipsters' purple uniform T-shirt.

"So where's the next stop on this tour?"

Ty got out the book again. He opened it to a map that he'd drawn all over and traced the route with his finger. "Well, the tour I sketched out will take us down Montague Street. Then we turn here and go south. If you're hungry, there's a restaurant on Atlantic I've been wanting to try, or else we can go a little farther and have a late lunch at one of the places I've marked with an X."

"You really thought this out," Ian said.

Ty grinned. "Well, first, I was trying to avoid another Central Park Incident."

Right. Of course. "Oh."

"Not because I was, like, embarrassed or anything. I just didn't want to make you so uncomfortable that you panicked again. The goal is to have fun, not freak out. So, map." Ty held up the book. "Plus I know this part of Brooklyn well enough. I lived in Carroll Gardens for a bit and used to walk up here along Court Street when I got bored."

Ian was touched that Ty had been so thoughtful. "Oh," he repeated. "Thank you."

"Plus I always hate it when you're in a neighborhood you don't know that well and get hungry but don't know where to eat. I planned ahead for such a possibility."

It struck Ian that Ty was trying pretty hard to be fun and impressive, going the extra mile to set up these dates/persuasive field trips. That meant that he probably really liked Ian, and Ian felt like a heel suddenly because he'd been treating Ty so indifferently. But how could he get invested when he knew he was leaving?

Because Ty was trying to convince him to stay.

Ian wasn't sure they had that sort of relationship. Not yet, anyway.

But as they sat on a bench in the middle of a long promenade overlooking the East River, with the breeze brushing against their faces and the noise of the city filtered out by the trees and the river, Ian was almost persuaded that this was a place he belonged.

He turned to Ty, who was looking out at the water.

"Ty?"

Ty turned and gave Ian a sad smile.

Ian leaned over and kissed him. As their lips slid together, he had a fleeting thought that everyone in the city could see them, but he wasn't sure if he cared.

He pulled away and said, "Thank you for all of this. I do appreciate it."

Ty lowered his eyelids. "Am I chipping away at your resolve?"

"Maybe a little."

But Ty's argument would have to be more persuasive, because even looking at the beauty of the city from this vantage point was not enough to convince Ian that this was where he should be. Other cities were more beautiful. Other cities had things to offer him.

New York City had Ty.

But was falling for a great guy enough of a reason to stay?

"In my adult life, I've never lived anywhere longer than two years," Ian said.

Ty balked, perhaps surprised by the abrupt subject change. "I couldn't do it," he said. "I moved across the country when I was eighteen. That was enough." He shook his head. "Although, I'm curious. If your anxiety is so bad that you get panic attacks, how can you handle all the new cities?"

"Don't know. I just do." Ian couldn't explain it. "I mean, I research the hell out of any place I'm about to work. If the location makes me uneasy, I turn down the job. Luckily I can afford to do that now. And, you know, the first few weeks in a new city are nerve-racking, but once I get into a job and start working, I'm fine."

Of course, he'd been running from New York for years, and he was fully aware of that. That he'd wound up back in the city was one of the great ironies of his life.

Ty fiddled with Ian's hair and then they both sat back on the bench. Ty put his arm around Ian.

"Which Woody Allen movie starts with that montage of the city with *Rhapsody in Blue* playing?" Ty asked.

"Uh. *Manhattan*?" The abrupt subject change surprised Ian.

"Yeah, I think so. I get *Manhattan* and *Annie Hall* confused. Don't ask me why. The view here kind of makes me think of that, though, you know?"

"Yeah, I get what you mean."

"I mean, Woody Allen. Say what you will about his personal life. I don't really get his movies either. But there's a guy who loves this city." Ty put his hand above his eyes like a visor and looked around again. Then he turned back to Ian. "You ready to move on?"

"Yeah, let's go."

THEY STOPPED for a meal at a pub on Atlantic Avenue that was supposed to serve some of the best food in the neighborhood, at least according to the signage out front, though Ty was a little underwhelmed by the menu. Allegedly their brisket was served "genuine Texas BBQ style," but Ty would be the judge of that.

He watched Ian look over the menu. His lips still tingled from the kiss Ian had given him on the Promenade, which was such a silly thing to think about. It was a kiss. He'd kissed many men in his life. He'd kissed Ian dozens of times too. Hundreds of times, maybe. But there was something special about this one. Maybe he was getting through to Ian.

"Are you ordering the Texas barbecue brisket?" Ian asked.

"I sort of want to, if only to shame the restaurant when it turns out to taste inauthentic."

Ian laughed. "I'll split it with you."

"Deal. And shall we order a couple of these craft beers?"

"Why do you sound so skeptical?"

"I always thought 'craft beer' was a dumb phrase. It just means the beer was made at a small brewery, right? But 'craft' always makes me think of, like, little kids in a playroom with glue sticks and construction paper."

"Says the artist."

Ty bristled. "Hey, I paint and draw. I don't craft."

Ian raised an eyebrow. "I can't really verify that without seeing some of your art. For all I know, you spray-paint macaroni and make necklaces."

"Then I'll show you when we get back to my place later."

The words were out of Ty's mouth before he thought about it. Ian looked so surprised that Ty realized he'd have to follow through. So he'd show Ian his paintings, and then Ian would probably judge him mediocre, and then Ty would die.

He tried to put that thought out of his head after they ordered so that he could just chat with Ian like a normal human on a date and not like a mental case.

The brisket arrived a while later. Ty scrutinized it, seeing that it seemed to have a rub on it and was cooked to the correct amount of pinkness. The waiter gave them little ceramic bowls full of sauce too. Ty stuck his fork in the sauce and tasted it. Molasses dominated the flavor, but it wasn't bad. He reached over and used his fork to cut into the meat. It cut like butter, so that was a good sign. He stabbed a piece of meat with his fork, dunked it in the sauce, and tasted it.

"Well, Texas?" Ian asked.

"It's kind of a hybrid of different barbecue styles. See, where I'm from in east Texas—"

Ian started laughing. "But is it good?"

Ty took another bite and paused to taste it. "It's not really authentic, but it's nice."

"I'm a Yankee, remember? Taste is all that matters."

So they split the brisket, and yeah, it was sort of a blend of styles, but the meat was tasty and well cooked and the sauce was tangy in the right way. By the time they finished eating—and Ian seemed to have tired of Texas jokes—they were both full to bursting and a little sleepy from the beer.

"Guess we better roll home now," Ty said as they waited for the check.

Ian nodded. "You want to split it or...."

"My treat."

Paying for dinner made it feel more date-like. Although it wasn't like there was any ambiguity here. They were dating. Ian had kissed Ty on the Promenade. They'd been sleeping together for weeks.

But Ty had felt as they held hands while crossing the Brooklyn Bridge that they'd crossed over into new territory, like something between them had become more serious than just a casual summer fling.

So he paid for the meal and he put a hand on Ian's back as they exited the restaurant, and Ian—skittish as he was about PDA—let him, and that was good. Ty pulled out the book again to work out the best path back to his apartment. He was tired and drowsy now, but they were still almost a mile away, by his calculation. He wanted to be home, though. He wanted to be curled up in bed with Ian. And how fluffy and romantic was that?

Ian walked ahead of him as they turned the corner to walk south again, giving Ty an excellent view of Ian's ass, which looked great in the weird high-water pants he was wearing. Though Ian wasn't quite a fashion plate, it was clear he put some effort into his wardrobe, and Ty appreciated a man who at least tried. Ty certainly tried and had lots of nice clothes, but he just didn't see the point in dressing up most days. He dressed well for client meetings or when he had to go work in an office, but otherwise he kept things casual.

But Ian. He had a day's worth of beard growth on his face, which was super sexy, and he had a bit of a swagger in his step as he walked ahead, something he did most of the time and was probably unaware of. Ty loved his confidence in the face of his anxiety disorder.

Ty jogged ahead to catch up and slipped an arm around Ian's shoulders. He liked the proximity of their bodies, and attraction zinged between them even when Ty kept it casual. Ian shot him a sly smile.

"So?" Ty said. "The tour of Brooklyn was not an unmitigated disaster, right?"

"No. I had fun. You have almost succeeded in convincing me that Brooklyn is an all right place."

"Your family still lives in Park Slope, right?"

"My mother, yeah. My dad moved to the suburbs when they divorced."

"So you go visit him, or—"

"No. My father and I don't really talk."

Ty wanted to laugh. So they both had daddy issues.

"I've been going to see my mother every other week or so since I moved back," said Ian. "I, uh… I mentioned I was seeing someone the last time I saw her."

That surprised Ty. "Really?" Trying to cover his shock, he purred, "So what's his name?"

"Oh, he's this burly redheaded Texan named Tyler. He's pretty hot. I mean, I didn't tell my mother that, just that I was seeing someone and he was fun."

"Burly, huh? Is he good in bed?"

"Oh, yeah." Ian snaked a hand around Ty's waist. "Didn't tell my mother that either."

"Fair enough. Don't traumatize the woman."

Ian laughed. They got to a corner and had to disentangle in order to cross the street without getting hit by a gaggle of bikers who chose then to zoom by.

Ty figured if Ian had mentioned Ty to his mother, maybe there was some hope after all.

"So can I ask the obvious question?" Ty said.

Ian paused to look at a display in a store window. "I really like that shirt," he said, pointing. Then he turned back to Ty. "What's the obvious question?"

"I hate to be all 'let's define the relationship,' but what are we doing? Is this just a summer thing? Are we seeing other people? Are we boyfriends? Are we just going to keep getting more involved until the inevitable heartbreak?"

Ian frowned. "Well, I'm not seeing anybody else."

"Okay. Me neither." Ty looked into the window. There was a maroon-and-white plaid shirt in the window that was not Ty's style but would look pretty great on Ian. "I don't know if that's an answer."

"Well, what do you want?"

The situation called for honesty. "I don't know exactly. I'd like to keep seeing you and see where it goes. I like you a hell of a lot more than anyone who has come around in a while."

"Okay." Ian made a weird face.

"You look unconvinced."

"You know that you've been kind of... closed off... with me."

Well, that was certainly true. What the hell was the point if Ian was leaving? "That's where the inevitable heartbreak comes in. If you're definitely leaving, how invested should I get?"

"Ah, we're back here again." Ian looked at the sky for a moment, then back at the store window.

It was a little strange to be having this conversation out in the middle of the street. This was probably a behind-closed-door conversation, but Ty kind of wanted to have it out now.

"Let's walk," Ty said.

Ian nodded and fell into step with Ty.

"What is it that you want?" Ian asked, apparently on the same page as Ty. "Like, if you could have anything you wanted with me. Long term, short term, forever, until August, what?"

Ty sighed. "I'm not sure, but it sure feels like you've taken the option away from me. You're moving at some point. You hate this city and you took a temporary job that is, apparently, ending sooner than you thought, so when does that mean you leave? A year? Two? You've necessarily cut this off at the pass, yeah? So you can see why maybe I wouldn't want to be the most forthcoming with you."

Ian nodded. He kept walking while mostly looking at the sidewalk.

"What do you want?" Ty asked.

"Well, I... you have to understand...." Ian literally stumbled then, missing a step on the sidewalk. Ty snagged his arm so he wouldn't fall. When he was back upright, Ian said, "Look, I was... when I signed up for the baseball team, I was kind of thinking that maybe I'd meet a guy. I'm too fucked up for sex to be that easy, but I thought maybe this time, I could put some of my anxiety aside and just have fun, but it's of course not that easy for me. And you know how I was at the beginning. So, like, for me to have slept with you, I had to really trust you, and I do. You have to appreciate how important that is."

Ty hadn't really considered that.

"And now we're both holding each other at arm's length, aren't we?" Ian went on. "Because yeah, my plan is to leave when this contract is up and I get another job at another hotel. Because I never intended to stay in New York very long. That's just... that was always my plan."

"You've been holding out on me too."

"Yeah, maybe. I really like you, Ty. I *really* like you. I could see us together for a while yet, you know? I keep thinking that I want this to last longer than the baseball season, because I'd hate to have to say good-bye to you at the end of the summer."

Ty kicked a stray rock. "Is that really so much harder than it would be to say good-bye when you move out of the city next year?"

"I don't know, but the end of the summer is sooner, and I wouldn't want to face that. Not yet. I keep thinking, damn, if I have to get through the rest of my time in New York without Ty, what the hell am I going to do?"

Well, shit. "I mean, look, I've been resisting you, I won't deny it. Not even in the spending time together way, because obviously we've been spending a lot of time together, but it's been hard to talk about, you know, my personal stuff with you."

"Your art?"

"My other baggage too. I've got a whole matched set, babe."

Ian laughed softly. "I find that hard to believe."

"Well. You show your anxiety on the outside. I've got plenty of stuff that makes me anxious. Like, showing you my art? Just, like, one of my paintings. I'm sweating like a pig thinking about it. I want to show it to you, but I also kind of don't."

"Do you think I won't like it?"

"I don't know what to think."

Ian was silent for a few moments. They crossed a street and rounded a corner before he spoke up again. "We like each other, don't we?"

"Yeah. I like you a lot. I already told you that."

Ian nodded. "I really like you too. This summer, this has been... you know, I think it's been one of the best summers of my life. Just between the baseball and you and this silly tour through the city and all of it. I can't remember when I had this much fun."

"Really?"

"Yeah. I don't want it to end."

"It doesn't have to. I mean, the baseball season will end, but we can still keep having fun."

"Can we? Didn't you just say—"

"I know what I said." Ty let out a breath. "I mean, obviously this would be different if there were even some possibility of you staying here."

Ian pursed his lips. "I know. I...."

They were back in familiar territory, in the northern part of Park Slope. They had not taken the most direct route, but Ty at least knew where he was now. They were still a good half mile from his apartment. Hopefully Ian still wanted to go there.

But at least they were talking.

"This whole campaign of yours," Ian said. "You want to prove to me that New York City is great because you want to convince me to stay here. With you."

Ty shrugged. "Yeah. I'm not sure that's been the plan all along, but that's what it is now."

Ian nodded. "Look, it's hard for me. I can't really convey how intense my childhood was, all the reasons I have for not wanting to stay here. But I... what if I agree to think about it?"

"What are you saying?"

Ian walked ahead a few paces and then turned around and walked backward. "If we're holding out on each other because I put an end date on the relationship, why don't we take away the end date? Pretend it's not there. Get to know each other, open up to each other, no holds barred. Then, when my work at the hotel is done, who the hell knows? Maybe I get a job at a nearby city. Philly or Boston, you know? Or maybe I stay in New York. Or maybe I move to Barcelona. I don't have a job lined up, so it could be anything. Hell, maybe we won't even make it that long. All I know is that it seems foolish to not try to make a good thing work if it's what we both want."

Ian was about to plow into a dog whose leash was tied to a No Parking sign, so Ty reached over and grabbed his arm to keep him from tripping. Then he pulled Ian into a shady spot and kissed the hell out of him.

"Really?" Ty said when they came up for breath.

"Yeah. We like each other. Why try to fight that?"

"You might revise that opinion when you get to know me better."

"Or maybe I won't. But we won't know if you don't let me get to know you."

Ty nodded. "You're right. Let's go to my place. We're only about six blocks away now."

"Good." Ian shook out his shoulders. "What, ah, what do you think about all this? About what I just said?"

"I promise to try, okay? You want us to open up, and that's hard for me, but I will. I'll stop keeping you at a distance. For you, I can do it."

"That's all I ask."

"Come on. Let's go."

Chapter 17

NO QUESTION, Ty was nervous as he unlocked the door to his apartment.

Uncomfortable now, he went for a joke. He lowered his voice. "Hey, baby, can I take you inside to see my etchings?"

Ian laughed. "Okay, that's creepy."

Ty smiled.

His ground-floor apartment was basically three rooms, railroad style, with a tiny kitchen wedged between the front and middle rooms. Ty used the front room as a living room, the middle room as a bedroom, and the back room with its big window that overlooked the backyard and let in a fair amount of light as the art studio. He kept that door closed most of the time.

Now he tried to stall before opening it, offering Ian a drink, inviting him to sit on the sofa or stretch out his legs—they had just walked four miles, after all—and he even considered seducing Ian, distracting him with sex, but no, it was probably better to get this over with.

"I don't show my art much," Ty said. "I mean, most of my paintings are commissions, so the clients see them, obviously. You've probably seen a few if you spend any time in bookstores, actually."

"Right. What else have you done?"

Ty took a deep breath. "I'm a graphic artist. I do some design work too, but book covers and ads are my bread and butter. But I'll paint anything. I've also done sets for Broadway shows and props for movies. Did you see that movie *Brushstroke* that came out a couple of years ago about the creepy painter who's accused of being a serial killer?"

"Oh. With, um, what's the actor's name? With the big eyes? Yeah, I saw that one."

"The paintings hanging on the walls of his studio are all Tyler Arnold originals."

"Oh, wow. Cool."

Yeah, Ty thought, anything having to do with the movies was usually a pretty good hook for the boys.

Ty stalled outside the studio door and glanced around his apartment. Ian had, of course, seen the rest of the space before. Fancy it wasn't, but it was clean and functional. Most of the chaos was limited to the studio.

Ty put his hand on the doorknob. "Just... you're special, okay? I don't like showing this to people generally."

"Okay," Ian said, nodding solemnly. He touched Ty's arm and then ran his fingers down to squeeze Ty's hand. "I understand."

Ty pushed the door open.

He'd forgotten that the painting on the easel closest to the door was another clutch cover.

"So," Ty said, backpedaling, already regretting this decision. "I do a lot of genre fiction covers. Usually the text is added by the art department at the publisher. I just do these paintings."

Ian stared at it. This one wasn't quite finished. It featured a woman in a billowing green ball gown with her shoulders bared, clutched from behind by a man who was kissing her neck.

"That's pretty racy," Ian said.

"It's for a romance novel."

"I gathered."

Ty's heart was pounding and his stomach had suddenly gone sour. He said, "So, classic romance novel covers all look like this, but most of the covers recently are basically just photos of actors dressed up like historical characters and photoshopped to look like paintings. But for a select few authors, they still do these paintings. I'm more expensive than a photo shoot, so I only do these for the big-name authors who will sell enough books to justify my fee. Sometimes the publisher sends me some photos of actors to use. Sometimes they just send me specs and I use stock photos or get my friends to model. But pretty much I just do genre fiction. Romance novels, fantasy, that kind of thing." Ty took a deep breath, realizing he'd spewed all of that quickly. Ian looked a little dizzy. Ty walked across the room. "I mean, sometimes I do things on the computer. The trend in mainstream book covers is to do these minimalist things with just, like, a single object in the middle, or else a solid-colored cover with just the title of the book in a fancy font. And I do some advertising work too. My computer-designed stuff is very clean and modern, kind of minimalist. I don't love it, but it pays the bills. But see, I've developed a style, I have five or so companies I work for regularly, and basically when their art department is like, 'We need this thing in this style, let's call Ty,' I get a job."

Ian squinted at the painting. "That's interesting. I had no idea book covers still got made this way."

"For some of the lower-budget projects, I just draw it, scan it, and do the 'painting' on the computer." Ty made finger quotes. "I did a couple of gay covers that way."

That seemed to snag Ian's interest. "Can I see those?"

"Yeah, okay." Ty pulled out the big binder where he kept scans or printouts of all of his work. He flipped through it to his favorite gay romance cover. It was a painting he'd done mostly on his tablet—it was faster to do it that way, cost less money in supplies—of two men in Victorian garb embracing and about to kiss. He'd been hired to do a classic clutch cover, just with a second man instead of a woman, and that was what he'd done.

"That's pretty sexy," Ian said, bending to peer at it. "You painted this?"

"I did, yeah."

"Do you paint for yourself? Like, not for a commission?"

Ty sighed. "Yeah. Not as much as I used to, mostly because I don't have time, but I need the outlet, you know?" He walked over to his second easel, tucked into the corner away from the sunlight. "This one I've been working on just for me. It's not done yet, but it's getting there."

It was a cityscape done entirely in blues and yellows, the skyscrapers rendered in precise geometric shapes, all of them clean with sharp lines. In the foreground, though, was a rough figure, a man with a round head and a rounded body, hunched forward.

It was how he thought of loneliness.

Perhaps the metaphor was too on the nose. One man in the foreground juxtaposed against a bustling city, different from everything else around him. But it was how Ty had often felt as a kid, so there it was.

Ian stared.

It bothered Ty now that he'd put so much of himself on display but gotten almost no reaction back from Ian. He resisted the urge to start pacing, or to shake Ian while asking him to just say what he thought.

Finally Ian said, "It's beautiful."

"Really?"

"Yeah. You're really talented. I had no idea."

"Oh."

"I mean, when you mentioned you went to art school, I thought, oh, he does graphic design on a computer. I didn't realize you painted this way. I don't know much about art, but I can tell you're really good. Even the book covers." Ian walked back over to the clutch cover easel. "Like, if not for the subject matter, this could be in a museum."

Ty laughed. "Yeah, that'll be the day." He walked over to stand next to Ian, wondering if he could figure out what Ian saw in the painting. "I've gone racier. I did one that was just a guy standing in front of a castle with his leg propped up on a rock. The client said, 'Make him hot,' so I did. He was the alpha of all alpha men. This big brute with huge muscles." Ty held up his hands to show where his muscles would be if he were this guy. "I hate long hair on dudes, so I didn't give him the flowing locks that the client asked for, just a pretty standard short haircut, but I did give him a pretty nice bulge." Ty gestured over his own crotch. "The publisher wound up putting the title of the book over his midsection, effectively blocking out the bulge, but *I* know it's there."

Ian lowered his eyelids in a sexy way. "Is that what you like? Big alpha strongmen?"

"Eh. I could take or leave the really butch ones. I like 'em a little thinner, generally. And the skinny guys always have the biggest cocks."

Ian laughed and put his hands on Ty's shoulders. "So you like guys like me, is what you're saying."

"Baby, I was attracted to you the first time I set eyes on you." Ty put his hands on Ian's waist.

"Seriously, though," Ian said, sliding his hands to the back of Ty's neck. "I do appreciate your showing me this. I know it was hard for you. But you really are unbelievably talented, and I'm super impressed. I'm not even just saying that to get laid."

Ty closed his eyes and savored the compliment. "Thank you."

"This was what I wanted, Ty. To see a more complete picture of you. Because on the outside, you're this brash, funny, seemingly promiscuous guy, but there's a lot of depth to you, and I like that. That painting with the skyscrapers, I don't know. Something in it spoke to me." Ian ran his fingers up into Ty's hair. "Without making it sound too cheesy, I want to thank you for showing me this."

"I wouldn't do it for many others. I mean, Josh is basically my best friend in New York, and he's barely seen any of it."

"But you like me."

"I do like you." Ty tugged on Ian's waist a bit, pulling their hips together. Ty was becoming aroused by their proximity but didn't want to act on it just yet.

"I like you too," Ian said. He leaned in for a kiss.

And Ty was just… gone. Their lips met and slid together, fitting well as they always did, and intimacy and a certain rightness that was hard to find were always there when he kissed Ian. Because yeah, a few dozen men had paraded in and out of this apartment in the five or six years Ty had been living in it, but none of them mattered enough to get past Ty's outer defenses. Ian mattered.

Ian, with his colorful wardrobe and invisible eyebrows, his developing muscles and his tight little butt, his pouty lips and his long legs—he was gorgeous, no question about it. But that almost seemed beside the point. He was twitchy and anxious sometimes, totally relaxed other times, but he was an open book when it came to his anxieties. He was smart and successful. Ty enjoyed his company. And he was also harboring a great deal of pain, enough childhood trauma to send him running from the city he'd grown up in. Ty wanted to explore that, to get to know Ian better, for the two of them to spend more time together, in and out of bed.

Ty pushed Ian out of the studio, and though he thought about closing the door, he left it open. He kept kissing Ian as he pushed him toward the bed. They tumbled onto it together, and Ian let out an "oof" when he hit the mattress, but then laughed and continued kissing Ty.

Ty reached between them. He removed buttons from their holes, lowered zippers, pushed and pulled at the various layers of clothing that separated them. He was hungry, suddenly, craving Ian, needing him now. When they were naked, he took Ian into his arms and kissed him hard. Ian groaned into his mouth and snaked his hands through Ty's hair.

"I want you," Ty groaned against Ian's lips.

"Just like this, Ty."

That suddenly seemed ideal. The two of them lay on their sides, facing each other, their bodies pressed together. Ty hooked his leg around Ian's and tugged until they intertwined. He shifted his hips so that he lined up their cocks and pressed them together.

"Just like this," Ty agreed.

They shifted closer and humped together, groaning and digging their fingers and nails and hands into each other's skin. Then Ian sighed and pressed his wrists against Ty's shoulders and splayed his hands out, grasping at Ty.

"God, I'm so close," Ian said.

"So come. Come, baby. I want you to."

Ty pulled back far enough to see panic flash across Ian's face.

"Are you worried about the bedspread?" Ty asked with a chuckle.

"Yeah, I'm sorry, I just—"

Ty didn't give him time to explain. He pushed Ian away and then dove to take Ian's cock in his mouth.

Ian groaned and arched off the bed. "Oh, God," he sighed, thrusting a hand into Ty's hair.

Ty loved the texture of Ian's cock against his tongue. It was hard and smooth and tasted a little salty. Ty relaxed his throat to take Ian in farther, and he pressed his nose against Ian's pubic hair. The scent was intoxicating and arousing and it surrounded Ty. He thrust a hand between his own legs and wrapped a hand around his cock, stroking lightly at first, not wanting to come just yet. But as Ian groaned and gripped Ty's head harder, Ty knew he was close.

"Ty, God, Ty!" Ian shouted.

Then his come flooded Ty's mouth.

Ty stayed put, sucking gently until Ian started to go limp. He swallowed as he sat up, wiping the excess off his lips.

"Dear Lord," Ian said, sagging against the pillows. "I should help you."

He started to sit up, but it was clear Ian was pretty well sapped, and Ty was getting close anyway. He shifted closer to Ian, straddling his chest. He took Ian's hand and wrapped it around his cock. Ian took the hint and started to stroke. He increased the intensity, tightening his grip and picking up speed, and Ty's body responded. He thrust into Ian's grip, though his legs were starting to give out. He was shaky and aroused and so very close. Then Ian looked up at Ty and their gazes met. The plaintive look in his eyes combined with the flush of his body was beautiful.

Suddenly, Ty was there. His balls drew up, his body tingled, and then it was just light and nothing for a moment before he was shooting over Ian's chest and his hand. A bit hit Ian in the chin, but he gamely wiped it off with his free hand and put his fingers in his mouth. The nonchalant way he did it was so fucking sexy.

Before his body gave out entirely, Ty grabbed a tissue from the side table and wiped them off. Then he tossed the tissue at the wastebasket without checking to see if he made it before he collapsed next to Ian on the bed.

Ian leaned over and kissed him. Ty welcomed it, opening his mouth to let Ian in, and they explored each other with their tongues, tasting each other's seed. For a moment Ty thought he could go for another round.

But his body had other ideas, and soon enough they lay tangled together, panting.

Ian ran a hand over Ty's chest. "Thank you, Ty."

Ty laughed softly. "What are you thanking me for now?"

"I don't know. For showing me your paintings. For the good sex. For being you."

Ty put his arm around Ian and tugged him close. He kissed the top of Ian's head. "Thank you too, then."

Ian laughed.

"What's so funny?" Ty asked.

"We sound a little silly, I dunno." He sighed. "I'm just gonna sleep for a few minutes, I think."

"Not a problem. Me too. Sweet dreams, babe."

"Only if they're of you."

Ty laughed. "That was a really lame line."

"I know. Shut up."

Chapter 18

MASON WATCHED the little pretty boy dance around the jukebox in the corner, occasionally grinding up against one of his teammates. The guy was hot. He was small, yeah, maybe five foot five tops, with long limbs and a thin body—athletic, though, not skinny—and a tight little ass. He moved like he was made for sex. Topping it all off were those big blue eyes, the strong jaw, the high cheekbones…. This guy could model if he were taller, basically, and if he cut his hair, an insane blond mop kind of styled as if the guy were a rooster, with hot pink and purple streaks. That hair, it was a lot of look. So was the ring in his nose and the gauged earlobes. But Jesus. Mason was lusting hard.

Time to face facts, he thought. He kept dating these butch assholes who were hot in their own way, but this guy, the pretty one with the piercings and the hair, he really turned Mason's crank. Especially when he moved like that. Christ on a crutch.

Mason turned back toward the bar and signaled Tom that he wanted another. As Tom slid a pint glass in front of Mason, the guy flounced over and leaned on the bar.

"Well, hello," he said to Mason. "Nice hit you got in the seventh. Mason, right?"

"Uh-huh." Mason was dumbstruck. This much sexual energy was probably bad for his health.

"I'm Patrick," said the guy. "You're the one who used to be a Yankee, right?"

"Yes." Wow, it was hard to make words suddenly.

Patrick bobbed up and down, still dancing to the music from the jukebox. "You're not, like, some retired straight guy who joined the league just for the love of the game or whatever, right? 'Cause I know Will lets people like that join. A sports league for gay athletes can't possibly be exclusionary, right?" Patrick rolled his eyes.

"Nope. I'm gay. I got a lot of ink when I came out. Do you not remember?"

Patrick shrugged. "Like I pay attention to the news. If it wasn't in *People*, I don't know it happened."

"I was on the cover of *People*."

"Oh." Patrick squinted. "I suppose I do remember there being a little tizzy a few years ago. Some major leaguer who came out of the closet after he retired, yeah?"

Mason pointed at himself.

"Well, look at you, darling. You're practically a celebrity!" Patrick playfully poked at Mason's arm. "No wonder your team beat ours today."

Mason debated making a move. This guy talked a lot, but he was so fucking hot that it kind of didn't matter. Besides, Mason didn't want a romantic dinner or a long date, just a quick fuck somewhere nearby.

Patrick ordered a fruity cocktail, something that came in a martini glass and was garnished with a maraschino cherry. He took a careful sip. "You sitting here alone, big guy?" he asked.

"Yeah, just… taking in the scenery." He gave Patrick what he hoped was a meaningful look.

Patrick laughed. "I shall take that as a compliment."

Mason gave Patrick a closer look. He seemed to be wearing eyeliner, and his sneakers had hot pink laces in them.

"No offense, but how does a guy like you end up playing baseball?" Mason asked.

A frown flashed across Patrick's face, but he recovered quickly. "Well, before I became all this"—he gestured toward himself—"I was a little boy in the suburbs. I played Little League ball until I was fourteen or so. That was when I figured out that I wanted to play with the boys in different ways. I moved to the city and was looking to meet people, and this friend of my mother's mentioned this league, and I told some coworkers who thought it sounded like a lark, like, how hi-lar-ious would it be if Patrick the Sparkle Pixie did something so butch as play baseball. I was all, 'Challenge accepted.' Then I grew to really love playing again. Guess I showed them." Patrick winked.

"Your coworkers? What do you do?"

Patrick ran a hand through the messy rooster-comb hair on top of his head. "I'm a hairdresser, darling."

Of course he was.

"And you?" Patrick asked.

"I write feature stories for a sports website."

"How literary of you." Patrick grinned. "Look at this, we're getting to know each other. And here I thought all your leering at me was just to get me into bed."

"Who says it wasn't?"

Patrick's eyes went wide with surprise for a moment. He took a healthy sip of his martini and then leaned closer to Mason. "Can I ask you a rude question, darling?"

"Yes."

"Is it true what they say about black men?"

Mason mentally reeled from that hard enough to nearly fall off the stool. He grabbed the edge of the bar. "Is what true?" He steeled himself for whatever bullshit nonsense was coming.

Patrick pointed downward.

"Did you really just ask me that?" Mason said. And just like that, erection sapped.

"I meant no offense," Patrick said. "Merely curious. I've only been with white guys. Well, and this one Chinese guy at beauty school who…." Patrick held his thumb and forefinger about an inch apart. "I'm not a size queen, but come on."

Mason bristled. He didn't have time for this bullshit. It figured that the pretty white boy was treating him like a novelty item; he often found this to be the case. The butch assholes mostly wanted him because he'd once graced the field at Yankee Stadium. The pretty boys mostly wanted him because he was big and black and different from what they were used to. And oh ho, here came Patrick, peddling stereotypes. Chinese guys had small dicks, black guys were hung like horses. That was the conventional wisdom, wasn't it? Ha-ha. What fucking bullshit.

He slid off the stool. "Well. Nice talking to you."

Patrick reached over and wrapped his hand around Mason's upper arm. "No, wait, I'm sorry. I've offended you. I didn't mean to."

"You know, men are not all the same. They come in all shapes, sizes, and colors. I'm not here to be your experiment. I mean, how would you feel if I said, 'All twinks are bottoms and airheads who are silly and superficial.'"

Patrick pursed his lips. "All right. Point taken." He looked up at Mason. "You're taller than I thought."

"Are you intimidated?"

"Not at all."

Their eyes met. There was a sizzle in the air. No, Mason realized, Patrick was not intimidated. He was even more attracted than he had been before. Mason wondered if it was worth it to abandon his principles for the sake of a quick fuck, or at least a blow job in the bathroom at Barnstorm, which would prevent any messiness with trying to negotiate whose place they would go to. Hell, there was a condom vending machine in the bathroom. Mason didn't usually top, but he'd do it for this pretty twink, who despite being crass had Mason's whole body humming in a way it hadn't in a long time.

Patrick kept his hold on Mason's arm and leaned in. He stood on his toes to whisper, "I'm not intimidated and I'm not a bottom either. You want to go bust up some stereotypes with me in the men's room?"

Mason's brain totally shorted out. He just stood there staring at Patrick for a long moment.

"My mama used to say if you make a face, it'll get stuck like that," Patrick said, tapping on Mason's chin, prompting Mason to close his mouth.

Mason glanced around the room to see if anyone would miss him. Ian and Ty were full-on making out at one of the tables in the corner, shoving their tongues into each other's mouth in a way that was more vulgar than sexy; Nate and Carlos were sitting on the other end of the bar yukking it up about something; pink-haired Joe was across the room, hitting on some guy by flailing his hands around.

Everyone else from the Hipsters had left. And now Mason had lost the thread.

He looked back at Patrick, who just… yeah. So sexy. "Yeah, let's go," he said.

"Oh good. I thought I'd lost you for a second there." Patrick smiled. He had really nice teeth too.

On the way to the bathroom, Mason said, "Just because something is an unfair generalization doesn't mean it's not true in some cases." He raised an eyebrow at Patrick.

Patrick practically jumped with glee. Well, he did literally hop and clap his hands once. "Oh, baby," he said, "this is going to be fun."

Chapter 19

IAN LEFT the hotel with a sense of accomplishment. The renovation was proceeding at full speed, customers had been responding positively to the changes he'd already made, and the hotel was getting some buzz from the local press. He'd gotten three job offers that week from other hotels in New York, though he thought the New Amsterdam would require at least another year.

Still, he was smiling later as he walked from the subway to East River Park for the last regular season game of the Rainbow League. The Hipsters were currently in fourth place in the league and wanted to win this one to advance to the playoffs.

Ty was already there, lacing up his cleats. He smiled when he saw Ian. He finished tying his shoes and stood. When Ian arrived, Ty gave him a brief hug. "Hey, babe. How was work?"

"Good. Very good. Positive progress."

"Excellent. You ready to play ball?"

"As I'll ever be."

Ty gave Ian a kiss on the cheek and then ran over to talk to Scott.

What Ian would later come to think of as The Moment happened in the sixth inning. Somehow they'd managed a three-run lead over the SoHoMos. Nate was on fire, eight strikeouts under his belt already, which was exciting but didn't give the infield much to do. Ian kept glancing over at Ty, who was just far enough away not to be able to talk to but close enough to see well. Every time Ian looked over, Ty made a face at him. Sometimes it was goofy; he'd stick out his tongue or crinkle his nose. Sometimes he'd just wink. In the sixth inning, Ian looked over and Ty blew him a kiss. Ian laughed and then looked around to make sure Scott wasn't watching. Well, probably Scott was watching—he seemed to have eyes everywhere—but Ian didn't much care because the worst that could happen was a stern lecture after the game. He was having too much fun to stop.

He looked back at Ty, who grinned.

And then it hit Ian all at once: *I love Ty.*

The thought distracted him enough that, when one of the batters did manage to get a hit off Nate, sending the ball directly toward third base, Ian probably would have been beaned if Nate hadn't shouted his name. He managed to get his glove in front of himself in time to catch it, but it hit his hand so hard he almost dropped it. He danced a little, trying to regain his equilibrium, and then he threw it back to Nate. The toss went wide, but Nate leaped to catch it.

Ian was so going to get a stern lecture from Scott later.

Not that he even cared. Because somehow, over the course of this crazy summer, he had met a cocky artist named Ty and fallen stupidly in love, and now what the hell was he going to do?

Their victory put them in a playoff game against Coney Island, scheduled in two weeks. Everyone was in a pretty festive mood on the walk to the bar, though Scott did, of course, pull Ian aside to say some nonsense like "I can't have you and Ty making eyes at each other all game" and "You have to pay attention or you'll fumble more plays" and so on. Ian mostly ignored it. Scott was the least of his problems.

At the bar, Ty was all smiles. Ian supposed he should join in the celebration, and really, why should the realization that he had fallen in love cause anguish? Wasn't love something to celebrate?

So Ian did shots with the rest of the team, participated in a lot of toasts, got hugged and kissed and groped by most of his teammates, and then later leaned on Ty when he got a little too tipsy. Ty got pretty handsy as the evening progressed, though Ian didn't mind one bit.

"Okay," Ty said eventually. "You seem like you've had enough. I'll put you in a cab."

"Come with me."

Ty hesitated. "You've had a lot to drink, babe. You sure you want that?"

"Yes. Always. I want you all the time. Don't want to be alone tonight."

"All right."

So Ty managed to hail a cab, and on the way uptown, Ian let the alcohol overwhelm his system, making the streetlights swirl outside the window. He was getting a little nauseous, no doubt about that, but he was still doing okay when they got to his building. Ty had been the one to give the address because Ian suddenly couldn't remember it, but it worked out. There was Armand, lingering on the sidewalk.

Ty helped Ian out of the cab, put an arm around him, and walked him to the sidewalk. "I've never seen you this drunk before."

"I was celebrating!" Ian declared. "Go Hipsters! Woo!"

Ty laughed. "You're also slurring your words. You sure there isn't something else going on? A problem at work?"

"Nope. Work is great. I just wanted to celebrate."

"Because we won tonight? Because of the playoffs?"

"Because I love you, Texas."

And then, suddenly, everything went horribly wrong. Ian's stomach flopped as soon as the words were out of his mouth.

He threw up all over the sidewalk.

AS DECLARATIONS of love went, this one was boggling for Ty.

Ian groaned. Luckily most of the vomit was limited to the sidewalk, though the smell was already making Ty feel nauseous.

"You finished?" he asked Ian.

Ian nodded and groaned again.

The doorman looked alarmed.

"I think he's done for now," Ty said. "Let me get him upstairs. Then I'll come down and hose this off."

The doorman waved his hand. "Don't worry about it. It's fine. Super will take care of it. Not the first time it's happened."

So Ty pulled Ian toward the elevator and up to his apartment. Ian was pretty out of it, grunting instead of speaking, his face ghostly pale. Ty had to frisk him to find his keys and unlock the door. He managed to get him into the bathroom, where he stripped Ian of his clothes and washed off any remaining vomit. Then he put him to bed.

Ty got a glass of water, which he placed on the nightstand with an entreaty for Ian to drink it. Ian seemed to ignore him. But as Ty was pulling the sheets up to cover Ian, Ian reached out and grabbed his arm. "Stay with me?" His eyes were wide with worry, and his tone was urgent.

"You need to sleep this off."

"I know, but stay?"

"I will."

Ian nodded, apparently satisfied. "I meant what I said."

"Which thing?"

But Ian was asleep.

Ty got up and paced around the apartment. Perhaps there was something to the "in vino veritas" idea, though Ty was also certain he'd said and done things while drunk he never would have under other circumstances. Did Ian love him? Had he meant it? Did Ty love him back?

Ty didn't know the answers to any of these questions.

He still smelled a little vaguely of spilled beer and vomit, so he hopped in the shower, hoping to get his head screwed on straight while Ian slept. This was a challenge while he was in Ian's immaculately clean bathroom, particularly when his only options for cleansers were the minty body wash Ian used instead of having a decent bar of soap and the softly floral scented shampoo Ian's hair always smelled like. Being surrounded by Ian's regular scents distracted and aroused Ty, as if his body knew the mere presence of that clean, minty smell meant sex was imminent.

Maybe that said something about Ty's feelings for Ian, though. They had spent a lot of time together that summer. Ty had enjoyed it, had felt himself getting more emotionally entangled. Ian inspired and aroused him, as both an artist and a man, and really, it was sort of a miracle that Ty hadn't started painting Ian's face on every romance hero he created for those book covers. Ian had a cover-worthy face, and Ty certainly knew it well enough now to paint it without a reference photo.

He got out of the shower and grabbed a towel from the closet in the corner where Ian kept his linens. The towel, of course, smelled of the detergent Ian used, which was what most of his clothes smelled like. But this was not the essence of Ian, this was just the covering on the outside. Still, if Ian was determined to leave New York, he sure was ruining a lot of products for Ty, because he'd never be able to smell any of these things without thinking of Ian and longing for him. Hell, he was longing right now, and Ian was simply sleeping off a hangover in the next room.

Ty groaned in frustration, dragging the towel over his body.

He didn't want to be in love. That hadn't been the point of this interlude with Ian. He hadn't wanted to get involved with someone, hadn't wanted a relationship; he just wanted to float through life having fun.

But was that even true?

Well, the truth was that Ty had run to New York at the tender young age of eighteen, and he'd been a wide-eyed innocent, basically, even though he'd been torturing himself for years already by then for not being able to live up to the ideal his father had set for him. In New York, he'd felt like he could make a man of himself, a man his father could be proud of even if he was gay, but then his father had died and Ty had just been adrift.

He needed an anchor. There had been Ryan, a million years ago, a guy Ty had fallen for but who was not terribly invested in Ty. For whatever reason, Ty had held on to Ryan as the platonic ideal of relationships for far longer than was prudent. They'd been bad for each other and Ty knew it, and he'd shoved that damn photo of Ryan in a drawer about the time he and Ian started seeing each other regularly.

Now Ty had Josh and his other friends, he had the Rainbow League, he had his work. But he also had an empty apartment and the sort of insecurity that only bravado and anonymous sex could cover up. He'd derived satisfaction from all of those things, but not enough to make the ache in his gut go away.

The truth was that deep down, Ty was lonely.

And the weird thing about the past couple of months was that since he'd started spending time with Ian, the ache that had followed him through most of his adult life had eased. Sometimes he even forgot it was there. He could be walking around with Ian, or just talking to him on the phone, or in bed with him, or watching him from across the baseball field, and he felt something stir within him, a happiness that could make that ache go away.

If that was love, well, Ty was head over heels, because he wanted that in his life, wanted Ian's presence, wanted the ache to go away.

He and Ian were close in size, and he considered borrowing some of Ian's clothes, but he couldn't decide if that was kosher as he walked into Ian's bedroom with just the towel around his waist. Ian was fast asleep on the bed, rolled over on his side and tucked into the fetal position, the covers Ty had pulled over him wrapped around his waist. Something in Ty softened as he watched Ian sleep.

Was that love?

Ty pulled off the towel and draped it over the chair in the corner that he knew Ian often used to set out the clothes he intended to wear the next day. It wasn't OCD, Ty knew that, but Ian was damned particular about things. He had routines, little things he did each day to keep the anxiety at bay. If he picked out his clothes for the next day, he wouldn't worry about what to wear the next morning. If he kept his apartment clean and everything stayed in its place, he could find it easily when he needed it. He kept a grocery list on a magnet on his refrigerator, and he dutifully put an item on the list as soon as he was close to running out of it, unlike Ty's strategy of going to the store and just buying whatever struck him. These things had amused Ty at first, but they were so integral to Ian, to his way of coping with the world. He wasn't shy or secretive about them either. He had presented himself to Ty as he was: a neurotic, troubled man who had also been lonely because he'd been running from his past for almost fifteen years.

Ty wanted to be honest with Ian, though he struggled with it, because he worried that once Ian saw what a scared, messed-up man Ty really was, he'd keep running.

But showing Ian the paintings had been a step toward something, that was certain. Ty wanted to show Ian more of himself so that Ian would care for Ty the way Ty was coming to care for Ian, and then maybe they'd be all right.

Ty slipped naked into the bed. He lay on his back for a moment before rolling over to curl against Ian.

Chapter 20

THE HANGOVER was epic and most of the night before was still a blur. Ty had been sweet and accommodating, helping Ian pick out clothes and brewing coffee and kissing him and generally just being the greatest.

As they were sipping coffee at the kitchen counter, Ty said, "Right before you fell asleep, you told me you meant what you said, and I asked which thing, but then you fell asleep. Do you remember what it was you meant?"

Ian thought that over. He honestly couldn't remember saying much of anything. "Basically everything after that last shot is lost to the ages."

Ty raised an eyebrow. "Do you remember ralphing on the sidewalk outside?"

That memory came back to him suddenly. "Oh, God. I did do that, didn't I? Poor Armand."

"Armand?"

"The doorman. I'm never going to be able to look him in the eye again."

Ty laughed, though there was an uneasy quality to it.

"Are you okay?" Ian asked.

"Yeah. I had much less to drink than you did. You're lucky I was sober enough to get us here."

"I'm so embarrassed. I never drink like that."

Ty leaned over and kissed his cheek. "Happens to the best of us. I've been known to tie one on now and again. We were celebrating, you got really into it, and you got a little carried away. Now you'll spend the rest of the day groaning about how you'll never drink again, but a week from now you'll be back at that bar, a beer in your hand. That's how these things go."

"You think you're so smart," Ian said.

"I am so smart. And now you have to go to work. Come on, put your tie on. I'll walk with you to the subway."

Ty rode the train downtown with Ian and gave him a quick peck before Ian got off the train. It was such a sweet gesture, so domestic and ordinary, and yet it threw Ian off so much he forgot his head was pounding.

Until he got to the hotel, of course. He walked into the lobby and right into a dispute some guests were having with the front desk staff. He figuratively rolled up his sleeves and threw himself in to intervene before someone tore someone else's head off—or at least before someone caused damage to the newly renovated lobby.

Ian rode the elevator up to his office a short time later, satisfied that he'd successfully resolved the dispute. Mostly the solution involved giving the guest some free meal vouchers for his trouble, since apparently the argument was over the great cost of the hotel breakfast, given that half the building was under construction and all the noise kept it from truly being a *luxury* hotel. Ian shook his head, happy to turn his thoughts back to Ty, who… well, he'd been acting a little strangely that morning. Not in an obvious way, but something about his face had been unsettling. Had Ian said something in his drunken stupor that Ty had taken the wrong way? Ty had asked that odd question about Ian meaning what he'd said. But what had he said? He couldn't remember.

He had three meetings in rapid succession, the last one the worst, trying to work out what to do about a convention that had been scheduled for the hotel right when Ian had decided they should shut it down to finish the renovation. The owners wouldn't stand for the loss of revenue if they canceled, so the only thing to do was postpone construction, although that, of course, meant that the convention attendees would have to put up with the half-renovated convention space and the not-quite-finished lobby.

He was quickly stuffing a chicken Caesar salad into his mouth midafternoon when it came to him all at once.

He'd gotten crazy drunk the night before both because he'd been celebrating the Hipsters' victory and because he'd been elated and terrified by the realization that he loved Ty. Then Ty had asked what had motivated him to get so drunk, right? As they had gotten out of the cab and Ian was trying to talk Ty upstairs because the idea of spending a night without him had become suddenly unbearable.

Why?

Because he loved Ty and told him so right before throwing up all over his shoes.

Oh, good fucking goddamn.

No wonder Ty had been acting weird.

Ian rode the elevator from the staff cafeteria in the basement back up to his office and wondered the whole time if it was better to play dumb and pretend he didn't remember saying it or tell Ty he remembered—and confess that he had indeed meant it. Every damn word. Because he was in love with Ty, there was no question in his mind. The fact that Ty had been so sweet that morning, taking care of Ian even though the hangover was Ian's own damn fault, had made him want to spend all mornings with Ty. He wanted to return the favor, to take care of Ty when he was sick or hungover. He wanted to wake up next to Ty, to go to bed with him every night, to spend their days together as much as they could.

"Phone message, Ian," said Joy, one of the assistants, as Ian walked back into the staff offices.

"Thanks." He took the message and glanced at it. Joy had written, *Some dude named Victor from Hotel Something in Rome.* Below that she'd added, *(Italy)*. Ian laughed, though he was annoyed and wondered what it could be about.

TY SIPPED his beer and watched the warring expressions on Nate's face. He followed Nate's gaze across the bar and saw Aiden kissing Carlos, which was what he was doing at a bar after a very arduous Sunday practice.

Kiss was too mild a word for it, though. Carlos and Aiden were full-on making out, standing over in a corner of the bar where they thought no one could see them, looking like they were trying to climb into each other's mouth.

Ty had suggested this place. It was a Western-themed gay bar that had just opened around the corner from his apartment, and since it wasn't really that much farther from the Prospect Park ball fields than the bar they always went to in Park Slope, everyone had been all "Sure, let's try it out." Coincidentally, Aiden lived a few blocks away, so he'd come by as well, probably to do exactly what he was doing right now.

"I like a gay cowboy as much as the next guy," Nate said, "but the music here leaves something to be desired."

Ty nodded, agreeing. The speakers piped in soft country music and there were a couple of guys in tight jeans and cowboy boots dancing together. Something about it appealed to Ty's sense of Texas, and he watched the couple dance while daydreaming about teaching Ian to two-step. He thought about heading into Manhattan to do just that, at least once Nate finished having this nervous breakdown.

Because Nate was staring at Aiden and Carlos quite intently. He said, "I mean, they're making out like having sex in the next ten minutes is necessary for the propagation of the whole species."

"Well aren't Aiden and Carlos cozy," Mason said as he meandered over.

"Fuck everyone," said Nate.

Josh walked over. He leaned on the bar as he tried to get the attention of the pocket-sized bartender who was slinging drinks that night. "You look like you're about to stab something," Josh said to Nate.

"Many somebodies," Nate said.

Josh followed Nate's gaze and a comical look of openmouthed surprise struck his face as his gaze settled on Aiden and Carlos. "I didn't even know Aiden was here," he said.

"He's like a fucking vulture. Haven't you noticed? He's been circling around all of our social events all summer, waiting to get Carlos alone so he can swoop in and, well, do that." Nate gestured toward the new couple.

"I'm so sorry, Nate."

Nate sighed. "I mean, it's not like it's not my fault. I'll grant you that. I should have said something and I never did. But Aiden? Really? That asshole? I could make him so much happier than Aiden ever could."

"Nate," said Ty.

Nate slid off the stool on which he'd been sitting. "No, it's all right. Like I said, my fault."

Ty felt a little lost himself. Ian hadn't been able to make practice that day because his hotel was hosting a conference and he'd had to be on hand to help out, or so Ty had explained to Scott earlier as he groveled and apologized on Ian's behalf. Scott seemed to buy it and then had told Ty to relate to Ian that he'd have to run twice the laps next time. Ty was looking forward to joking about that with Ian. It was pretty weird to be here now without him, though. Hipsters practice wasn't the same without him.

"Welcome to the Broken Hearts Club," Josh said.

"Huh?" said Ty.

Josh grinned. "You know that movie with Timothy Olyphant about the gay guys on the softball team? I was making a joke."

Ty shook his head. "Never saw it."

"Oh, you should. Everyone on the team is gay, including Olyphant, and he's *hot* in the movie. Your character is played by Dean Cain."

"My character?" asked Ty.

"The slutty one," Nate supplied.

Ty let out an exasperated sigh. "Don't know if you guys noticed, but I think my slutty period is behind me. I've been a one-man guy all summer."

"So you and Ian are still—"

"Yeah." Ty couldn't keep the smile off his face. "Yeah, we're still together."

Josh elbowed him. "I knew it."

Ty rolled his eyes. "Oh, what did you know? You pretty much introduced me to Ian as the slutty one. Like, hey, Ian, you need to get laid and Ty will sleep with anything, so have at it."

Josh laughed. "Nah. You did some of that yourself. I wanted Ian to join the team because he's a good guy and a decent ballplayer, plus I thought it would be fun for him. He's been away from the city so long that he doesn't know many people here, and I thought it would be good for him to get to know a few of you. But I knew, somehow, that you and Ian would get along splendidly."

"You did, did you?"

Josh cracked his knuckles. "Live in fear of my matchmaking abilities."

Ty rolled his eyes again. "Oh, sure. You know, just because you live in wedded bliss doesn't mean you have to force the rest of us into it."

Josh just grinned. "I was right, wasn't I? You and Ian are going to ride off into the sunset, aren't you? And now I know engraved invitations are a great expense if you decide to just get married at City Hall wearing jeans and T-shirts. It's *tacky*, but totally something you would do. Tony and I expect to be there bearing witness, so start putting money aside."

"I hate you," Ty said.

"I know, darling." Josh turned his considerable charm toward Nate. "Now, as for you, I figure you have three options. You love him, I know you do, and that sucks right now."

"Is this supposed to be a pep talk?" Nate asked.

"Hush. Listen to Uncle Josh. He is wise in the ways of men."

Ty scoffed. "Since when?"

Josh crossed his arms, looking injured. "Which of us is married? I snagged a man, thank you very much." He turned back to Nate. "Three options. You either tell him how you feel now, before he gets more involved." He held out his thumb as if he were counting on his fingers.

Nate glanced over at Carlos and Aiden, who were now basically just dry humping each other.

"Well, maybe not *right* now," said Josh. "Wow, they're really going at it."

"When I make out with Ian in public, does it look that gross?" asked Ty.

"Yup," said Nate.

"Oh. Yikes. So noted."

"So, okay, maybe don't tell him how you feel right now," said Josh. "Your other two choices are to hope that Carlos comes to his senses and ditches that guy. Otherwise you find somebody else. Plenty of other fish."

"Basically," Ty said, "stop pining. Put up or shut up. Shit or get off the pot."

"Ugh," said Nate. "I don't know if I can... I mean, I want him to be happy. And if Aiden makes him happy...."

Josh was on a tear. "Tony has a gay cousin who lives in Queens. He owns a super fabulous pizza place in Astoria. Like, one of those locally sourced artisanal places. I'll totally set you up."

Nate gave Josh a dirty look. "Yeah, no thanks." He took a deep breath. "If I have to let him go, give me a little time to do it."

Chapter 21

THE FIRST playoff game, which occurred during the first week of September, was the Hipsters versus the Mermaids. Ty wasn't totally thrilled about having to play against Rachel again, but she was a good sport about it, ribbing him as they stood around shooting the shit before the game started.

"You're lucky I like you," Ty said. "We'll try not to kick your ass too hard."

Rachel laughed. "Nice words, pretty boy. I've got your number. The girls and I have been practicing hard-core the last three weeks. We're unstoppable. And as I recall, we whupped your ass in the regular season game."

Ty shrugged. "A fluke."

"How go things with your new beau, by the way? He's the blond over there, right? With the blue cleats?"

"Yeah. Well. I mean, things are going really well with him." Although Ty wasn't sure how true that was. Ian had been acting strange ever since the night he'd declared his love before vomiting on the sidewalk. Ty was still trying to wrap his head around what had happened too. They'd gone out to dinner a few nights ago, and that had gone well enough, but Ian had begged off going back to Ty's place afterward on account of work, and Ty had gone home disappointed.

Rachel nodded. "Glad that's working out for you."

"Thanks."

Scott yelled at Ty to stop fraternizing with the enemy, so Ty gave Rachel a quick hug and then ran over to his own team. The game got underway five minutes later.

And it wasn't pretty. The Mermaids were operating like a well-oiled machine. Maybe they didn't hit as hard as some of the male players, but they had a great rapport with each other and easily fielded the ball, preventing the Hipsters from scoring a single run until the seventh, and that was likely only because the pitcher was getting tired. The Mermaids, meanwhile, kept hitting what Nate threw at them. Nate seemed confounded by that.

Scott was basically ripping his hair out.

"Do you guys *want* to lose?" Scott said at the beginning of the eighth, when the Hipsters were down 5–1.

The Mermaids were unbeatable, though. It was not for lack of effort on the part of the Hipsters, who really were playing some of the best ball they had all season. They collectively had quicker reflexes. They hit the ball hard when they could get their bats to connect and they hit it farther— and right into the gloves of the Mermaids' outfielders.

Ty wondered if Scott found this game especially frustrating because they were losing to a bunch of girls.

It didn't much matter, though, because even though Mason got a run in the eighth and Carlos got one in the ninth, it wasn't enough to close the gap, and the game finally finished 6–3, a resounding defeat for the Hipsters.

And with that, the season was over for the team representing Brooklyn.

They all dragged themselves to the bar afterward. Tom gave everyone a round on the house, given that one team was celebrating while the other wallowed in defeat.

Really, all Ty wanted to do was take Ian home and hide under the blankets for a while, having sex until he forgot what baseball was.

Ian had been quiet the entire walk to the bar, and he was still quiet now, turning his mostly full pint glass around in his hands. Ty couldn't tell if he was mopey about the game or if this was a symptom of whatever had been plaguing him for the past couple of weeks.

"Game aside," Ty said, because it bugged him, "is something going on? Because you've been a little weird."

Ian pursed his lips. "I'm not sure this is the place to—"

"Just tell me."

Ian sighed. "I, ah, I got a job offer. A really good one."

"Yeah? Where?"

"Italy."

Ty supposed that normal people got a job offer in Italy and were ecstatic. Ty wondered what he would do if offered a job in Italy. Probably jump for joy. Unless, of course, he had a boyfriend whose whole life was in New York.

Shit.

"When would it start?" Ty asked.

"Negotiable. Probably not until next spring."

"Christ. Italy?"

"Rome, specifically. They're willing to pay me a shit-ton of money. The owner also owns a place in Paris that I worked on a couple of years ago, so he really wants me for this job because he trusts my work, and he's willing to pay me double what he paid me in Paris. I'd probably be there six months, maybe longer depending how far gone the hotel is. It's... it's an incredible offer."

Ty's heart sank. "It sounds like it."

"I'm sorry, Ty. I didn't want to tell you like this, in public with everyone, especially not on a day that's already been kind of disappointing."

Ty nodded. Ian did seem genuinely remorseful. Ty shook his head and then took a long sip of his beer.

Ty didn't know what to say or do. The temptation of Italy for six months or longer along with a bucketful of money? And that was also paired with the prestige Ian undoubtedly received for doing a job like this, for being the guy the big hotels turned to when they started losing money and needed to modernize and revamp. Ian would keep getting offers like this, certainly. But how could he turn down this one? In Ian's shoes, Ty didn't think he'd be able to say no, even with a boyfriend he... felt very strongly about.

No, fuck it. Ty was in love with Ian. And Ian sitting there telling him that he was leaving in six months, give or take, pretty much broke Ty's heart.

"So you're taking the job," Ty said.

Ian turned and looked at Ty. "I told them I'd think about it. I haven't made a decision yet either way."

That surprised Ty. "What's to decide? Rome? A good salary? I'm surprised you didn't just jump at it."

"There are other considerations."

"Like?"

Ian let out a breath slowly. "Well, I want to finish the work I'm doing at the New Amsterdam, first of all. But also...." Then Ian shook his head and looked away.

"What?"

Ian pressed his hands to the bar. Then he turned and looked back at Ty. "Do you really have nothing else to say?"

Ty balked. "What the hell are you talking about?"

"Did you not just spend the whole fucking summer trying to convince me that New York City was a place I should consider living? Weren't you trying to get me to stay so that we could see where this relationship between us went? Are you really just going to sit there while I tell you that I have a job offer halfway around the world and not... I mean, do you really just...." Ian shook his head and bowed a little. "Shit."

"What do you want me to say? 'Please stay'?"

"Don't you want me to?"

"Of course I do. But this is a good offer, isn't it? Don't you want to take it?"

"Ty."

"What? I don't know what you want me to say. Yes, I had a great time this summer, and yes, I want you to stay. But... Italy. I mean, what were you hoping to hear?"

"Give me a reason to stay, Ty. Why do you want me to stay?"

"Because I like you?" Ty tried, still not understanding what Ian was asking of him. "Because I like spending time together?"

"Is that all?"

"What else is there?"

"So... have I just been wasting my time all summer getting to know you? Going on your strange outings? Letting myself be convinced that maybe I don't want to run screaming from this whole fucking city? Because I swear to God, this place has only ever brought me misery, but I thought maybe after this summer that there was some hope for it. Was I wrong?"

Ty sighed. "No. The time wasn't wasted. Not for me."

"Then why are you actually... I mean, you are actually pushing me to take this job, aren't you?"

"I don't...." Ty slid off the stool, because he couldn't have this argument while sitting with Ian's discerning gaze on him. He still had no idea what he could possibly say that would convince Ian to stay. Ian hated New York and had a dream job waiting for him in Italy. Why the fuck would he stay? "If you want to take the job, take the job."

"Really? You have nothing else to say?"

"What could I say? Could I really stand here and make a case for staying in a place you hate even for my sake? You just said yourself, this city has only ever brought you misery. Well, I'm tired of fighting against that. I put forth what I thought was a pretty good case for staying, but apparently it wasn't persuasive. I'm not persuasive. So what the fuck do you want from me, Ian?"

"Indeed." Ian slid off his stool. "There it is, I guess." He rubbed his forehead. "I'm getting the hell out of here. I'll see you around, Ty."

"Oh, so it's over? Just like that?"

"What the hell's the point?"

Ian looked so pained, so devoid of hope, that Ty wanted to reach out and hug him, to comfort him, to tell him that yeah, he should stay, but… how the hell could Ty compete with Italy?

What was the point?

I love you, Ty thought. That was the fucking point.

But he couldn't say that. Not when they were both this upset. It wasn't the time or place. Love should be joyful, not full of pain like this.

"Don't go," Ty tried weakly.

"Don't go home or don't go to Italy?"

"Either. Both."

"Why? Give me a reason, Ty."

But what reason was there? It wasn't like Ty was even worthy of the love of a guy like Ian, a handsome man who was smart and successful, and who, yes, had issues with anxiety but had his shit in order in a way Ty never would. What the hell could Ty even have to offer Ian that would get him to stay? A lifetime spent in a city he hated? Time to realize that Ty wasn't good enough for him?

"I have nothing," Ty said.

Ian pursed his lips and nodded. "Yeah. Well. Like I said, I'll see you around, Ty."

Ty stood at the bar and watched him go, wanting the whole time to grab him and pull him back. But, no, he let Ian go.

IAN WALKED into his apartment, still smarting from the conversation with Ty. Had Ty really had nothing to say? Did Ty not love him?

Because Ian had been preparing to decide to stay. He'd been coming around on New York City for the past month or so. Because yeah, this city held a lot of bad memories, but he'd made a lot of good ones with Ty, enough that he was seriously considering sticking around and making more. He and his mother had been reconnecting during their biweekly lunches too. It had finally sunk in that New York was not the city he'd run from but an almost entirely new place, with new people, with friends, with

Ty. He'd come to love the Rainbow League somehow, over the course of the summer, loved the physical activity and the competitiveness and all the baseball. Even though they'd lost that night's game, it didn't matter because they were all friends and comrades and they'd see each other next season.

Unless Ian went to Italy and there was no next season.

But even putting all that aside, he loved Ty, and he was willing to stay for love. He knew he couldn't take Ty with him to Italy, that with his job and his energy, he was as much a part of New York as the Empire State Building or the Brooklyn Bridge. Ian had given some thought to the practicalities of taking Ty and his art studio across the Atlantic. Maybe Ty would appreciate the art in Italy in a way Ian never would—maybe he'd find inspiration there—but maybe Ian would also be dragging Ty away from his real work, from his friends, from the city he loved.

So he hadn't even asked.

And Ty hadn't given him a reason to stay in New York.

Ian moved to toss his keys in the little glass bowl he kept on a table near the door reserved for this purpose, but instead he threw the keys at the bowl with as much force as he'd throw a baseball to get an out. The keys hit the side of the bowl, knocking it on the hardwood floor, where it shattered.

Ty hadn't given him a reason to stay.

Ian sank to the floor just inside his door, leaning his back against it, probably sitting on broken glass, but right then he didn't give a shit, because for the first time all summer, he didn't want to leave New York because the man he loved was here, but apparently that man didn't love him enough to ask him to stay.

What the hell was the point, indeed?

Ian began to weep. Because his heart was breaking. Because everything he'd ever wanted was in easy reach, just not at the same time, and he had to make a terrible choice: love or his career? Love or his continuing adventures? New York or Italy? Ty or misery?

He let himself cry for a few minutes before he got up off the floor and grabbed a broom to sweep up the parts of the broken bowl. He would figure a way through this; he always did. He hadn't been sure that Ty would try to get him to stay, but he hadn't expected it to hurt this much when Ty didn't.

Chapter 22

AFTER DELIVERING his most recent cover to the client, Ty took the subway straight home. He always found it a little strange to no longer have baseball at the end of a season. The adjustment to not going to practice and to lightening up on his gym routine was always a little weird. Probably he'd gain weight during the off-season, which he had last year, and which Scott had berated him about until he dropped the extra pounds.

He hadn't really talked to Ian much since that night at the bar. He'd called to apologize and gotten nothing but a stilted conversation for his trouble.

But dear Lord, he hated that this was how things were between them. Could they not even make the most of the time they had remaining before Ian moved? Was that too much to ask for?

Apparently so, if Ian was now barely talking to him.

Ty got home and walked back to the studio. He had another commission to fulfill, but he decided that could wait. He had a stack of newly stretched canvases in the corner, done a few weeks before in anticipation of the work he'd have in the fall. He picked up the smallest one and considered it for a moment. He called to mind Michelangelo's famous saying about how the sculpture emerged from the marble, not the other way around. Ty looked at the canvas and could perfectly imagine what should be there.

He set the canvas on the easel he usually reserved for work, near the door. He wanted the better lighting that this part of the room provided, and he felt an urgency to paint that he hadn't felt in a long time. It was the kind of urgency he'd often felt as a kid, when he was convinced if he didn't commit what he saw in his mind to paper that instant, the vision would leave him. When he worried that drawing in the corner instead of playing outside would disappoint his father.

Well, his father was gone and Ty was alone, and he was going to paint if he goddamn well felt like it. And now he felt like he had to because he'd just let the love of his life slip through his fingers without putting up much of a fight, because he hadn't known how to make Ian stay.

First it had been about sex, then about giving a good thing a chance, but now it was about love. He didn't just want to see where a relationship with Ian would go; he knew where it *could* go, had seen and felt it firsthand, had known they would be great together. And he'd let it end because he'd felt unworthy. Ian deserved better.

He grabbed his paints and started mixing colors. The sandy yellow of Ian's hair, the greenish blue of his eyes. The gray of the shadows of Ian's white sheets in the morning. The pale peach of Ian's skin—just enough green added to tint it naturally, not like a peach crayon. The white invisibility of Ian's body hair, the perfect ivory of his teeth, the pink of his face when it flushed. The dark pink of Ian's lips, the red of his blood. The paleness of Ty's own skin by contrast, the red of his own hair, the brown of his freckles. Ty didn't intend to paint himself, but it felt like he should be represented somehow.

It started with a red slash across the canvas. A white field with a red slash like blood smeared, like someone had indeed taken a thin knife and plunged it right into Ty's heart, because it sure hurt that bad sometimes. He'd paint over it, because the metaphor was too obvious and not what he wanted to convey anyway, but that red slash was cathartic in a way.

Ty took a deep breath. Then he started to paint.

AT DINNER with Josh and Tony, Ian felt like he might actually be on trial, although what he had done wrong, he could not fathom.

Well, Tony didn't seem to be in on the interrogation. He, in fact, looked just as confused as Ian felt. Tony sat at the head of his dining room table with a furrowed brow, staring at Josh as if he expected the mystery to unravel right there on the table.

"So you and Ty broke up," Josh said, a "let me get this straight" tone to his voice.

"Uh, well, not, like, *formally*, but it seems to be over. He won't really talk to me now. I mean, he called me, and I didn't know what to say, so I tried calling him again and just... got nowhere. He doesn't want to talk to me."

"Because you're going to Italy."

"I was willing to stay."

"Did you say that?"

"I told him to give me a reason to stay."

Josh and Tony exchanged a look. "Honey," Josh said to Tony, "what would you say is the key to a successful relationship?"

Tony seemed confused by the question. "Good sex?"

Josh guffawed. "Communication. No?"

"Communication while we're having sex?" The expression on Tony's face indicated he was joking, but Josh still looked offended.

"Darling, you are always open and honest with me, are you not?" Josh said.

"Of course."

"See, all of these relationships that are falling apart, it's bad communication."

"Oh boy." Ian fought not to roll his eyes. "Okay, Professor Josh. Teach away."

"You may regret that," Tony said.

"Shut up," Josh said, reaching over to slap Tony on the arm. "Look, take poor Nate, for instance. There's a boy who is cowardly because he's in love with his best friend but is so terrified of losing him that he's never said a word about it. And now Carlos has taken up with Aiden and they're hot and heavy. You know why?"

Ian wondered if he was supposed to answer. He looked to Tony for help. Tony shrugged. Since Josh wasn't talking, Ian said, "All right, I'll bite. Nate lost Carlos because he didn't communicate."

"Yes. Now. You and Ty are at odds because you're both obviously in love with each other but you're afraid to say anything."

Ian sighed. "I don't think he's in love with me."

"Did you tell him you love him?"

"Well, no, but… look, I told him I was willing to stay. For him."

"Did you really say that?"

"I—" Wait, had he? Ian had intended to tell Ty that he was willing to stay in New York for Ty so they could be together, because Ty had become more important to him than a job, particularly when there would be other offers. But Ty had backed away so easily that he couldn't possibly…. But….

Ian sighed. "I implied it."

That time, Tony exchanged a knowing look with Josh.

"Sweetie," Josh said to Ian, "you're a man. You should know better. Men are not good at subtle. You should have said directly, 'Ty, I love you. I want to stay.'"

"What good would that do?" Ian said, sick of Josh being patronizing. "I want to stay, but only if he loves me. If he doesn't, well, what the hell is the point?"

That seemed to give Josh pause, finally.

"Why can't we talk about something else?" Ian said. "How are you guys? How is work? How is any goddamn thing that does not involve Ty?"

Josh held up his hands. "Fine." He launched into a story about work, and Tony kept butting in to add his two cents, and it was almost normal for a few minutes. That was until Ty started drifting back into Ian's thoughts. Had he really fucked up by not communicating clearly? He didn't think so; Ty should have fought for him if he really wanted him to stay.

Right?

AFTER BEING somewhat unceremoniously uninvited to the couple-y dinner party thrown by Josh and Tony, Ty was feeling kind of done with his friends, but he agreed to meet Mason for a "freelancer's lunch" at a café near Mason's apartment in Manhattan anyway. Mason was always a good time, and one of the few friends Ty had who didn't work in an office during the day. As far as Ty knew, Mason was still living off the money he'd saved from his Yankees salary and whatever pennies the sports website he wrote for decided to toss his way, but he supposed it didn't matter if Mason was free for lunch.

Mason had mentioned something vague about the décor at this place, and as Ty sat with him at a table in the corner, he realized that Mason had been referring to the two guys working behind the counter. "Whoa. The one with the mohawk has ridiculous hair, but Lordy, he's smoking," Ty said.

"I know."

"Not the type you usually go for, though. Don't you mostly date meatheads?"

Mason smiled. "Just because the beef is always available doesn't mean you have to eat it at every meal."

Ty laughed. "Truer words." He clinked coffee cups with Mason.

They ordered sandwiches and chatted about their jobs. Mason asked what Ty was working on, but Ty was reluctant to admit that he'd spent the past week painting Ian instead of his commission. So he said, "Oh, you know."

Mason was too smart not to see through that. He raised his eyebrows.

"Look, don't... since Ian and I have been on the outs, it's been hard to concentrate on work, okay? I have a cover commission, but I haven't done anything more for it than some initial sketches, and even those were just so I'd have something to send to the client."

"That sucks, man."

No joke. Ty didn't want to get into it because he wasn't prepared to have an emotional conversation about all the ways he'd fucked up this summer. He had, in fact, agreed to bow out of the dinner with Josh and Tony in exchange for Josh doing some reconnaissance on Ian and what the hell Ty was supposed to have done before everything fell apart.

Ty had a hunch, though. He'd been turning over their last conversation in his head for a week, trying to figure out what he should have said. Ian hadn't actually taken the job yet; he'd wanted Ty to give him a reason to stay. Ty had reasoned at the time that Ty himself was reason enough. But perhaps he had to make a stronger case. In fact, in retrospect, that was that Ian seemed to be pleading with him to do.

Ty's first instinct was to plan a grand romantic gesture, but he knew he'd have to think this one through carefully.

"I'm sort of sad the season is over," Mason said. "Not devastated, because my foot was killing me the last few weeks." The injury that effectively ended Mason's career had been a pulled tendon. It had apparently healed quite well but still bothered him sometimes.

"I know what you mean. I always kind of hate when the summer ends. Cold weather is on its way. The summer fling is over."

"I'm surprised," said Mason. "I guess I thought you and Ian had more staying power. You seemed really great together."

Ty shrugged. They had been great together. But. "He got a job offer in Italy. I don't want him to take it, but honestly, we've been together all of four months. Why should I get to dictate what he does with a career he's been developing for more than ten years?"

"He took the job?"

"By now he probably has."

Mason furrowed his brow in confusion. "Wait, did he ask you if he should take the job? Did you say yes?"

"What was I supposed to say?"

Mason reached across the table and smacked the back of Ty's head.

"Ow! Asshole."

"Tell him you want him to stay."

"I did tell him that. He told me to give him a reason, whatever the fuck that means." Ty picked at the table varnish with his thumb, unwilling to look at Mason because he didn't want to be having this conversation. No, sir.

"Do you love him?"

Ty sighed. "Of course I do."

"Did you say that?"

"No, I did not. But I should have, right? I should have told him." Shit.

Ty didn't know what he'd been expecting or what he wanted. Saying "I love you" to someone was so fraught. Maybe he and Ian had both been playing chicken, neither willing to be the one who put himself out there and got his heart stomped on. But if they both felt the same way... had that been what the pleading at the bar on the last night of the season had been about?

Mason sipped his latte.

"I hate when you're right," Ty said.

"Did I say anything? No."

Ty caught Mason smiling from behind his cup.

Ian wanted Ty to give him a reason to stay. So Ty would give him one.

Chapter 23

IAN WAS at his desk at the hotel, reviewing the renovation contracts, when he got a call from the front desk. "There's a Mr. Arnold down here to see you," the desk agent said.

Ian thought of Ty, his own Mr. Arnold, and briefly entertained a fantasy that Ty was waiting for him downstairs. It seemed unlikely; he and Ty hadn't really spoken in nearly two weeks, and Ty had never come to the hotel. Probably this Mr. Arnold was a guest Ian had helped earlier in the week who just wanted to thank him for whatever he had done. That happened sometimes. Ian believed strongly in good customer service, the sort of above-and-beyond service that turned one-time guests into repeat customers. He took it upon himself to model how to deal with disputes or help customers, hoping the staff would adopt the behavior.

So he adjusted his tie, thinking he'd probably just say hello to Mr. Arnold and then go back upstairs to keep moping about Ty.

He took the elevator down to the lobby, thinking about Ty but also starting to panic a little, and then his mind was off to the races. What if it was Ty? What if it wasn't? What if something had happened to Ty? What if all those missed calls on his phone had been Ty trying to get in touch with him because something bad had happened? What if he was in the hospital right now? What if he'd been accosted by a homeless man or hit by a subway train?

The doors dinged, opened, and right there, standing in the middle of the lobby, was Tyler Arnold himself, in the flesh.

Ian was elated. And also kind of furious. And feeling completely insane and unable to cope.

Ian crossed the lobby in three great strides. "What the hell are you doing here?" His bafflement came across in his voice.

Ty rocked on his heels and looked a little sheepish. "You haven't been returning my calls the last couple of days."

"We didn't really have anything left to say to each other." That was the resigned truth Ian was now confronting. He'd seen a bunch of missed calls from Ty but hadn't wanted to respond. Ty would just hand him the same feeble arguments he had the night they had sort of broken up, if that mess could even be called a breakup. Now that Ty was standing here, at least Ian knew he was alive and well and nothing bad had happened, so really, those missed calls had probably just been Ty doing his Ty thing and making jokes or not saying what he really felt or wanted.

"See, that's where you're wrong," Ty said. "I have a lot I still need to say, actually."

Ian wanted to say something snide, like *So you thought barging into my place of business was a good idea?* But he held his tongue. Besides, he wasn't officially an employee of the hotel. Technically, it didn't much matter what he did during business hours because he was the only one who would hold himself accountable.

"All right," Ian said, taking a deep breath and trying to calm down. "What is it you have to say?"

Ty's face was hard to read. It looked like a parody of solemnity. "I broke a promise to you."

Ian hadn't remembered Ty making any particular promises. "What are you talking about?"

Ty pressed a hand to his heart. "I promised you that I would be totally open and honest with you. That day in Brooklyn? When we walked over the bridge? Remember? You're such an open book, Ian, but I tend to keep things close to the vest. And I kept something important from you because I was afraid of what you would say."

Ian moved to protest, but Ty held up his hand.

"I'm not afraid anymore, Ian, at least not as much as I am of losing you for good, so let me tell you this. Okay?"

Ian looked around, suddenly aware of their audience. He looked back at Ty, who seemed sincere. Ian had no earthly idea what Ty wanted to tell him, though he wanted to find out. Still, if Ty was about to cause a scene, the hotel lobby was hardly the right place for it. Besides, most of his employees didn't know he was gay—although he imagined they probably suspected—and airing this much of his dirty laundry with this many witnesses would hardly put him in the right light.

"Come with me," Ian said, walking past Ty toward the hotel restaurant, which wasn't open and wouldn't be for another few hours. No one was even there; Ian chose a key from his ring and opened the door to let them inside.

"Look at you, Mr. Hotshot With All the Keys."

Ian turned and looked at Ty with a raised eyebrow. "Right."

"Sorry, trying for a joke. I didn't want it to get too heavy in here."

Ian nodded and walked through the door.

Inside, the half-renovated restaurant was dark, lit only by the neon lights over the bar. Ian reached for the light switch, but one of the bulbs popped when he flipped it, leaving the light low.

"Sorry," Ian said. "Everything in this place is busted."

"S'all right," Ty said, sounding every inch a Texan.

Ian had missed that accent in the three weeks or so they'd been estranged. He'd missed Ty's warm skin and his low voice and his fiery red hair. He'd missed walking around the city and talking about nothing and gently teasing each other. He'd missed sex, missed making Ty howl, missed being pressed against Ty's body in the night.

Was Ty here to make amends? Was he here to apologize? To ask for Ian back?

"What didn't you tell me?" Ian asked, hoping to keep on target.

Ty took a step back and half sat on a table. "I promised you I'd be totally honest with you. I wasn't. I withheld things."

Ian wanted to tell Ty to quit stalling, but he waited.

"Okay, total honesty." Ty said this mostly to himself. He looked up at Ian. "I don't want you to go to Italy."

Ian moved to open his mouth, but Ty held up his hand again.

"Just let me say this," said Ty. "I don't want you to go to Italy. Okay? I don't. And I didn't want to say that very forcefully, because honestly? Deep down, I'm kind of fucked up. I didn't think that I was worthy of you. Because why would a smart, successful guy like you want to be with a guy like me?"

"What?" Ian was so surprised by this little speech that he reacted with confusion instead of processing the words. He came back and said, "What kind of guy are you?" He started cycling through the possibilities in his mind. Did Ty have something horrible in his past? Did he have some kind of illness? It was hard not to go to all of the worst-case-scenario places when Ty was just standing there hedging.

But then Ty swallowed and said, "I'm not... I'll never be my father, you know? He was a goddamned hero, the most perfect man who ever lived, and I say that not at all sarcastically. Like, he really was a great guy, and he had expectations for me that I'll never meet. Hell, by rights I should be back in Texas, a fireman or an Army colonel or a football star or something, but instead I'm an artist in New York, a million miles from Texas, and all I've got is my art."

It was starting to become clearer to Ian what Ty was talking about, but still he waited.

"See," Ty went on, "I'll never be what my family wanted me to be. Instead, I'm the froufrou artist cousin in New York. The gay one. The slightly effeminate one. The one who…." Ty closed his eyes and shook his head. "You put it all out there. You were totally honest with me about your anxiety right when we first met. You trusted me enough to fall apart in front of me."

"Well, that wasn't quite how it went—"

Ty took a deep breath. "I'm not…. It's all a front. Being the slutty one. I'm… I'm not that attractive. I'm not that successful. So how could I expect you to stay for me?"

Could this be true? Was Ty really saying these things? "I had the front part figured out," Ian said, "but the rest of what you just said is not true. How can you even say that? You're gorgeous. And you're obviously successful if you can paint and have the career you want but still pay for your apartment and take care of yourself. You're remarkable, Ty."

Ty bit his lip and looked down.

So Ian reached over and put his hand under Ty's chin. He lifted Ty's face. Their gazes met. "I think you're amazing," Ian said, "and right now, in this room, mine is the only opinion that matters."

Ty looked like he didn't believe it.

But that was what this was about, wasn't it? For all his bravado, Ty was really masking a deep insecurity and a lot of old pain where his father was concerned. Ian had gotten hints of it all along, but he hadn't realized how deep those old wounds cut, how much Ty still struggled against familial expectation. It was enlightening.

"So what?" Ian said. "Your self-esteem is lower than it should be. Happens to all of us."

"You told me you were going to Italy, and I thought, what the hell can I even say to make you stay? You've got this amazing job opportunity, and the alternative is to stay in New York for me. But why would you do that?"

Why, indeed. Ian didn't answer. He sensed that Ty had more to say.

He did. Ty pushed off the table and started walking around it. When he'd made the full circle around the table, he turned back to Ian and said, "I couldn't live with myself if I didn't at least try, you know? Because I don't want you to go to Italy, but if I didn't tell you the whole truth or try to argue why you should stay, you'd go anyway. So, yeah. I have issues. I decided to put them aside so that I could give this a shot."

"Okay. But Ty—"

"I love you, Ian. I'm in love with you. Totally, butt-crazy, head over heels in love with you. And I couldn't let you leave for Italy without telling you that. So you want me to give you a reason to stay? There it is. I love you. You should stay with me in New York because I love you."

Ian couldn't process Ty's words at first. He had wanted to hear exactly this all along. He'd wanted to know how Ty really felt. Well, there it was. There it all was. A shiver of happiness went through him. He had the whole picture of Ty, from the handsome bravado on the surface to the insecure kid stuck in Daddy's shadow underneath. But this was Ty; this was a man who was sweet and artistic and beautiful, who was capable of making whole stories come alive on a canvas. And sometimes with Ty, Ian felt a little less panicky.

Ty leaned back against the table. He looked like he was sulking. "So?" he said.

Ian couldn't speak for a moment. All of it, everything, welled up inside him, and he wanted to shout and jump for joy and run from the room all at the same time. Instead he did what instinct told him to do, which was to take the wounded-looking Ty into his arms and hug him tightly.

"Ty," he said. Then he repeated Ty's name over and over, rocking them both gently, petting Ty's back. "Ty, I love you too. So much."

Ty let out a breath and sagged against Ian a little, though he also lifted his hands and wrapped his arms around Ian's shoulders. "Really?"

"Yeah, I do. That's… I didn't know how to tell you. Was it not clear when we were fighting it out in the bar? I guess it wasn't. All I really wanted from you was for you to tell me you love me."

Ty huffed out a breath that ruffled Ian's hair. "Oh, was that all?"

"That's not a small thing."

"No, it isn't." Ty laughed softly. "So don't go to Italy. Stay here with me. Unless I'm too late and you've already said yes."

Ian almost didn't know how to respond. "Well," he said.

Ty pulled away and looked him in the face. "Oh God. You did, didn't you? You already took the job. Oh my God, no. You can't go. You can't. Not after all this. What the hell will I do without you?"

Ian petted Ty's head. "Actually, I haven't given them an answer yet."

Ty tilted his head. "How can that be true? Have you been stalling for two weeks?"

"I told them I had something in New York that was very important to me that was up in the air and I had to get it straightened out before I could make a decision."

"What did you... wait, are you talking about me?"

Ian sighed. "I don't know what happened at Barnstorm after that last game. You just seemed so determined to let it end when I announced my news. I honestly wasn't sure at all that I even wanted the job. I mean, yeah, Rome. I'd love to move to Rome. I've never been. I've been to Venice and Milan and Florence but never Rome. I've worked for these hotel owners too, so I know what they're like. I didn't love every minute of the job I did for them in Paris, but that was mostly the city, not the hotel people."

"So you want to move to Rome."

Ian extricated himself from Ty, whose proximity was becoming too distracting. "Actually, no. When I got the offer, I was initially set to turn it down. Because I figured, well, I'm giving things a shot with Ty and his whole life is in New York. Like, I thought about asking you to come with me, but I wasn't sure if I could. How could I ask someone I've only known for a few months to uproot their life for me?"

"I would have."

Ian believed that Ty believed that now, but the practicality of the situation told him otherwise. "No. Your job is here. I know you freelance, but how would you bring your paintings to your clients?"

"I could mail them."

"Ty. Come on. It's not like I'd be coming back to New York after Rome. There'd just be other cities. I could go anywhere. After Rome it could be Moscow or Prague or London or Vancouver or Los Angeles. Once I move on, I'm gone. But you belong here in New York. This is your home. You love this city. It's a part of you and you're a part of it. So no, I wouldn't ask you to move. You deserve better than that."

"I would do it for you. Only for you, though."

"And I appreciate that, but the thing is...." Ian paused, trying to work out what he wanted to say. He stepped back and paced a little, finding the rhythm soothing to his frayed nerves. "The thing is that all summer, while you were trying to convince me that New York was a place worth staying, I started to believe it."

"Really?"

"You can be pretty persuasive. You started trying to convince me that this was the greatest city on earth, and well... I don't know if I believe that quite yet, but I do believe it might be worth it to stick around to see what happens with you and me, because you are worth it, Ty. You are so worth it. And you're worthy of me because I love you and I want to stay with you." Ian sighed and shook his head. "These past few weeks have been so hard without you. But we hadn't quite broken up, right? I was working up to figuring out how to tell you I love you before I made a final decision about Rome."

Ty rubbed his head, sending his crazy red hair askew. "Were you? You sure took your sweet time."

"I figured you'd want a grand romantic gesture. That's kind of your thing, right? But I couldn't figure out what to do or what would work, so I was just paralyzed." Ian took a deep breath. "Like you said, I figured I should put myself out there one more time. I'd tell you I love you and if you didn't return the sentiment, well, then I'd have to leave for Rome because certainly there wouldn't be anything for me here."

Ty reached over and traced the back of his fingers along Ian's cheek. "You would stay here just for me?"

"Well, not just for you. For the Rainbow League too. For the Brooklyn Hipsters." Ian tried for a smirk.

Ty laughed. "So is that it? Are we back together? Are we going to live happily ever after? Please say yes, because I want for the answer to be yes, and then I want to kiss you."

Ian smiled. "Yes. Yes, Ty, I want for us to be together. The deeper stuff, the stuff you just shared with me, your insecurities and my anxiety, those are things we can work on and hopefully help each other with. Okay? And yes, I want to stay in New York. I want to stop running. I want to be in one place long enough to be in love and have a family and have everything work out the way it should instead of me just… I don't know. Running in circles."

"I want that too. Well, I want for you to stop running so that we can be together here and… all of that. Yes. We'll work on it together. Can I kiss you now?"

"You can kiss me whenever you want."

So Ty kissed Ian, sliding their lips together, and it felt like coming home. Ty's scent surrounded Ian, as did his strong arms, and Ian hugged Ty back and touched all that crazy red hair. They kissed and they fit together and this was the way it was supposed to be. Ian could sense it. He knew that he'd made the right choice in that moment, that he belonged here with Ty, that they would live happily ever after, or at least for a long time to come.

"When do you get off?" Ty asked.

"Oh, baby."

"Get your mind out of the gutter, dirty boy. What time do you get off work?"

"Anytime you want."

"Good. Get your stuff. Let's get the hell out of here."

TY WASTED a long time just running his hand over Ian's blond head as they lay tangled in bed. Well, not "wasted"—it was time well spent as far as Ty was concerned, since Ian had such lovely hair.

Part of him wondered what had just happened. He knew, intellectually, that he had gone to the hotel where Ian worked and bared his soul and that Ian had taken him back, but even with Ian there in his arms, he still didn't quite believe it.

"Ian?"

"Mmmph." Ian might have said something, but it was muffled due to the fact that Ian's face was pressed against Ty's side near his armpit.

"Would you have come for me if I hadn't come to you first?"

Ian lifted his head. "Yeah. I was cooking something up. Like maybe getting Josh to invite you somewhere and then ambushing you and then… that was as far as I got."

Ty laughed. "Really? That doesn't seem like your style."

"I would have done it for you. Something big and brash that you'd appreciate." Ian sighed. "I wish I wasn't such a goddamn coward sometimes. The whole thing was making me so nervous. Literally every time I started to think about possibly going to Europe without you, I started to feel panicky."

"That's an interesting reversal. Didn't you used to get panicky about being with me? Now you're panicky being without."

Ian rubbed Ty's chest. "I know. It's true, though."

"Wow." Ty wrapped a lock of Ian's hair around his finger. "I should have told you I loved you sooner."

"No. I mean, maybe it's better this way. Us not seeing each other for a few weeks let us see how much we mean to each other."

Ty lifted his head and kissed Ian. "And here you thought you were just joining the Rainbow League to get laid."

"Uh, mission accomplished, Red."

Ty laughed. "Well, you know. This ended up being more than just getting laid."

Ian rolled his eyes and rested his head against Ty's chest again. "Don't know if you were paying attention, but I was never just going to get laid."

And Ty knew that. Ty knew that Ian had had to trust him before they could sleep together. Ty was grateful Ian trusted him so much. He stroked Ian's back. "We're the only ones who know that."

"True. Although I think the rest of the team was kind of onto us."

"Yeah. They were."

Ian snuggled closer to Ty. "If I stay in New York, I'm going to have to get a new job next year."

"In case you haven't noticed, there are a few hotels in this city. Didn't you tell me the New Amsterdam is not the only one who wants your services?"

"Yeah. I'll find something. And maybe I could take a few short-term gigs. Spend a couple of weeks in Paris or London and take you with me."

"I'd like that. I've never actually left the States, you know. Well, I went to Toronto one time, if that counts."

"What were you doing in Toronto?"

Ty smiled to himself. "Got a job as a set designer for a dinky little indie movie nobody saw. They filmed it in Toronto, but they try to pass it off as New York in the movie."

Ian laughed softly. "Figures."

"Hey, it was work. And I had to get a passport and everything, so it was like visiting a foreign land where everything was sort of like home and the people spoke your language."

Ty thought of the painting in the next room. He spared a moment to let possible ideas for what to do with it cycle through his head: he could hide it, he could sell it, or he could destroy it. Ian would never know. But he could also show it to Ian and risk... everything.

Well, no, not *everything*. Ty believed that Ian loved him, that they'd have many more afternoons lounging together in bed like this, that they would travel together and play baseball together and spend a lot of their idle moments together. But showing Ian the painting might put a blemish on an otherwise wonderful day.

Or it might not.

Before he could lose his nerve, Ty said, "In the interest of full disclosure, I want to show you something."

Ian groaned. "What now?"

"Unfortunately, we have to get out of bed for me to show you."

Ian burrowed into Ty's side. "Do we have to?"

"Just for a minute. Come on."

Ty untangled from Ian and donned a pair of boxers. It was too weird to walk around his apartment totally naked. Ian eyed his clothes where they still lay on the floor of Ty's bedroom.

"We're not going outside or anything, are we?" Ian asked. "Or does this thing you want me to see involve me standing near a window your neighbors can see into?"

"Nope."

"Then fuck it." Ian waved his hands at his clothes and moved to follow Ty, still stark naked.

Ty led Ian into the studio. "Um, close your eyes? No, open them. It's fine. Just… if you hate it, don't tell me."

"What should I be—" Ian stopped speaking so abruptly that Ty was afraid to look at him. But he did and saw that Ian was staring at the painting of himself, awe on his face.

Ty had decided to paint him as he most wanted to remember him, smiling and in bed with white sheets around him, his blond hair a little wavy and mussed up from sleep, his eyes sleepy but seductive, his shoulders exposed but the rest of his body cut off. It felt vulgar to paint Ian naked, though Ty supposed he could have. But no, it was Ian's face he was treasuring when he couldn't see it. He'd kind of just painted what was in his heart. It was in the same style that he usually did the covers, more realistic than abstract, soft around the edges. But Ty had always thought that those covers showed men and women at their most ideal, and thus he painted Ian as the ideal male, because that was what he was to Ty.

"That's… that's remarkable. You painted this?"

"Yeah, I… I mean, after we had that fight at the bar, I really missed you, you know. So I just painted what I was thinking about. Which was you."

"It looks like me. That's crazy."

Ty started to relax. Ian seemed to like it, so that was something. "Has no one ever thought to immortalize you in paint before?"

"Nope. Pretty sure you're the first."

"Well. You're gorgeous. You deserve to be immortalized."

Ty looked at the painting, feeling self-conscious about it. It was weird to put his heart out there, to bare his soul, to be this open with anyone, but it felt good too. He wanted to do it for Ian. He didn't think he could have for anyone else.

"Ty?"

Ty turned to Ian. Ian kissed him hard. It was brief but intense.

"So you think it's okay?" Ty said.

"Yeah. I'm... no one has ever done anything like this for me. It's sort of narcissistic to say I love it, but... I love that you did it."

"I love you," Ty said.

"I love you too." Ian put his arm around Ty's middle. "You're... how could you have ever thought you weren't worthy of me? You're completely amazing, Ty. I'm so in awe of you."

Ty knew he was probably blushing, but he didn't much care. "Well, if I knew all I had to do to get my ego stroked was to paint you, I would have done it a long time ago."

"You know what would be awesome? If you painted us together like on one of your covers. We could be all sexy and muscular and wear, like, white shirts open to the navel that are tucked in for some reason. And I'd hold you like this." Ian moved behind Ty and grasped his arms tightly. "And I'd kiss you like this." Ian leaned down and kissed Ty's neck. Ty realized Ian was imitating the poses from a cover Ty had painted. "And then, of course, we'd live happily ever after."

"Of course." Ty leaned back against Ian and laughed. "Don't say things like that. I might just do it."

"I'd totally hang it in my apartment."

Ty hugged Ian.

Ian sighed. "Only you could have gotten me to stay in this city."

"I'm glad. Now as to that happily ever after...."

"We're most of the way there, wouldn't you say?"

"Yeah." Ty put an arm around Ian and steered him out of the studio. "I just noticed that you're not wearing any clothes. I do know of a clothes-less activity that will definitely make you happy."

"Yeah?"

"Yes. Let me show you."

Ian smiled. "After that? You can show me anything."

"Oh, baby," Ty said, peeling off his boxers.

Keep reading for an exclusive excerpt from

Thrown a Curve

The Rainbow League: Book Two

By Kate McMurray

Mason made headlines when, after his professional baseball career was sidelined by an injury, he very publicly came out of the closet. Now he's scratching the baseball itch playing in the Rainbow League while making his way through New York's population of beefcakes, even though they all come up short. Plus, he's still thinking about last summer's encounter with hot, effeminate, pierced and tattooed Patrick—pretty much the opposite of the sort of man he has long pictured himself with.

Patrick hasn't been able to forget Mason either, and now that baseball season is back upon them, he's determined to have him again. Mason is unlike any man Patrick has ever been with before, and not just because he's an ex-Yankee. All Patrick has to do is convince a reluctant Mason that their one night wasn't just a crazy fluke and that they could be great together…if only Mason could get past his old hang-ups and his intolerant family.

Coming Soon to
http://www.dreamspinnerpress.com

Chapter 1

MASON SIPPED his beer and watched Odell mack on some girl. She was pretty, with smooth, dark skin and a petite frame. Not Mason's thing, but he could see the appeal.

He turned his attention to the TV over the bar, which was showing *SportsCenter*. The hot topic of the evening was the Yankees and their abysmal season to date, a discussion Mason could have done without. When the show broke for commercial, he looked for the bartender, who fortuitously seemed to be headed back in his direction. The bartender was a cute, dark-haired white guy with a gym-sculpted body, obvious under the black tank top he was wearing. Mason kind of wanted to lick his arms, just because they were there. He smiled at the bartender and motioned that he wanted another beer. The bartender winked.

That was more like it.

Of course, just as the bartender slid another pint toward Mason, Odell leaned over and slapped Mason on the back. "And this here's my brother, Mason," he said to the girl. "He used to be a Yankee."

And here they went. Mason was mostly unfazed by people using his past notoriety for their own personal gain—this certainly wasn't the first time they'd done this act so Odell could pick up a girl. But still, it grated on him a little.

"You used to be a Yankee?" said the girl, her eyes wide. "Do you know Derek Jeter?"

Mason sighed. "I played with him for a couple of seasons, yeah. But we're not, like, best friends or anything."

That seemed to satisfy the girl, who nodded and hooked her arm around Odell's. "Jeter is so hot," she told Odell, who probably didn't care. Then she turned back to Mason. "Why did you stop playing? Did you get injured?"

Mason had answered this question many times in the four years since his contract had ended. For whatever reason, people thought it was noble to give up a career as a professional athlete because of an injury.

Odell shot him a warning look, but Mason didn't much care what he thought and also hoped Odell would go away so he could flirt with the cute bartender.

"I did get injured," Mason said. "It wasn't debilitating. I fell badly when I was running toward first base during a postseason game. Tore up the tendon in my foot." He pointed at his foot as if that would be enlightening. "It healed pretty well and I probably could have played a few more seasons in the minors at least, but I left when my contract was up."

"Why?" asked the girl. "How could you give that up?"

This was where it got dicey. For one thing, most people assumed that if you played ball professionally, you must have made millions of dollars. This had never been the case for Mason, who had been drafted right out of college and bounced around the minor leagues until he got called up to the Yankees. His first contract wasn't bad, and he'd made enough smart investments to keep him supplied with beer at sports bars with cute bartenders well into the future, but a millionaire he was not.

Also, Odell was now giving him the "I don't know what this girl's deal is, so tread carefully" look.

Fuck it, though.

"Well," Mason said, "I decided not to re-up my contract so that I could come out of the closet."

Odell rolled his eyes and gave Mason the finger behind the girl's back.

The girl's eyes went wide. "You're gay?"

It was hard to read her tone of voice. Surprised, yes, but it was not clear whether she thought this piece of news was good or bad. Mason inwardly braced himself for either possibility.

"Yes," Mason said. "I'm gay."

The bartender was hovering and seemed very interested in this piece of information.

The girl turned back to Odell. "It's really cool that you have a gay brother and that you two get along so well."

Score one for Odell. He grinned. "It *is* cool."

They flirted, so Mason turned back toward the bartender.

"My shift is up at ten," the guy said, sliding Mason a bar napkin. The name *Travis* was scrawled across the top above a phone number.

"Excellent," said Mason. "I live three blocks from here."

"How convenient," said Travis.

"I'm Mason, by the way."

"Yeah, I got that." Travis smiled. He had a dimple in his right cheek.

"I need to powder my nose," the girl said. "I'll be right back, sweetie."

When she was gone, Odell turned his triumphant smile back on Mason. Travis slid down the bar to help another customer.

"That could have gone badly," Odell said.

"Or it could have gone the way it did, which is that now your lady friend thinks you're sweet and sensitive because you're friends with your gay brother."

"Hmm."

"And honestly, do you want to go out with a girl who hates gay people?"

Odell shrugged. "Date, no. Hook up with tonight, doesn't matter."

Mason suppressed a tired sigh. "What's the girl's name?"

"Bettina. Pretty name, right?"

"At least you have that much figured out."

She came back a few minutes later and smiled beatifically at Odell. When Odell suggested they leave, he gave Mason a fist bump and wished him luck with the bartender. Once Odell and Bettina were gone, Mason turned back to watch Travis work.

This guy Travis was basically every guy Mason had dated since last summer: athletic, muscular, too much testosterone. Every last one of them had been unfailingly wrong for him. Mason's friend Nate kept suggesting it was a sign that Mason should stop dating meatheads. He had a fair point; the parade of butch guys had not helped him forget that he'd had the best sex of his life in the bathroom at a gay bar in the East Village with a small, femme-y guy named Patrick the summer before. Mason didn't have high hopes that Travis would break the slump, but it might be fun to try anyway.

Still, the central problem was Mason thinking he should be with a guy like Travis but his dick thinking he wanted a guy like Patrick.

Mason's family had had a hard enough time with the gay thing, completely mystified that a guy as masculine as Mason could possibly be gay. Odell was better than their mother and her extended family, for the most part, but he grudgingly approved of guys like Travis. What the hell would any of them say about a guy like Patrick?

Patrick didn't lack athleticism. Hell, they'd met because they both played baseball in the Rainbow League, an LGBT amateur sports league in New York City. But Patrick had piercings and tattoos, and he talked too much. So even though that encounter had been awesome, once the baseball season had ended, Mason had—literally—kissed Patrick good-bye. They hadn't seen each other since. Mason had never bothered to reach out.

And in Mason's defense, Patrick hadn't tried to get in touch with him either.

So when Travis's replacement showed up and Travis shrugged into a very nice leather jacket, Mason was game, though he knew this couldn't last.

"Did I overhear you say you used to be a Yankee?" Travis asked as they walked outside.

Mason hated trading this bit of trivia about himself in exchange for sex, but since it was only for the night, he nodded.

THE WOMAN at Patrick's station had amazing hair. It was thick and wavy, naturally a bright caramel color, and the sort of hair many women spent a lot of money trying to achieve. It made the crimes perpetrated against her hair such a shame.

He ran his fingers through it. God, it was healthy and silky too. If only all of his customers took such good care of their hair.

"They really butchered you," he said.

"I know. I said to leave it long in the front and short in the back, which is the opposite of what happened, and the layers are so uneven. Last time I'm going there."

"You came to the right place, girl. I can fix it. It'll be on the short side because I have to cut a lot to fix these uneven layers, but it'll look great, I promise."

"Cut as much as you need to. You are a lifesaver," said the woman. She frowned. "I literally cried when I looked in the mirror after I got home from the salon."

Her name was… Michelle? Patrick was terrible with names. He tended to remember his customers by their hair, and he liked to remember some bit of trivia about each so he could bring it up with his repeat customers. This one, with the thick caramel-colored waves, was a first-timer, here to fix the wretched haircut she'd gotten at some discount salon. Dimensions, where Patrick worked as a stylist, wasn't cheap, but it was a fantastic salon.

He spent the next twenty minutes repairing Thick Caramel Waves' hair, giving her a kicky bob that was trendy enough to be interesting but not so edgy that corporate America would balk. He learned as he was cutting her hair that she worked as a paralegal at a huge law firm in Midtown, so nothing too strange for her.

As he was finishing, his next customer—Black Dye Job, Color #315—came in. The whole day had been this way, back-to-back appointments, which was great for Patrick's wallet, but he was starting to get tired.

After he got Color #315 set up at a sink to get her hair washed, he checked in at the front desk. Valerie was on the phone, but she said, "Oh, he's right here, hang on." She put her hand over the mouthpiece and said, "You free next Tuesday night? It's for Melissa Schneider."

He had no idea who that was. It was irrelevant, though. "Baseball starts Tuesday. So, no, I'm not free."

Valerie tilted her head and looked at him quizzically. "Oh, right. I keep forgetting you do that baseball thing." Patrick knew his appearance didn't exactly scream "athlete."

He couldn't deny that he'd put on a few pounds over the winter, but not enough that he'd gone to waste. His fatigue was making him irritable, and he knew it, so he opted not to get defensive. "Well, I put my schedule in the computer, so the days I have games or practices should already be marked."

"Can you see Melissa on Friday, then?"

"Yeah, that's fine."

He left to go check on Color #315 and then slipped into the back room to mix up the color. It was nice to get out of the salon for a few minutes, although the mention of the impending baseball season was a reminder of what else this summer could bring. He was most looking forward to seeing Mason again, although he was a little worried about that too. Mason had made it pretty clear at the conclusion of their encounter at Barnstorm, the East Village bar Rainbow League members frequented, that it was a one-time thing. Which was a damn shame, because sex with Mason had been mind-blowing.

So, okay, they'd gotten off on the wrong foot. Patrick had put that foot right in his mouth, saying some pretty stupid things. Mason had rightly called him on something racist he'd said. Patrick had wanted a second chance, especially after he'd availed himself of Mason's amazing body. But then the season had ended without them exchanging contact information.

Patrick had pushed the encounter out of his mind. He'd spent part of the winter warming his bed with a sexy personal trainer who worked at the gym up the block next to Dimensions, but that had ended as soon as the snow finally melted.

And still Patrick hadn't been able to stop thinking about Mason.

Which was really fucking stupid, because all they'd had was a quick fuck—a spectacular, sensational fuck, but a quick one nonetheless—in a bar bathroom, and yeah, Patrick had never had a hotter encounter, and Mason was so goddamned sexy, but they didn't know each other at all. Probably they had nothing in common. And at the end of the day, what business did Patrick have with an ex-Yankee?

Patrick sighed and finished with the dye. Then he rejoined the chaos in the salon.

Coming Soon

The Long Slide Home

The Rainbow League: Book Three

By Kate McMurray

Nate and Carlos have been the best of friends since their childhood playing baseball together in the Bronx. For the last few years, Nate's been in love with Carlos, though he's never acted on it, and Carlos has never given any indication that he returns Nate's feelings. Nate has finally given up, determined to move on and find someone else, especially now that Carlos has shacked up with his boyfriend Aiden.

Carlos doesn't understand why Nate has suddenly gotten weird, acting cold and distant at team practice for the Rainbow League. But if that's how things are going to be, Carlos is done trying to figure Nate out. But then Aiden starts to show he might not be the man Carlos thought he was, and Carlos needs his best friend's support. Worse, he starts to realize his feelings for Nate might not be limited to friendship. But in the aftermath of his relationship with Aiden, and with Nate having problems of his own, the timing is all wrong to make a real relationship work. As emotions run high, both have a hard time figuring out what is real and what is just convenient.

http://www.dreamspinnerpress.com

KATE MCMURRAY is an award-winning romance author and fan. When she's not writing, she works as a nonfiction editor, dabbles in various crafts, and is maybe a tiny bit obsessed with baseball. She is active in RWA and has served as president of Rainbow Romance Writers and on the board of RWANYC. She lives in Brooklyn, NY.

Website: http://www.katemcmurray.com
Twitter: http://www.twitter.com/katemcmwriter
Facebook: https://www.facebook.com/katemcmurraywriter

Blind Items

By Kate McMurray

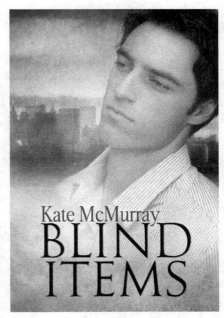

Columnist Drew Walsh made his career by publicly criticizing conservative, anti-gay politician Richard Granger. So when a rumor surfaces that Granger's son Jonathan might be gay, Drew finds himself in the middle of a potential scandal. Under the guise of an interview about Jonathan's new job teaching in an inner-city school, Drew's job is to find out if the rumors are true. Drew's best friend Rey is also Jonathan's cousin, and he arranges the meeting between Jonathan and Drew that changes everything.

After just one interview, it's obvious to Drew that the rumors are true, but he carefully neglects to mention that in his article. It's also obvious that he's falling for Jonathan, and he can't stay away after the article is published. Still, Jonathan is too afraid to step out of the closet, and Drew thinks the smartest thing might be to let him go—until Jonathan shows up drunk one night at his apartment. The slow burn of their attraction doesn't fade with Jonathan's buzz, but navigating a relationship is never easy—especially in the shadow of right-wing politics.

http://www.dreamspinnerpress.com

Four Corners

By Kate McMurray

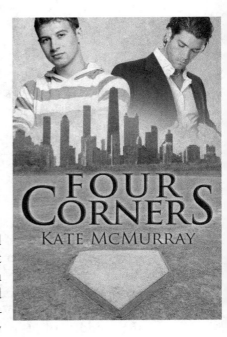

Since childhood, Jake, Adam, Kyle, and Brendan have been teammates, best friends, brothers. Then one day, when they were twenty-five, Adam disappeared without a word, devastating his friends— none more so than Jake, who had secretly loved Adam since they were teenagers.

Now, five years later, Adam is back, and he has his mind set on Jake. But those years of anger, hurt, and confusion are a lot to overcome, and Jake doesn't find it easy to forgive. He isn't sure they'll ever fit together the way they did. Jake, Kyle, and Brendan have moved on with their lives, but Adam's high-profile career keeps him in the closet—the same place he's been for years. Still, his apologies seem sincere, and the attraction is still there. Jake desperately wants to give him a chance. But first he has to find out why Adam left and if he's really back for good.

http://www.dreamspinnerpress.com

Kindling Fire with Snow

By Kate McMurray

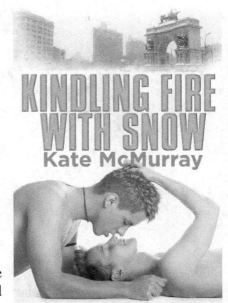

Weathermen are predicting an incredible blizzard for New York City, but with old snow melting on the sidewalk, Seth Roland is a little skeptical. Despite moping over his ex-boyfriend Evan, who recently dumped him, Seth pretends all is well as he steps into his regular local bar, where he's surprised by a blast from his past. Enter Kieran O'Malley, Seth's very first boyfriend, in the city for a conference.

It might have been just a chance meeting, but first a train derailment and then the predicted blizzard keep Seth and Kieran in close proximity. It's enough time for old feelings to surface, rekindled attraction to take hold, and new hopes for a future together to fill them both. But once the storm passes, the real challenge begins. Will Seth and Kieran work to make the relationship last, or will they let it melt away like snow in the sun?

http://www.dreamspinnerpress.com

The Stars that Tremble

By Kate McMurray

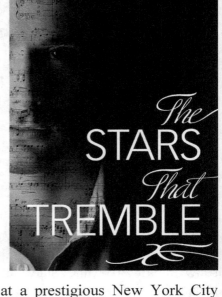

Giovanni Boca was destined to go down in history as an opera legend until a vocal-chord injury abruptly ended his career. Now he teaches voice lessons at a prestigious New York City music school. During auditions for his summer opera workshop, he finds his protégé in fourteen-year-old Emma McPhee. Just as intriguing to Gio is Emma's father Mike, a blue-collar guy who runs a business renovating the kitchens and bathrooms of New York's elite to finance his daughter's dream.

Mike's partner was killed when Emma was a toddler, and Gio mourns the beautiful voice he will never have again, so coping with loss is something they have in common. Their initial physical attraction quickly grows to something more as each hopes to fill the gap that loss and grief has left in his life. Although Mike wonders if he can truly fit into Gio's upperclass world, their bond grows stronger. Then, trouble strikes from outside when the machinations of an unscrupulous stage mother threaten to tear Gio and Mike apart—and ruin Emma's bright future.

http://www.dreamspinnerpress.com

The Silence of the Stars

By Kate McMurray

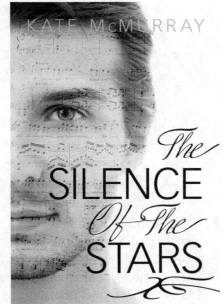

Sandy Sullivan has gotten so good at covering up his emotions, he's waiting for someone to hand him an Oscar. On the outside, he's a cheerful, funny guy, but his good humor is the only thing keeping awful memories from his army tours in Afghanistan at bay. Worse, Sandy is now adrift after breaking up with the only man who ever understood him, but who also wanted to fix him the way Sandy's been fixing up his new house in Brooklyn.

Everett Blake seems to have everything: good looks, money, and talent to spare. He parlayed a successful career as a violinist into a teaching job at Manhattan's elite Olcott School and until four months ago, he even had the perfect boyfriend. Now he's on his own, trying to give his new apartment some personality, even if it is unkempt compared to the perfect home he shared with his ex. When hiring a contractor to renovate his kitchen sends Sandy barreling into his life, Everett is only too happy to accept the chaos… until he realizes he's in over his head.

http://www.dreamspinnerpress.com

What There Is

By Kate McMurray

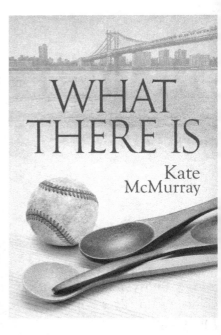

Former professional baseball player Justin Piersol needs a new life after a career-ending injury, and his job as a high school baseball coach isn't exactly fulfilling. Still, things are looking up: he finds the perfect room in an apartment in Brooklyn with Mark, who writes a popular column on sports statistics.

Mark is nerdy and socially awkward and intensely shy, and he immediately develops a terrible crush on Justin, who barely seems to notice him. As they get to know each other, Justin admits he misses playing baseball, that coaching doesn't scratch the itch. Mark confesses he thought he'd be married by now, that he wants a serious relationship. So they make a pact: Justin will help Mark find a man, and Mark will help Justin find something he loves more than baseball.

They put their plan into action… and then life gets complicated. Mark meets a nice guy named Dave, and Justin is suddenly crazy with jealousy. Justin realizes he wants to let go of the past and focus on the present, but as Mark and Dave become an item, Justin fears he's too late.

http://www.dreamspinnerpress.com

When the Planets Align

By Kate McMurray

Best friends Michael Reeves and Simon Newell always lived within ten minutes of each other, but somehow they're never in the same place at the same time.

Brash, outgoing Michael's unwavering confidence that he and Simon are meant to be carries him through some hard times. When Simon moves to New York, Michael dutifully follows. Quiet, practical Simon loves Michael as a dear friend, but he's not ready for anything romantic.

Several years and several failed relationships later, Simon realizes he's been in love with Michael all along. Only now Michael has moved on. Though Simon offers everything Michael's ever dreamed of, the timing is all wrong. Confusion, betrayal, and secrets from the past threaten their friendship until it might be time for them to go their separate ways. Or maybe the planets will finally align, and Michael and Simon will find themselves in the right place at the right time to take the next step.

http://www.dreamspinnerpress.com

Playing Ball

By Shae Connor, Kate McMurray,
Marguerite Labbe, & Kerry Freeman

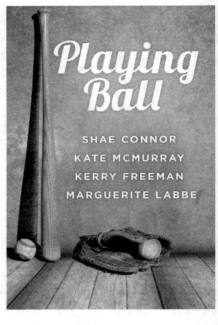

Baseball—America's favorite pastime—provides a field wide open for romance. A Home Field Advantage may not help when Toby must choose between the team he's loved all his life and the man he could love for the rest of it. In 1927, Skip hides his sexuality to protect his career until he meets One Man to Remember. Ruben and Alan fell victim to a Wild Pitch, leaving them struggling with heartache and guilt, and now they've met again. And on One Last Road Trip, Jake retires and leaves baseball behind, hoping to reconnect with Mikko and get a second chance at love.

Home Field Advantage by Shae Connor
One Man to Remember by Kate McMurray
Wild Pitch by Marguerite Labbe
One Last Road Trip by Kerry Freeman

NO PLACE LEFT TO RUN

ZARAH DETAND

http://www.dreamspinnerpress.com

CPSIA information can be obtained
at www.ICGtesting.com
Printed in the USA
LVHW081940170319
610981LV00022B/1081/P

9 781632 169679